Praise for *The Last Manly Man*

"Welcome back to Sparkle Hayter—and to her sparkling heroine. Robin Hudson is . . . feisty, funny, sexy, and entirely believable. In *The Last Manly Man*, she mediates wittily on issues of gender, and even gets close to answering the question that has puzzled—and frightened—men over the centuries: what do women really think of us?"

—Simon Brett

"A clever, careening romp through New York City streets and the backbiting, bureaucracy-ridden world of corporate media, interspersed with callow eco-terrorists. . . . Fast-paced plotting, witty dialogue, fleshed-out characters and enough red herrings to distract from the real villains and maintain suspense."

—*Newsday*

A PENGUIN MYSTERY
THE LAST MANLY MAN

Sparkle Vera Lynnette Hayter was born in Pouce Coupe, British Columbia. She has worked for CNN in Atlanta, WABC in New York, and Global Television in Toronto. As a freelance reporter, she lived in Washington, D.C., and in Peshawar, Pakistan, where she covered the Afghan War. She has also performed stand-up comedy. She created Robin Hudson with her first mystery, *What's a Girl Gotta Do?*, which won the Crime Writers of Canada's Arthur Ellis Award for best first mystery novel. She is also the author of *Nice Girls Finish Last*, nominated for the Arthur Ellis Award for best novel, *Revenge of the Cootie Girls*, *The Last Manly Man*, and *The Chelsea Girl Murders*. The creator of the tartcity.com Webzine for the Tart Noir group, co-founded by Lauren Henderson and Katy Munger, Sparkle Hayter now lives in New York City.

THE LAST *Manly* MAN

A ROBIN HUDSON MYSTERY

SPARKLE HAYTER

PENGUIN BOOKS

PENGUIN BOOKS

Published by the Penguin Group

Penguin Putnam Inc., 375 Hudson Street,
New York, New York 10014, U.S.A.
Penguin Books Ltd, 80 Strand,
London WC2R 0RL, England
Penguin Books Australia Ltd, 250 Camberwell Road, Camberwell,
Victoria 3124, Australia
Penguin Books Canada Ltd, 10 Alcorn Avenue,
Toronto, Ontario, Canada M4V 3B2
Penguin Books India (P) Ltd, 11 Community Centre, Panchsheel Park,
New Delhi - 110 071, India
Penguin Books (N.Z.) Ltd, Cnr Rosedale and Airborne Roads, Albany,
Auckland, New Zealand
Penguin Books (South Africa) (Pty) Ltd, 24 Sturdee Avenue,
Rosebank, Johannesburg 2196, South Africa

Penguin Books Ltd, Registered Offices:
Harmondsworth, Middlesex, England

First published in the United States of America by William Morrow,
an imprint of HarperCollins Publishers Inc., 1998
Published in Penguin Books 2002

1 3 5 7 9 10 8 6 4 2

PUBLISHER'S NOTE

This is a work of fiction. Names, characters, places, and incidents either are the product
of the author's imagination or are used fictitiously, and any resemblance to actual
persons, living or dead, business establishments, events, or locales is entirely coincidental.

THE LIBRARY OF CONGRESS HAS CATALOGED THE HARDCOVER AS FOLLOWS:
Hayter, Sparkle, 1958–
The last manly man : a Robin Hudson mystery / Sparkle Hayter.—1st ed.
p. cm.
ISBN 0-688-15517-0 (hc.)
ISBN 0 14 20.0039 6 (pbk.)
I. Title.
PR9199.3.H39L37 1998
813'.54—dc21 97-40943

Printed in the United States of America
Set in VanDijckMT / Designed by M. Kirsten Bearse

To my dad, who wrote the real polio letter,

and

Mr. Chicken, RIP

I am Tarzan of the Apes. I want you. I am yours. You are mine. We will live here together always in my house. I will bring you the best fruits, the tenderest deer, the finest meats that roam the jungle. I will hunt for you. I am the greatest of the jungle hunters. I will fight for you. I am the mightiest of the jungle fighters. You are Jane Porter, I saw it in your letter. When you see this you will know that it is for you and that Tarzan of the Apes loves you.

EDGAR RICE BURROUGHS,
Tarzan of the Apes, 1914

THE LAST *Manly* MAN

PROLOGUE

For weeks after my reported death, I made light of it with friends, asking them, "Where were you when you heard I died?"

My mother didn't hear about it, thank God, but the news traveled like wildfire over the Internet to my far-flung friends. My ex-husband Burke was hanging around the state department, looking for a story, when he heard the news from a producer who worked at ANN, the All News Network.

Immediately, Burke E-mailed my old friend Claire Thibodeaux, a White House correspondent, who was on the phone with a spokesman for the Saudi embassy when she read Burke's E-mail: "Just heard. Robin killed in explosion."

"Holy shit," Claire said out loud.

"Pardon me?" said the Saudi spokesman.

"I'll have to call you back," Claire said, and she got to work forwarding Burke's E-mail to various friends, former colleagues, and ex-lovers of mine around the world.

My former colleague Susan Brave-Druper was in L.A., nursing her infant daughter, when she heard.

Tamayo Scheinman, an anarchic Japanese comedienne, was

asleep in Tokyo after attending a relative's wedding when Susan called her.

My ex-boyfriend Eric joked that when he heard, he was in a hotel room in Budapest whacking off—and thinking of me. He was always saying sweet things like that.

None of them, not even the best journalists among them, thought to check out the story before spreading it. Why? "Even though I was stunned by the news," Claire explained to me later, "I wasn't surprised. Do you understand?"

Yeah, I understood. Most everyone said the same thing. Because of my history of getting into jams, my premature death was all too easy to believe, kind of like the Clinton intern story.

It would have been fine if the story had merely spread among my friends, but unfortunately, the story made our air, and things went horribly wrong. If you were watching the 3:00 P.M. (EDST) news on ANN that particular July day, you, too, heard anchorman Sawyer Lash announce that ANN executive and reporter Robin Jean Hudson had died in an explosion at an abandoned warehouse in Long Island City, just a few weeks shy of her fortieth birthday.

"Correspondent George Jerome looks at Hudson's all-too-brief life," was the last thing Lash said before the tape rolled on what was supposed to be my prepackaged video obituary.

But instead of seeing and hearing a report on the life of a TV newswoman, our viewers got something else, and the shit really hit the fan.

A bit of background: Obits of famous people and ANN television personalities are kept on file to be run quickly to air when required. A few years ago, my friend and producer Louis Levin and I put together a fake obit for me, which shows me Gump-like in a number of different historical scenes. For example, it has me leading an infantry charge at the Battle of the Bulge, jetting off to Scandinavia to pick up my Nobel prizes for literature and peace with Sam Shepard on my arm, floating outside *Mir* with a big wrench and a hammer, and so forth, all while dressed in a minidress and high heels, my red hair coiffed 1940s-style to enhance my already remarkable resemblance to Rita Hayworth in her scene-stealing, glove-peeling performance in *Gilda*. This is followed by testimonials from folks like Joe, the retired autoworker who, when asked what Robin Hudson did for him, says, "Cured my male itch."

The idea was, when I die, this tape would be on the obit shelf instead of my real obit, and would run on ANN worldwide, and I'd get the last laugh.

But that isn't what ANN viewers saw.

Louis Levin was one of the few people at ANN who did not hear of my death. Every now and then, Louis would update the tape, which is what he was doing when news came through that I had died.

He was hiding out in a back edit room, adding an improved version of the scene where millions of grief-stricken North Koreans in Pyongyang are prostrate before gigantic pictures of me.

So when the playback assistant went to the shelf to retrieve my obit, it wasn't there. Louis had it.

Stunned by the news and in a hurry, the playback kid mistakenly grabbed the wrong tape, and though Sawyer Lash announced my death in the intro, what the world saw was the obit of Robert Huddon, a deputy secretary of state and a close personal friend of the president. If you're up on the news, you may recall that Huddon was involved in delicate Mideast peace negotiations at the time, and that word of his death sent shock waves throughout the world and beyond, all the way to the White House. The oil markets went nuts. Huddon himself had to appear in public on live TV to put the rumors to rest. Even the president had a comment, which we have since added to my fake obit.

"Robert Huddon is not dead," the president says with visible relief. "A reporter by the name of Robin Hudson is dead."

That's the only *real* moment in the whole obit, but it's my favorite. I just get a kick out of that, the leader of the free world saying my name on national television. I'm kind of starstruck that way. It's the small-town girl in me, I guess. Sometimes, late at night, when I'm feeling lonely and insignificant, I pop a dub of that sound bite into my VCR and play it over and over.

Before the day was done, ANN would retract the story of Huddon's death, and of mine, and report that I wasn't dead, I'd been revived and heavily sedated and was in critical condition, albeit heavily bandaged.

I'm the girl behind the Robert Huddon mistaken death story, which shook the world for a moment. Ten years from now, someone may ask you that in a trivia game. I'm also the girl who broke the Last Manly Man case wide open, but as is too often the case, I didn't get my due credit for that. No biggie. All I did was save the world, sort of. But I'm not too bitter about not getting full credit, since I haven't had to take my due blame for a lot of bad things in this lifetime.

My name, as I said, is Robin Jean Hudson. Born after *Sputnik* and before color TV transmission, I am divorced and I live on Manhattan's Lower East Side with my cat, Louise Bryant, who is now retired from a lucrative career in cat food ads. Until recently, I was the boss, and a reporter, in the Special Reports Unit at the All News Network, not to be confused with the new Investigative Reports Unit, which does *60 Minutes*–style pieces for its weekly newsmagazine show.

Special Reports does three- to five-minute rating grabbers that run repeatedly during regular news programming. Our content tended toward the sensational and absurd, e.g., evangelical Christian preachers who claim to have been abducted by UFOs; and low-grade consumer fraud, e.g., the shady side of the hairpiece industry. But we tried to do these pieces intelligently and with wit and we tried to do a few serious-minded pieces too. That had been harder to do once Investigative Reports, headed by former foreign correspondent Reb "Rambo" Ryan and his shrewd and sneaky Cardinal Richelieu, Solange Stevenson, came on the scene and stole every good hard news story out from under us, leaving us with the fillers and the features. All this at a time when I was trying this new thing, Taking the High Road.

But back to reports of my death, which, as Mark Twain once said of his own, were exaggerated.

The whole mess began in late spring, when I went barhopping with Jack Jackson, the CEO and fearless leader of Jackson Broadcasting and its subsidiary networks.

Every once in a blue moon, Jack comes down from his penthouse to Keggers, the bar in the basement of the Jackson Broadcasting Building, to mix with his employees. After hanging out for a while, he picks one employee to go barhopping with, and that fateful spring night it was me. We got really drunk, hit some of his favorite joints, then some of mine, all the while talking about two things: men and women.

We both had a lot to say and ask on the subject. Jack was one of the sponsors of a big women's festival being held in the city that summer and was to give an "important speech" at the end of it. He was trying to "figger out wimmen," he said, and though he didn't say it, he meant one woman specifically— actress Shonny Cobbs, who had recently dumped him after a two-year relationship. The man was a canny visionary who slew dragons daily in the business world, but he couldn't figure out how to keep his woman happy.

As for me, some primal urge was pushing me to figure out men and work it out so I wouldn't end up spending my dotage alone, except for the male nurse I'd pay to change my diapers and listen to my life story. Did I mention I was about to turn forty? I figured if I couldn't make this man thing work for me now, when I was still young and energetic, it was only going to get harder down the road as my various internal organs started to shut down.

But I had another agenda: impress Jack and save my Special Reports Unit from the budget ax, as its fate at that time was iffy.

For hours and hours that spring night, Jack and I asked questions about each other's gender, exchanged loopy theories, admitted sexist notions, and drank a lot.

Sometime around 6:00 A.M., at a gritty, unlicensed waterfront bar on West Street that caters to men coming off the night shift, I suggested a series on the Man of the Future, looking at how far men had come and where they might evolve to in the future. In this context, I was sure, I could pinpoint exactly what it was that made a man a man, beyond anatomy, through all times and all fashions. I would pinpoint that mysterious quality good men have that makes them so attractive, despite how annoying they sometimes are. Whenever I try to give this mysterious thing a name—call it courage, strength, whatever—I think of a bunch of women with the same quality. This thing is something I find only in men, and not in all men.

It was a crazy fool idea, fueled by vodka and the attention of a famous man. Crazier still, Jack believed in me. The next day, he gave me his personal go-ahead for the series and a more important-sounding title: senior executive producer.

That booze-filled night with Jack started the ball rolling that led to my prematurely announced death and all the trouble in the worlds of fossil fuels and international diplomacy, among other things.

Between the booze-filled night and all the trouble came a man in a hat, a pack of Doublemint gum, and a bunch of crazy people.

CHAPTER ONE

It was a hot July evening in New York, the steamy post—rush hour, and in addition to the harried office workers streaming away from their offices toward subways, midtown was crawling with feminists and bees.

The feminists were arriving to set up for a corporate-sponsored conference on women's rights, ten days of symposiums, films, art shows, and rock bands, culminating with a big bash the last day.

Why the bees came here was still a mystery. The local media made a big deal out of the fact that the bees flocking to New York City were country bees seeking flowers, as opposed to our native New York City bees, who are lazy and tend to congregate around doughnut shop Dumpsters.

Why would so many tens of thousands of bees suddenly, spontaneously, decide to make a—forgive me—beeline for Manhattan? Not that New York doesn't have a great deal of greenery for enterprising bees to feast upon, tucked away in a million window boxes and rooftop gardens as well as in a couple of parks. But it takes a lot more work to find pollen sources here than it would in a rural field of clover, and the hazards of city life—pollution, taxicab windshields, and marauding youth gangs—meant there was also a great deal more risk involved for these greenhorn bees.

But as one newspaper pointed out, bees follow their queen, and evidently some queens had a taste more for the risky city than for the bucolic country life.

A couple of confused bees evidently had a taste more for me, or maybe just for the floral notes in my scent, L'Heure Bleue, which I had sprayed on a little too heavily as I was leaving my office. In addition to dodging large groups of women pulling wheeled suitcases and walking abreast, I was dodging two bees as I crossed Third Avenue, heading toward Wingate's restaurant. Once people saw the bees, they gave me a wide berth. Couldn't help thinking how handy these bees would come in during management meetings, salary negotiations, and Saturday night movie lines.

Because of the bees, and because, as usual, I was completely self-involved, I didn't notice right away that there was a man in a hat following me until I heard him say, haltingly, "Ex . . . cuse . . ."

I turned and gave him a quick glance, decided from his rolling eyes that he wasn't talking to me and tuned him out, though I put my hand in my jacket pocket and grabbed onto my pepper spray because I've been stalked before and learned the hard way that—duh—it's better to be safe than sorry. I was in a hurry. I had places to go, people to meet, a butt to kiss.

Kissing butt with grace is one of those adult skills, like telling believable lies, that are almost essential to success. There's an art to it. As the old line goes, when you can fake sincerity you've got it made, but it's not an area of expertise for me. In fact, I was pretty lousy at it and normally I'd rather hammer a railroad spike up my nose than kiss ass. But in one of those compromises grown-ups are required to make every now and then, I was on my way to meet with a flack for the anthropologist Wallace Mandervan and lay a big wet one on his rosy behind. This was especially humiliating—I wasn't going to kiss Mandervan's ass, but the ass of a snotty proxy who would then report back to the man himself.

At the end of another hard day, all I wanted to do was go home, take off my clothes, and kiss the ass of a mad Irishman I'd been neglecting lately. It was Wednesday, and Mike, the mad Irishman, was leaving the next day. I'd been all set to leave my office at the stroke of five, and then Benny Winter, Power Publicist, called and said he could meet me for dinner tonight, and tonight only, to discuss getting Mandervan for my Man of the Future series.

Just as I was about to go into Wingate's, I heard, "Miss . . . miss," behind me.

That's when I really noticed the man, an older guy, maybe in his sixties, wearing a dark brown suit with a matching hat, walking erratically. Before I could get into the restaurant, the man had moved in front of me and stopped, barring my way, while the bees buzzed above me. A strange look crossed his face. He walked a few steps one way, stopped and turned around, walked a few steps the other way, and stopped again. He looked around himself, scared, as if he was trying to recognize his surroundings and couldn't. It was almost like he was drunk, but he didn't smell of liquor. Then he looked down at his feet and took a few more tentative steps away from me, still looking down, as if his feet might remember the way home and all he had to do was follow them.

If it wasn't for the feet thing, I would have thought he was just your garden-variety loony toon and abandoned him right there. Call it coincidence, whatever you like. My witchy neighbor Sally calls it my Alzheimer's-finder karma. Three times in as many years, I'd happened upon someone who had Alzheimer's and helped them find their way home. Two of them did the same thing with their feet. (The third kept smelling his hands, one after the other, as if they smelled bad. They did not. He had worked for many years in the Fulton Fish Market.)

The other times this happened, I was free and able to help the lost people, do my bit for my fellow man and feel like a big hero afterward. But I was in a hurry now—Benny Winter was a notorious stickler for punctuality—and I resented this stranger's intrusion upon my time. How I wished I could just look away, move past the lost man, and put him out of my mind. How well I know that no good deed goes unpunished, that stopping to help a disoriented stranger can cost you your life. It's a heartless city sometimes, but you have to look out for yourself. Since I'd started this new thing, Taking the High Road, one of the central questions of life—my life, at least— had been: How do you walk out the door and be a good person without getting the shit kicked out of you?

On the other hand, if I didn't help this poor slob, something terrible might happen. Even if it didn't, I'd worry later and feel guilty—and construct terrible fantasies about what had happened to him—all because I would not take the time to help in my hurry to kiss up to some jerk in order to further my career.

"Do you have a wallet?" I said, sighing, as I danced about to avoid the bees, which he was completely oblivious to.

He felt his pockets, but turned up nothing except a half package of Doublemint gum. His eyes rolled back and then rolled forward again. He took off his hat and handed it to me.

This was the second hat-wearing lost man I'd encountered in my life. The last one, Dr. Seymour Gold, a retired thoracic surgeon with Alzheimer's, had his name and address written into the inside of his hat by his wife.

Before I had a chance to look inside this man's hat, a thin trickle of blood dripped down the side of his head.

"Did you fall?" I asked, as I wiped the wound with a tissue

from my pocket. The cut was about a half inch long and not very deep.

The man gurgled a bit but said nothing.

"Want me to get you to a doctor?" I asked.

"P-p-p-pa-p-per . . ." he stammered, clumsily patting his pockets.

I handed him my notebook and a pen and he feebly wrote. The handwriting was very shaky but it looked like 7 Mill Street.

"It's an address," I said. "Is this where you live? Do you want to go to a hospital . . ."

A limo with smoked windows had pulled up beside us, and I was distracted for a moment, hoping maybe it was Benny Winter, and I wasn't late at all, and then hoping it wasn't, because I wasn't sure what he'd make of this tableau, me doing my bee-dodging Saint Vitus's dance in front of a man with a head wound. But nobody got out of the car.

"Ahhhhh," the lost man said, and then he gurgled again.

"I'm sorry, I don't know what you're trying to say, or what to do. Let me call someone." I dug in my purse for my cell phone.

"Dumb," he said.

"You're dumb? Are you a mute? Or practically a mute? You want to write some more?" I asked, holding out the reporter's notebook.

He didn't take it. Instead, some realization dawned on him and he suddenly turned, walking quickly away, the limo following him down the block.

I was about to follow also when two men got out of the limo. They wrapped the lost guy in an embrace and put him into the car. Before I could call out, "Wait! Your hat," they all drove off, to my great relief.

I used the hat to wave the bees away as I opened the door to Wingate's, ducked in, and closed it. One of the bees managed to follow me inside, causing a few moments of arm-flailing panic among a group of stout, well-suited men who had been exchanging business cards in the foyer. Big, strong men, probably captains of industry, reduced to a Jerry Lewis dance number by a little bee, until the maître d' and I were able to maneuver the bee to the door and wave it outside with the hat and a menu.

Needless to say, this did not endear me to the maître d', who gave me a dirty look, as if I had brought the bee in on purpose. Like it was my pet bee and I was walking it.

While the maître d' escorted me to Benny Winter's table, I checked the hat to see if the guy's name was inside it so I could return it to him, but there was just a store name, Harben Hats, Fifth Avenue, New York.

"I specifically asked you not to be late," Benny Winter said, not rising from his chair.

"Sorry," I said, sitting down. "This lost man stopped me and I was trying to help him. I think he had Alzheimer's . . ."

"Did you get his name? Perhaps you can return the hat," Winter said, as though the whole thing bored him. He was completely deadpan all the time, which is weird but effective. He was very pale too. Though I could not get past seeing him as a flunky, he was one of the best publicists money could buy. In addition to working for some of the world's biggest corporations, he had worked effectively for various nasty countries with nasty agendas who wanted to hang on to American foreign aid or obtain American weapons (often used against Americans later).

"I got an address . . . or something. It's hard to read," I said.

"Let me see." He took it from my hand, glanced at it quickly, and handed it back.

"So you can return the hat. So why are you telling me this? I don't have much time, Ms. Hudson. Let's order," Benny Winter said impatiently. "Do you know what you want?"

Quickly, I scanned the menu. Wingate's is a venerable and very pricey old steak house, a serious Male Power place, which is why I had chosen it. It was possible to have meat for almost every course, a meat soup, steak salad, and beef carpaccio as appetizers, and steak for the main course. If they'd had meat cake for dessert, it would have been the perfect carnivorous menu. I ordered a small filet, while Winter ordered the only nonmeat entrée, broiled red snapper.

After the waiter left, Winter said, "Let's hear it. Make your case."

"The bottom line is, I really want Wallace Mandervan for this series. I'm a great admirer of his work and . . ."

"What do you know of his work?"

I took a deep breath. "Wallace Mandervan is the man who pioneered commercial anthropology. Oh sure, almost every corporation has its own anthropologist now," I said. "But that's because, back in the 1960s, Mandervan blazed the trail—he predicted the antiwar movement, the breakup of the Beatles, designer jeans—he predicted disco! He was ahead of the demand for Cabbage Patch Kids . . . and aromatherapy! And all his predictions have a sound anthropological basis—he's pop culture meets the Royal Academy of Sciences. An original. His last article on how politics and sociology can force physical evolution was brilliant . . ."

On and on I went in this vein, listing the man's many achievements, demonstrating my scholarship in all things Mandervan, reciting Mandervan quotes and nakedly gushing. This, I'd been told by others who had dealt with him, was what Benny Winter responded to. Don't be real, I was told, don't be funny, don't be warm, and don't be late. Kiss up.

While I delivered a first-class kissing, Benny Winter ate his dinner and betrayed no emotions at all.

"You're quite right about Mandervan," Winter finally said, nodding, maybe not with approval, but with a lack of the earlier subsumed malice. "Who else are you talking to? Dr. Mandervan has to be careful about the company he keeps."

"We've got a biochemist who believes by the middle of the next century, men will live to be a hundred and forty. We've got Gill Morton, CEO of Morton Industries . . . you know him, of course. He's the one who referred me to you. We have Jose Blanca, the fashion designer, an automotive engineer, feminist scholar Alana DeWitt, some preschool kids, and that scientist who grows human hair in a test tube . . ."

"People pay Dr. Mandervan millions of dollars for his analysis. Why should he give it to you and your network for free?" Winter asked, seeming almost receptive.

My hopes rose and I blazed forward with renewed confidence.

"ANN has prestige and respectability—it means free publicity for whatever Dr. Mandervan is working on now. Rumor has it that he's working on a book about the New Man, so there's a strong thematic link with my report on the Man of the Future. And, more important, we have worldwide coverage. It's a chance for Mandervan to get his message to a much wider audience in the new global economy."

"Prestige," Winter said. He leaned over to his valise and pulled out a newspaper clipping, which I immediately recognized as a bad review I got from the *New York News-Journal*.

"Your special report on fatalities caused by childproof containers got slammed by the critics," Winter said. "And you had to make a public retraction after the mad cow story. . . ."

"But we've also won awards . . ."

"You won your last award for a humorous piece, didn't you?"

"Well, yes, for best short feature, but . . ."

"Let me see here . . . for 'The Bible Code Code.' "

The special report he was talking about was a feature in which we subjected Michael Drosnin's book *The Bible Code* to our own rigorous decoding, and revealed the secret messages found within the book about the code found within the Bible. We had a cryptographer go through *The Bible Code* using our own special skip code and then, just for fun, I went through a couple of chapters with my father's Little Orphan Annie secret decoder ring, which I found in the bottom of a box of his stuff sent to me by my aunt Maureen. Among the things we found in *The Bible Code* were cryptic predictions that Frank would step out on Kathie Lee and that the world would be destroyed in 2017 not by a giant apocalyptic comet, as some had predicted, but by a giant blob of space goo. It was a fun filler, but it wasn't a high point in broadcast journalism, that's for sure.

"You can understand that Dr. Mandervan doesn't want to appear in anything that might generate negative publicity indirectly, through no fault of his own, or trivialize his work in any way. So if we did agree to do this—and the chances are slim, I must be honest—we would require approval of the edited product."

"What I could do," I said, "is show Dr. Mandervan the final product, and get his feedback."

"We require approval, in writing, up front."

"I can't do that," I said. "It's against news policy."

He looked at his watch and said, "I'll get back to you after I speak to Dr. Mandervan and he tells me of his decision. But it's safe to say he won't go for it."

Then, before he left, he said, "You shouldn't have been late."

Damn. Mandervan would be a coup for me, and not only because he'd become a twitchy recluse and hadn't given an interview in more than two years. Landing Mandervan for my series would provide an exciting perspective on men, and it would shut up the network gossips, who were convinced our CEO Jack Jackson had saved my Special Reports Unit from the ax *not* because of my leadership abilities but because of my rumored ability to suck the dimples off a golf ball. As if Jack Jackson, multibillionaire, media mogul, dater of college-educated supermodels and actresses, would need to sexually harass middle-manager me to get off. Strictly speaking, sexual harassment wasn't his style in any event.

Outside, the bees were waiting for me. Now there were three. A couple more and it would be a Hitchcock movie. I didn't lose them until I got into a cab.

"Where to?" the cabbie asked.

"Tenth Street between B and C."

But as he pulled away, I changed my mind.

"Mill Street, in the Village. I'll only be a moment there. Then East Tenth Street," I said.

As part of my mission to talk to as many men as possible, I asked the cabbie what it meant to be a man these days.

"Work, work, work," he said. "Nothing but work. And no thanks for it."

"You married?" I asked.

"No. I'm single. I'd like to get married, but girls these days, they got a list. There's no romance to it anymore, it's all business."

Then he clammed up and cranked up talk radio to drown out any further questions.

CHAPTER TWO

Mill Street is a tiny, picturesque lane that curves off Christopher Street toward Barrow in Greenwich Village, so tiny a street that it doesn't even show up on most maps. Number 7 turned out to be some kind of storefront, but without a sign. While the cab waited, I hopped out and approached a man who was locking a front door festooned with stickers to save the whales, save the bonobos, improve the working conditions of egg-laying chickens, boycott Texaco and Mitsubishi, and ban bioengineered food (a DNA helix in a red circle with a slash through it made that point emphatically). There must have been twenty of them clustered on the glass door. I couldn't help thinking of this bumper sticker my friend Tamayo picked up in Japan when she lived there, which said in English and Japanese: Eat More Whale. Which I'm against, eating whales, but I thought it was a funny idea, if someone put that bumper sticker smack across this door.

"You work here?" I asked the man. He looked to be in his early twenties, with dark hair and a boyish face not quite grown out of its baby fat. If it wasn't for the sneer, he would have been very nice looking. He was sort of a runtier, younger, darker version of Brad Pitt.

Looking over his shoulder at me, he said, "Yes. Can I help you?"

"I dunno. I'm looking for the man who lost this hat and this is the address he gave me . . ." I handed him the crumpled piece of paper but he took the hat instead and examined it.

"This hat?" he said with scornful surprise, handing it back to me as though it was infected with Ebola. "I don't think any of our people would be wearing a Harben hat. It's some kind of animal felt. Harben traffics in animal pelts and has polluted the water supply in Guatemala, where it now operates its death mills."

"I did not know that. Hmmm. Could it belong to someone's dad or grandfather . . . the guy was older, late fifties, early sixties, nice suit. . . . Look, I'm just trying to be a Good Samaritan with a man who appeared to be lost . . . he left his hat . . ."

"Awright, awright. I'm sorry I snapped at you. I just got back from a bad trip to South America an hour ago, only to learn a friend of mine is in the hospital and that our offices were burgled today. I'm having a bad day."

To make it up to me, he took the crumpled slip of paper and looked at the address.

"That looks like a one to me," he said. "There is no 'one' on this street. It's an empty lot. Someone is about to build on it."

"Well, take my number and ask around the neighborhood, will you?" I said, handing him my card.

"ANN . . ." he said with deep suspicion in his voice. He seemed to be trying to remember what ANN's environment or animal crime was. Finally, he said, "Cultural imperialis s."

"Yeah, right. Whatever."

"That's a McQuarrie briefcase, isn't it?" he asked, and snapped firmly back into his self-righteous mode. "Did you skin the animal yourself? Perhaps you are unaware that

McQuarrie takes the youngest calves, barely weaned, still mew-ling for their mothers, and . . ."

"It's not a McQuarrie," I said, trying not to breathe in his direction, lest there was still beef on my breath. "It's a cheap vinyl knockoff. I bought it in Chinatown."

He wouldn't let up. "Was it made in China? And if so, how do you know it wasn't made by imprisoned pro-democracy activists? And your clothes . . . do you even know where your clothes are made?"

"No, I don't. Jeez. I'm sorry, but all my hemp-cloth cloth-ing is at the laundry," I said. "Don't you get tired of pre-tending to be perfect all the time?"

"Don't you get tired of wearing lipstick and high heels and playing into male sexual objectification fantasies?" he persisted.

If there's one thing I can't stand, it's a man who is more of a feminist than I am.

"I never get tired of that," I said. "Look, I'm just trying to do a good deed. . . ."

"Sure, you are, sure. I think I've told you too much al-ready. I think you're one of *them*," he said, and started backing away from me, then took off running.

Right, gotta go now, the microchip in my buttocks is beep-ing, I thought, as I always did when I encountered a loony. Vile young man. I had sized him up too—those cruelty-free natural-weave clothes don't come cheap and he couldn't make much working for animal rights or whatever the hell he did. Chances were, he was a trust puppy, a kid with a trust fund, probably the rebellious offspring of some meat-eating, hide-bearing conservative in a hat.

I stomped off toward the waiting taxi in my leather shoes, tripping slightly, which made me even madder.

"Tenth Street now?" the cabbie asked as I got back into the cab.

"Yes, thanks," I said.

What a weird day. Not the weirdest day I'd had by a far sight, but the weirdest in a while. Good thing the Econut didn't know that I was on my way home to, hopefully, have sex with an Irish cameraman with the blood of twenty-seven kamikaze Pakistani dogs on his soul, all strays mowed down at night on the unlit roads of Pakistan's tribal territories over a period of two years during the Afghan War. Hope Mike isn't weird too, I thought. He had been acting odd lately. Which Mike would be waiting there for me? The sweet, sensitive poet, or the dark, brooding dog killer? The former was preferable, but either way, we were sure to have good sex. It had been a while—I'm prone to long droughts, due to my prickly nature and, if not an outright fear of intimacy, sober caution in that regard. Though Mike had been here for about five days, every time we tried to have sex something interfered, either his daughter or this insane trapeze artist who was in his circus documentary and kept calling for him.

I sat back in the seat, toying with the hat until the cab pulled up to my prewar building on East Tenth Street, in the neighborhood locals call Alphabet City and Loisaida and realtors call the East Village. Along with the spicy smells of cooking, love gone wrong permeated the humid air in my neighborhood. From my neighbor Sally's window, I heard the final strains of Bix Beiderbecke's version of "There Ain't No Sweet Man That's Worth the Salt of My Tears," which she always played when she'd had a breakup.

Up in my hallway, there was a bigger commotion. Mr. O'Brien, who lived down the hall from me, was banging on his door. When he saw me, he said, "The woman put the board in the door again."

I nodded politely. Mr. O'Brien was a retired lawyer, about seventy, and "the woman" was little and foreign-born, Filipino, I think, late fifties or early sixties. He referred to her as his "housekeeper" when he was in a good mood, and as "the woman" when he was not. She called herself "Mrs. O'Brien" when he wasn't around. Because of her embarrassed fiction and because their apartment was a one-bedroom, there was probably more than housekeeping going on.

Their arguments always revolved around one contentious point, whether or not he would marry her, and followed the same script every time. They screamed at each other until he stomped out, sometimes disappearing for days on end. When he came home, she'd have inserted a board between the wall and the door so it wouldn't open, and he'd then stand in the hallway pounding and shouting until she finally relented and let him in.

"I saw you on Eighth Street today, Robin. How come you didn't say hello?" Mr. O'Brien asked.

"Must have been someone else. I wasn't on Eighth Street today, Mr. O'Brien," I said.

"Oh. How strange. Listen, watch out for Ramirez," he said, referring to my elderly downstairs neighbor, Dulcinia Ramirez, a blue-haired vigilante who had recently invested in a cellular phone and taken her job as crime fighter to the streets, where she was particularly zealous about calling the police to report "quality of life" crimes like public urinaters.

"I always do watch out for her," I said. Ramirez was not too fond of me, not too fond of any of her neighbors, in fact.

"I hear she has a gun now."

"How did she get a gun? Who would give her a permit?" I asked.

O'Brien just shrugged.

"Thanks for the warning. Have a good evening."

"You too," he said, and started hammering on his door again, shouting, "Let me in!"

Ain't love grand?

As soon as I popped the lock open, I heard the Waterboys on the stereo and knew the answer to my question—which

Mike would be there? It looked like it was the conscience-stricken dog killer, sitting in an armchair in the corner of the living room, in the dark, staring at an unopened bottle of Bushmill's. His suitcase was packed and near the door.

"Hey, Girl," he said, getting up without enthusiasm, as if he was weighted down with lead.

Chances were, if I asked him what was bothering him, we'd end up talking and drinking all night instead of having sex. Now, I like both those things, talking and drinking, but when Mike was like this, his stories would eventually get to the dead dogs, and they're a real mood killer. Then he'd be off on a plane, leaving me unscrewed and depressed, having absorbed his pain for yet another night.

So I didn't ask. I said, "Hi, Mike. God, it is so good to be home. What a day."

"Yeah. The meeting with *National Geographic* didn't go well. Lost the Tibet job. I need to talk to . . . whoa, nice hat."

"Yeah, it's a Harben hat," I said, putting it on his head. "Gee, it looks good on you."

The compliment perked him up a bit. He's a dark Irish guy, nice-looking, not too handsome, but in the hat he looked deadly and noir.

"Where'd you get this hat?" he asked.

"Long story short . . . some man lost it."

"Some man? Who . . . no, I don't want to hear about it. It's a nice hat all the same. Reminds me of this guy in Cork. Old Jimmy Riordon. Wore a hat like this. Worked at a boot factory, liked to go to the pub every night, get drunk, and write letters to world leaders telling them how to run their countries. I remember . . ."

"Mike, do we have to talk?" I asked, flinging my blue Anne Klein blazer onto a chair and kicking off my high heels.

The living room was a mess, on account of my maid being

in detox, but I was able to clear some junk off the sofa and pull Mike down onto it and kiss him.

While we were kissing, my phone rang and my answering machine picked up. Mike pulled away from me to listen to it.

"Lola? Gus," we heard. "I'm not sure if you got my earlier message. I might have dialed the wrong number because a strange man picked up as I was leaving it. Well, anyway, I lost my patient and it turns out I'll be in New York on Friday and maybe Saturday. I'm in Boulder, at the Boulderado Hotel, room 511. Call and let me know."

"Ah, poor Gus, lost his patient *and* then dialed the wrong number again," Mike said, sounding thoughtful. "Second time he called here today. I hope he finds Lola. Kind of too bad, isn't it? He and Lola might miss each other this weekend."

Gus had called here before and left messages for Lola, though not for a couple of months, and Mike liked to speculate on who they were, what they looked like, how their romance had unfolded. Mike's romantic for a nonwussy guy—it's an Irish thing, I think.

"How come you're so interested in talking, Mike?"

"We haven't had a chance to talk this week. We haven't had a chance to really talk in a while."

"You could always stay another day."

"Can't. I have to be back in San Fran tomorrow to set up for Saturday. There's lighting to worry about, crowd sound, we're working with three cameras, all those temperamental circus folk. The lion tamer Olga is jealous of Veronkya, you know, the trapeze artist, and . . ."

Veronkya. That name was a cold shower, and not just because it sounds like someone expelling phlegm. She was almost all Mike talked about lately, about how Veronkya, an eighteen-year-old East European, was flying without a net for the first time Saturday, how she had conquered a fear of heights to follow her family into the trapeze-flying business, how bloody brave she was. But as Mike and I were nonmonogamous, it wasn't my place to express jealousy.

"Let's not talk," I suggested, pushing up against him. Mike was definitely into it—or at least, he was responding. We kissed and sort of dry-humped lightly, when he suddenly stopped and pulled away from me again. He looked very serious.

"I have something to . . ." he started to say, and our timing being what it was lately, at that moment his beeper went off and I didn't hear the rest of the sentence.

"Damn," he said, checking the rolling message on the beeper's LCD screen. "It's my ex-wife."

"Felicia? She can wait," I said, trying to pull him back.

He threw my arm off him and read the message. "It's urgent, about Samantha. I'd better call her. I'll use the phone in the bedroom."

He talked real low on the phone and I couldn't hear what he was saying. When he came back, his pale Irish face was even paler, if that's possible. He said, "Samantha was supposed to come straight home after ballet three hours ago to go to her grandmother's place for a birthday dinner."

"Maybe she forgot," I said, suppressing the thought that Samantha had escalated her tactics. Lately whenever Mike and I were close to refinding our old intimacy, there was some emergency with Samantha requiring Mike to spend time with her and his ex-wife. You don't have to be a genius to see the Hayley Mills parent trap scenario there.

"Samantha loves Felicia's mom, she wouldn't forget the birthday," Mike said.

"God, maybe she is missing then," I said.

"I'll call you later. Sorry, Girl."

"That's okay," I said. "But you were about to tell me something . . ."

"It's . . . it can wait, really."

"Really?"

"Sure. Not enough time now. It's complicated . . . I gotta go, Robin."

"Not even a hint?"

"Gotta go . . . Samantha . . ."

"Yeah, of course. I hope Samantha is okay. Call me when you have the scoop."

He looked at me in a way he'd never looked at me before, kind of sad, kind of nostalgic, and kissed me. And then he was gone with his suitcase and my newfound hat on his head. It was a far cry from the man I used to know, who would read excerpts from pornographic books to my voice mail at work and then ravish me with chest-thumping gusto for a full hour when I got home.

Men leaving me in the lurch—just part of the curse I travel under, to be attracted to interesting men driven by a vision who just can't be counted on to stick around. But to be fair, I've left a few in the lurch myself. Still, it didn't feel good, standing there half-dressed, my black slip sticking to my skin, all sweaty and slatternly like Patricia Neal in *Hud*, having just been rebuffed by a man.

It wasn't until I turned on the lights that I noticed that Mike had taken some of his Mecca souvenirs with him, the best of his collection of cheesy Mecca knickknacks, including his Mecca snow globe and his Mecca cityscape carved out of cork.

The guy was slowly moving his stuff out of my place. I was losing him, I thought.

"Men! Why do I like them so much?" I asked Louise Bryant, who was scratching at the window. She wanted to go out to visit my neighbor Sally. Lately, she'd been spending a lot of time with Sally. It was like my cat was cheating on me too.

"Don't leave me tonight, Louise," I said to her.

As the Roman poet Ovid said, if you seek a way out of

love, be busy. I had plenty of other stuff to think about, i.e., the Man of the Future series and my interviews the next day with Gill Morton, CEO of Morton Industries, and incendiary man hater Alana DeWitt, who believed men were devolving to extinction.

Despite how lukewarm Benny Winter had been at our dinner meeting, I still hoped he would come through with anthropologist Wallace Mandervan. I had the old boys' network on my side—specifically, my CEO Jack Jackson and Gill Morton of Morton Industries. It was Jack who set me up with Gill Morton, who in turn set me up with Benny Winter. They were powerful allies.

For the next hour, I read through my research and pre-interview notes, until just before 11:00 P.M., when Mike finally called to say Samantha was home and she was okay. She had fallen asleep in the library at school (or so she claimed). He was going to spend the night out at his ex-wife's place in Jersey and fly out from Newark in the early A.M.

"What did you want to tell me?" I asked.

"I can't talk here. Someone's here . . ."

"Give me a hint."

"It can wait."

"Should I worry?"

"No, don't do that. Once you get started you don't stop. It's fine. No big deal. I'm going to be crazy the next few days, but I'll try to call you when I can. If Veronkya calls, will you give her Felicia's number?"

"Oh, I'll be sure to," I said, half wishing I'd replaced the condoms in his shaving kit with the promotional talking condoms a sex magazine sent me when we were doing a series on porn magazines featuring dominant women. I collect talking and singing condoms. A tiny microchip at the base of the condom is activated by body heat to make the penis appear to be talking, in this case, saying, "Bad boy! Baaad boy!" The Hungarian singing condoms were pretty good too.

A talking penis, that'd put the fear of God back into Veronkya. Not that I had any right to complain, not with Gus coming to town.

I'd almost forgotten about Gus.

Mike imagined Gus to be a short, blond doctor in his late thirties, married with two kids, and Lola a raven-haired mistress, or mister, Gus saw whenever he could get away to New York. He couldn't have been more wrong. Gus was a single, hetero, brown-haired actor, five eleven, thirty-eight years old, who liked rock climbing, simultaneously translating Tori Spelling movies into Shakespearean dialogue, and going to a dark restaurant called Mia Cara, where the tablecloths reach all the way to the floor.

I hadn't heard from him for a while.

I called the Boulderado and left a message, "Lola is free."

When I got off the phone, Louise was back scratching at the window.

Sometimes I think the only reason I have her is to keep me from talking to myself, though she also warms up the bed. Bed. That was a good idea. I grabbed Louise Bryant and crawled into bed to watch the news. The day had been jam-packed, my bones were tired, and my bed was criminally comfortable.

Just as I was about to doze off, an anchor intro to a breaking news story jarred me awake.

"The dead man had no ID on him," the anchorman said. "He was wearing a brown suit. The only thing the police found on the body was some Doublemint gum in the jacket pocket. We now go live to Archer Wilkie at Coney Island. Archer?"

According to Archer Wilkie, the body of a white man in late middle age had washed ashore on Coney Island, shortly after sundown, and been discovered by a gang of preteens, who, before they reported the corpse, put a blunt cigar in his mouth and had their pictures taken with it. And then, after they had squeezed all possible fun out of the dead man, they went for the police.

CHAPTER THREE

While we waited for the morgue attendants to locate and pull out the right corpse, Detective June Fairchild, public relations liaison for NYPD Homicide, asked a fair question: "Other than the Doublemint gum, what makes you think this might be the same man you saw on the street?"

"You know my history, June," I said. "I've had several run-ins with people who later ended up as corpses. . . ."

"So have I. It comes with my job, and with yours too, doesn't it?"

Fairchild was a well-pressed, very efficient, and unflappable woman, and just thirty years old. The local media knew her as the "Debutante Detective" because she came from a well-to-do family on the Upper East Side and had gone to Dalton before going on to the John Jay College of Criminal Justice and the NYPD. Despite her connections and fair looks, she had not been a deb, having opted out of the social whirl of the frivolous rich in favor of a career as a crime fighter. Naturally, this made the media love her and her boss, Detective Richard Bigger, resent her.

A logical sort of person, she didn't buy my theory that I was traveling under a curse. True, my job did take me into some hairy corners with some hairy characters, but the murders in my life went beyond that.

"The guy you met had a half package of Doublemint gum . . . not just one piece," Fairchild pointed out.

"The rest might have washed away, or those kids who found the body might have taken it," I said. "There was nothing else found on him?"

"No."

"Distinguishing marks?" I asked.

Fairchild consulted her notepad.

"Port wine birthmark shaped like a small banana on lower back. Tattoo on left bicep, the word 'Fraternité,' " she said with a perfect Parisian accent. "Oh, this is interesting. He only has nine fingers. He's missing the pinky on his left hand."

"Born that way or severed?"

"Not severed recently. But we won't know more until an autopsy is done. Did the man you met have all his fingers?"

"I didn't notice and I think I would have if he was missing a finger," I said. "Does it look like the John Doe was murdered?"

"This one hasn't been classified yet," Fairchild said. "Looks like death by drowning. Could be accident, suicide . . . Even if it is the same guy, I don't know how you can help. You don't remember the car make. You don't remember the license plate number, and you didn't clearly see the faces of the occupants." She sighed. "Robin, I'm reminded of the dead dry cleaner case. Remember that one? You were convinced you knew him and that there was some clue in your laundry receipt."

"That was an easy mistake! He even looked like my dry cleaner."

You wouldn't be a tad paranoid if you'd been involved in several unfortunate murder cases? Whenever a dead body showed up without explanation, I was compelled to find out if there was any connection at all to me, because in the past, if I'd been more alert, if I'd been smarter sooner, I could have saved a life or two, or at the very least, saved myself a whole lot of trouble. The other detectives got sick of talking to me, and Fairchild inherited me. Up to now, she'd been very patient, but today she sounded annoyed. This was what . . . my ninth, tenth such call in the last four or five months? Hardly excessive, all things considered.

"I really hope this is another of your mistaken hunches, Robin, because my boss will be much happier if you're not involved. If he's happier, I'm happier," she said.

"I'll be happier too," I said.

Her boss, Richard Bigger, and I had crossed paths before on homicides, always unpleasantly. He was a stick-up-the-ass guy, what my friend Tamayo would call a "cube," square squared, Joe Friday without the stylish wardrobe and erudite cocktail conversation.

"Bigger really, really doesn't like you," she went on. "Among other things, he seems to think you gave his home phone number to a crackpot neighbor of yours . . . a Mrs. Ramirez who, thank you very much, I have since inherited."

"Is he still pissed about that? I don't know how she got that number," I said.

"Mrs. Ramirez also sees murders everywhere," Fairchild said. "You two should form a club."

"But I have a history of actually being involved in murder cases. She's just nuts," I said. "By the way, I hear she has a gun and I'm fairly certain it's unlicensed."

"I'll have someone from the precinct check it out," she said.

We both knew nothing would be done until old Mrs. Ramirez shot someone. A uniform would inquire if Ramirez had a firearm, she'd deny it, and nothing would happen. It wasn't like the cops and ATF agents were going to storm her apartment to confiscate a gun from an elderly, churchgoing woman with no criminal record. A thing like that can too easily turn into a standoff and a PR disaster.

"We're ready," said the morgue attendant, wheeling in a stainless steel gurney. The body was covered with a pale blue sheet.

"Are you ready?" Fairchild asked me.

Just thinking about seeing a corpse gave me a chill, exacerbated by the morgue's heavy air-conditioning, which made me wrap both hands around my take-out coffee cup, trying to suck warmth out of it.

"Yes," I said.

Fairchild threw back the sheet, revealing the waxy, blue-white face of a bald man I had never seen before.

"Well?" Fairchild said.

"I don't know him."

"Remember, he was in the water for a while. He's slightly bloated."

"The guy I saw had brown hair, a lot of it, and a completely different face and build," I said. "He was wearing a different suit too."

"Well, good. I'm relieved you don't know him. Thanks for coming down, all the same."

"No problem," I said. "It's just such a weird coincidence, the Doublemint gum, I mean."

"A lot of people chew gum. When I learn more from Brooklyn Homicide, I'll call *you*," she said, which was her polite way of saying, "Don't call me."

Though Bigger and Fairchild saw me as some kind of murder fetishist, I was more than happy that the dead guy was a stranger. Not happy for him, poor slob. Whoever he was, he had lived and loved and died too soon. While I was heading to work, it was hard not to wonder about him, who he was and how he ended up dead. And it was hard not to be depressed after a trip to the morgue, with its bright lights, sterility—emotionally and otherwise—the chem lab smell and . . . what was that other thing? Oh yeah. Staring into the face of a dead man and confronting the chilly darkness of oblivion.

That face was hard to shake, but I managed to put it out of my mind as I went into the pink and granite Jackson Broadcasting Building in midtown Manhattan. As Wallace Mandervan wrote in his book, *The Natural Leader*, successful men leave their personal troubles and existential angst outside the workplace. No time now to contemplate the certainty of death and the uncertainty of an afterlife; I had to summon up enough of an air of authority to get me through another day as the Boss.

Just getting to my office these days involved a series of obstacles. To get into the All News Network part of the building, you have to go through a security desk ID check, a metal detector, a series of *Star Trek*–style airlock doors, and past Investigative Reports. There was always a risk of running into either Dr. Solange Stevenson—former TV psychologist and now Barbara Walters clone in the Investigative Reports Unit, whom my ex-husband once referred to as six feet of walking saltpeter, because of her great personal charm—or Reb "Rambo" Ryan, whose sartorial role model was Ernest Hemingway.

Fortunately, neither one was around that morning, so I felt safe stopping to see what was new on Democracy Wall, the ten-foot-long employee bulletin board in the hallway outside the newsroom. The state of Georgia had commissioned a study to select a second method of killing death row inmates, in addition to the primitive electric chair. Some dark-humored ANN wag had posted a contest soliciting suggestions. Topping the list were Batmanesque ideas involving conveyor belts, circular saws, and large, mutant Venus flytraps, along with the simpler, more whimsical methods such as "death by tickling." Near the bottom, one gentle soul had added, "Old age."

Someone else had posted a contest to determine the programming for Jack's new nameless worldwide network, formerly Millennial Broadcasting. This was fairly fresh; the only suggestions so far were the 24-Hour Home Video Network and the 24-Hour Test Pattern Network.

Normally, I'd cut through the newsroom on my way to my offices, but at the moment, I was trying to avoid the newsroom gossips and their peasant-king, producer Louis Levin, lest they try to pry information out of me about Jack Jackson, my "benefactor," as Louis Levin called him in the loaded way he has. So I took the long way, skirting around the newsroom through the warren of feature news offices, science, fashion, medicine, legal, the *Kerwin Shutz* show, to Special Reports, a room of partitioned offices off one of ANN's back hallways.

My miserable employees were waiting for me with questions, complaints, problems, complaints, paperwork, and complaints, which I listened to as I made my own morning coffee (light, four sugars, in a cup that said "Bitch-Boss").

Karim the tape editor had called in sick—again. The company accountants were getting anxious for the quarterly budget figures. During the night, the cleaning people had rearranged the conference area furniture and Liz the associate producer, who was legally blind and litigious, had almost hurt herself.

"Are you going to look after the cleaning situation?" Liz demanded. She was very aggressive for a blind woman, which would have seemed admirable if I hadn't been on the receiving end of it so much of the time.

"Robin, the cleaning crew must move the furniture back exactly where it was before they started cleaning. Otherwise . . ."

"I'll write a memo to maintenance. Anything else?" I asked.

Liz always had a long list of complaints. The air-conditioning was on too high. Her Opticon, the text-reading device she used, was not working properly. How come I hadn't done anything yet about the slippery tile outside the ladies' room?

It was hard work wearing two hats, boss and reporter, in the Special Reports Unit, or as the newsroom called it lately, Village of the Damned, because it had become a repository for every outcast employee the network couldn't fire for one reason or another. There was Liz, Karim, the hypochondriacal tape editor, and Shauna, the production assistant who either had really low self-esteem or no personality at all, I couldn't decide. Plus, I had all the interns rejected by the other units.

This cast of characters arrived after Investigative Reports had pillaged my unit for talent. This is the deal. Jack Jackson went to war with media baron Lord Otterrill for control of Millennial Broadcasting after Millennial's head, Reverend Paul Mangecet, went bankrupt. The company mandarins decided that the network had to be sleeker in order to do battle, and there was a lot of talk about Special Reports being shut down in favor of the higher-profile Investigative Reports Unit. Presumably, Human Resources thought they could replace my staff with the misfits and then fire them all indiscriminately in one fell swoop when my unit closed down, thereby protecting the company from lawsuits.

To the chagrin of the "serious" journalists and Human Resources, Jack Jackson saved Special Reports. Though we had been "saved," it was with the understanding that this reprieve was temporary, until budget time rolled around again in another month and our status was reviewed. By this time, the serious journalists hoped, Jack would have come to his senses. By this time, I hoped, the Man of the Future series would have aired and been a tremendous success.

This series and all my work on it was all that stood between my staff and the unemployment line. But did they appreciate it? No. It was no good telling my staff how lucky they were to have me as a boss, that it could have been so much worse: They could have worked for Jerry Spurdle. Spurdle, my former boss in Special Reports, had once made me pose as his wife for an undercover report on shoddy sperm banks. I avoided further embarrassment on that story by saying unflattering things on camera about Jerry to a nurse, forcing Jerry to cut me out of the edited piece. Then there was the time he had me pose as a "hopeful customer" of a computerized dating service. In this case, I made myself as unattractive as possible, claiming I was thrice widowed with four kids and my hobbies were tournament whist, Court TV, and making my own muumuus. I was looking for "lucky husband number four" and my personal quote was: "You got any money?" Oddly, I got no takers.

The point is, I was a good boss, relatively speaking, and my staff didn't appreciate me. Jerry would have made fun of all their tics and deformities and threatened them with his big drawer full of "résumés of all the people who want to replace you."

I'd tried being the "friend-boss," but that didn't work, because I was so much older than my employees—in their eyes anyway. They were embarrassed to be in the unit, and they took it out on me most of the time. There was not a one of them I trusted, and I suspected someone in the office was responsible for certain rumors about me and Jack Jackson that showed up anonymously in the companywide, computerized rumor file, known as Radio Free Babylon and run by my old friend, producer Louis Levin.

"I'd like you to think again about letting me bring my Seeing Eye dog into work," Liz said.

"Karim's allergic, but I'll talk to Human Resources about it." Whenever possible, pass the buck. "Any calls?"

"Yeah, you got a call yesterday, just after you left, from

some guy. He wanted to know where your dinner meeting was. You met up with him okay, right? Because I forgot to tell you about the call."

"Yes. Benny Winter. We met up. Has he called this morning?"

"No, but Jack Jackson called," said Liz, her voice laden with innuendo.

"Any other calls?"

"A guy named Jason called a couple of times already this morning."

"Jason? Doesn't ring a bell."

"Wouldn't leave a number." She lowered her voice to parody Jason's conspiratorial tone. " 'Phones might not be safe.' Is he a loony?"

"Probably."

"And a Dr. Karen Keyes called. She's presenting at the women's conference . . ."

"Not interested. We have two feminists for our series. If you count that file clip of Gloria Steinem, that's plenty. I'm more interested in what men have to say about their future. Anything else?"

"Here's your fan mail, all of it from that village in India."

"Balandapur." I didn't get much fan mail anymore, and what I did get came mostly from this little village in south India, where villagers had been watching ANN by satellite in their teahouses. Most of my fan mail talked about my carrot-red hair, which was evidently a great topic of conversation in Balandapur. My fan base used to be comprised mainly of masochists who wanted me to hurt them, but the masochists had all deserted me for meaner and/or more powerful goddesses like Xena, Courtney Love, and, inexplicably, Kathie Lee Gifford.

First thing I did was call back Jack Jackson, Our Fearless Leader, aka Daddy Warbucks due to a more than passing resemblance. Jack was working on a speech he was to give at the end of the women's conference and he was looking for "some feedback from some of my women."

"What was the thing you told me the night we went barhopping about urinating standing up?" Jack asked.

"Oh, a trick I learned from an old Girl Scout named Julie," I said. "That's a thing feminists say a lot, the only thing a man can do that a woman can't do is pee standing up. But a little technology—a simple funnel—and you've solved that problem."

"A little technology," Jack repeated. "And didn't we discuss how many names men have for masturbation, while women have none?"

Christ, I must have been really drunk that night. I didn't remember discussing masturbation with the Great Man.

"Possibly," I said.

"What were some of the names men had for it? I've got spanking the monkey, polishing the pipe, stretching the leather, and there was something about Bubba."

"Shucking Bubba," I provided.

"Shucking Bubba. Haw haw."

"What does this have to do with feminism?"

"You'll see, when I give my speech," he said.

He hung up without saying good-bye, as usual, and I turned my attention back to the administrative crap I had to look after before I went to my first interview of the day. While doing an isometric butt-tightening exercise, I speed-wrote memos to maintenance and accounting; then I gulped down my coffee and ran to meet the crew for the first of our Man of the Future interviews.

CHAPTER FOUR

"**W**ho are we shooting?" Sven the sound tech asked when I climbed into the back of the crew car.

"Alana DeWitt, the mother of modern feminism," I said. "Followed by Dr. Budd Nukker, and Gill Morton, CEO of Morton Industries."

"Gill Morton?" Jim the cameraman repeated after me, visibly thrilled. "No shit. My dad was a Morton Man for years. Did they have Morton Men in Sweden, Sven?"

"Yeah, my uncle was one."

When you hear the words Morton Company, you too probably think of the Morton Man, a guy with a sample case flogging cleaning products door-to-door. Of course, Morton was no longer just a door-to-door outfit peddling patent medicines and Morton Mopwash to the lonely and the housebound. After World War Two, it branched out into automotive products, plastics, and household appliances. According to the press packet, since Gill had taken over in the 1970s, the company had expanded into food products, pharmaceuticals, cosmetics, building materials, and tableware. If you look in your cupboards and medicine chest, you probably have something made by Morton or one of its subsidiaries. One sub had a defense contract to make electrical switches for guided-missile systems, another to set up private prisons in Texas. It was a long way from the original Morton Man, Hock Morton, who in 1887 started the company by selling soap and scrub brushes door-to-door in Brooklyn, dispensing his folksy wisdom for free.

"My dad was one for a summer," I said.

"Did he have the jacket? The suspenders?" Jim asked.

"I don't know. He didn't do it for very long."

"Jeez, my dad had all the crap, whaddya call it. Memorabilia. Some of it is worth money now," Jim said.

"But before we interview Morton, we interview Alana De-Witt. By the way, if she asks, you're both gay men."

"What?" Jim said. "I'm not gay. I have a wife and two kids. . . ."

"She hates men," I explained. "But she hates gay men less than straight men. I couldn't find an all-female crew and this was the only way she'd agree to do the interview."

As the antimatter Will Rogers—never met a man she liked—CUNY professor DeWitt was so paranoid and hated men so much that she insisted only women reporters interview her. That was a noble kind of gesture back in the days of Eleanor Roosevelt, when women journalists were denied access to important briefings, but these days it just seemed petty and mean, though totally in character for DeWitt. Among her other interview eccentricities, she didn't like discussing specific men, only men in general. This way, you couldn't confuse her or trip her up with examples of men who went against the "norms" that she railed against.

We were met at the door of her Greenwich Village town house by DeWitt's niece and personal assistant, a doughy-faced young woman with rimless glasses. After showing us into De-Witt's study, she excused herself and closed the door.

There was some muffled arguing outside—I couldn't make out the words—and DeWitt came in. DeWitt was in her sixties, of average weight, average height, with long hair dyed jet-black. All her wrinkles pointed downward. She scared the shit out of me.

"I have a question for you to begin with, Ms. Hudson," DeWitt said, usurping control of the interview immediately.

"Yes?"

"You're a woman. There's a big women's conference in town. How come you're doing a story about the *Man* of the Future?" she asked, suspicious. "Women are the story."

No doubt about it, women were hot, I agreed. The politicians had discovered the gender gap, companies had discovered women's megaspending power, and Soccer Moms swayed the presidential election. Employers were sponsoring on-site day care centers and parental leaves in record numbers to lure and keep talented women on their staffs and Madison Avenue was falling all over itself to play to dames. Though feminism was in disarray, women overall were doing well.

"It seems obvious that, generally speaking, women will just continue getting stronger, smarter, sexier, more secure, and more independent, wielding increasing influence over society and the world, from the workplace and from the home," I said, and I wasn't *just* spouting the party line. I believed it. "What I can't get a grip on is how all this will affect men, generally speaking, and how men will adapt to it or rebel against it."

"They'll do neither for very long," she said, and went into her usual rap, women were evolving, men were not, the Y chromosome was devolving, and women would rule the world in the foreseeable future. When Alana DeWitt talks, don't even try to interrupt her until she takes a deep breath, because she'll just talk louder and roll right over you. As she spoke her face grew redder and redder, in splotches, like a rash.

"But let's say we *don't* evolve beyond men. In that case, how do you see men evolving, and adapting to evolving women?"

"I don't. That is why we must evolve beyond them. They're brutes," she said.

"You can't envision any scenario where men will evolve enough so you could get along with them, just for argument's sake?" I asked. "What if they refuse to become extinct?"

"Nature will take care of it," she said. "The Y chromosome will grow smaller and weaker and I believe fewer and fewer male children will be conceived until men just disappear."

To lighten the genocidal tone of things a bit, she told a feminist joke from *Hysteria* magazine, about the army's new weapon, the estrogen bomb. You drop it and all the combatants throw down their arms, hug, and cry out, "I'm sorry. It's all my fault."

"Seriously, though," I said. "The estrogen bomb would only work if all the women had aligned menstrual cycles and were all postmenstrual and in Good Jesus mode . . ."

"Good Jesus mode?" she said.

Now I'd done it. Lost control of my tongue and blurted out the name of a very specific man.

"Humble, self-sacrificing, I-feel-your-pain Jesus," I explained.

"As opposed to . . ."

"Mean Jesus, turn the other cheek, and if that one gets slapped too, kick 'em where it hurts and run like hell. You know, tearing through the temple overturning money changer tables," I said. "Like when you're premenstrual . . ."

"I'm the same way no matter the time of month. And you were clearly warped by patriarchal religion. This interview is over now."

With that, she rose, her fists clenched, and stormed out of the room like a stevedore. Didn't much matter that she was pissed off—the woman was always pissed off—and we had what we needed, a few provocative sound bites from a so-called expert, a controversial, academic feminist.

DeWitt got me thinking about the John Doe again. Now there was one less man, or "testosterone-addled mammal" to use her preferred term, on earth for her to worry about. Somehow, I knew that DeWitt would have been cheered by this. For all her talk about the moral superiority and caring-sharing ethos of women, she was sure lacking in the milk of human kindness her own self. Speaking of violence . . . the woman was known to be a terror on a book tour and had allegedly bitch-slapped a small Mexican man in her Acapulco hotel last year because of a reservation mix-up.

Maybe it was as Wallace Mandervan had said in an article a couple years before, that people crazy enough to envision utopias usually design utopias they themselves could never live in because of their nutty individualism. If DeWitt got her all-woman world, it would just be a matter of time before she'd try to take power, purging disloyal women. Before you know it, it would be a full-fledged Reign of Terror, and women like me would end up with our heads in straw baskets.

Back in the crew car, Jim the cameraman said, "She's full of shit, isn't she? About that Y chromosome stuff?"

"Face it. You guys are going the way of the dodo and the passenger pigeon," I said. "Just kidding. Yeah, she's full of shit. The next guy thinks you guys will not only survive, but live longer than ever."

The next interview, Dr. Budd Nukker, was a biochemist, a nutritionist, and an Extropian.

"Extropians aim for nothing less than literal immortality," said Nukker, a muscular, healthy man who looked much younger than his seventy years. He was doing the interview while on a treadmill. He had wires running from his wrist and neck to various bodily monitors—our mike was wireless—and periodically he took big sips from a bottle of electrolyte-rich water.

"We believe a regimen of exercise, grain-based diet, vitamin, hormone, and enzyme therapies, along with advances in medical technology, will make immortality possible in our lifetimes," Nukker said. "Current research indicates that men with no vices who do only the exercise and diet part of the regimen could live to be a hundred and forty. By the time they are a hundred and forty, further advances will make immortality conceivable."

"But you have to spend almost all your free time working out and you eat nothing but macrobiotics," I said.

"Yes," he said, not seeing my point.

"Forever is a long time if you're not having any fun," I said.

"This is more fun than being dead," he said, turning off the treadmill and detaching his wires. While stretching, he talked about some of the hundred or so pills he took every day and then informed us it was time for his weekly hormone shot, which he gave himself in his ass.

This seemed a propitious time to wrap up the interview and break the crew for lunch at Tycoon Doughnut. Keeping with my practice of multitasking, I called in for messages on my cell phone while I ate. That Jason person had called again, and my friend Tamayo had called from Tokyo to say she would be returning to New York "in a few weeks," which could mean tomorrow or could mean next month, after a stop in Cairo or Budapest. With Tamayo, a comic actress and free woman . . . excuse me, "struggling demi-goddess on a great adventure," you just never knew.

Benny Winter had not called.

That was a good sign, I figured, a very good sign, because an outright refusal would have come much quicker.

June Fairchild of the NYPD had called. When I returned the call, she asked, "Is your unit Special Reports or Investigative Reports?"

"Special Reports. Why?"

"Because someone from the Investigative Reports Unit at ANN just called me, wanted to know why you were at the morgue this morning."

"What did you say?"

"That you came in to ID a John Doe, but you didn't recognize him, and I told him what I told you about the John Doe. I don't have any new information."

"Thanks," I said.

This was amusing. Reb Ryan and Solange Stevenson, those story stealers in Investigative, thought I was on to a story with the John Doe. Someone in homicide must have tipped them off about my visit. Ha. If I wasn't so, you know, mature, and Taking the High Road, I might aid and abet them by feeding them a few false leads. . . .

"Time to go," Jim said, wiping his mouth with the flimsy paper napkin. He was eager, which was unusual, but understandable. At lunch, after he finished trashing Alana DeWitt, he had talked to Sven about growing up with a picture of Gill Morton on the mantelpiece, as if Gill were one of the family. When we got to the Morton Building, Jim was like a kid in a toy store, bug-eyed and slack-jawed with fresh awe.

"Mr. Morton will be right down," the security guard said.

We waited in the pre–art deco lobby, a great hall with vaulted archways, brass and glass lamps, high ceilings, and lots of marble inscribed with the quotes of Teddy Roosevelt— "I am only an average man but, by George, I work harder at it than the average man"—and Hock Morton: "a man makes his own luck." It reeked of manhood.

One wall was hung with portraits of Morton men. The biggest of these was of founder Hock Morton. Hock Morton had bushy gray hair and a handlebar mustache. Judging by the expression on his face, he hadn't been having a good day when he'd sat for this portrait back in, according to the brass plaque beneath it, 1929.

His son, Gray Morton, on the other hand, looked blankly sober, Gray's son, Herbert, looked frail and sad, and Herbert's son, William, stern and sturdy. William's son, Gill Morton, robust and ruddy-cheeked, had chosen to be painted in out-doorsman gear, his retriever at his side. None of the men resembled one another in the least.

Below the portraits were display cases with the original Morton products: the Morton Mop, the Morton Scrub Brush, Morton Soap, and an antique bottle of Morton Mopwash.

At the other end of the hall was a statue of an angel holding a fallen doughboy under one arm.

Within five minutes, Gill Morton, a stocky, florid man with a blond brush cut, strode into the lobby. He seemed taller in his portrait, but maybe that was because the portrait was about twenty feet high. Behind him came his assistant, a young man named Ken Duffin, who handed me a packet of old press ads and some videos I had requested. Behind Duffin was Morton's security detail, five beefy guys in black suits.

I introduced the crew and Jim mentioned that he had met Morton before, when Jim was seven and his dad had won a big sales award which he had kept with his most private things until the day he died. Morton was most gracious. He seemed touched and gave Jim a two-handed handshake, and in keeping with my careful study of men, especially men in power, I noticed that Morton didn't feel the urge in the face of praise to immediately self-deprecate. Jim was tickled and I was glad for that too, because I was trying to be extra nice to Jim, on account of his wife having a second baby and . . . what was that other thing . . . oh yeah, because he was a lousy cameraman. Our several talks about improvements had yielded nothing, and I was going to have to demote him back to sound tech soon, a task I was putting off.

Morton had a weird voice, stiff, moderately deep, earnest, and totally fake-sounding. He sounded like the dubbed voice of Hercules or Sinbad in a cheesy foreign film from the fifties or sixties. You half expected to see his lips move out of sync with his words. It was hard to keep a straight face when talking to him.

After a few ham-handed pleasantries, Morton said, "Now, on to Phase Two."

With a half wave, half salute to the crowd, he strode off with his men, me, and the crew scrambling to follow him through steel doors and a long hallway to the Phase Two Annex, a building next to the Morton Building that Gill Morton had purchased in order to convert it into the workplace of the future.

Duffin put his hand against a laser reader of some kind and another big steel door opened automatically.

"After you," Morton said to everyone.

We went into a large office area, empty except for us. It was bright but not too bright—it had a soft, diffuse light—and clean, in pale cheery colors, with no sharp corners on any of the "ergonomically designed" office furniture. There were no windows.

As soon as Gill Morton stepped through the door, the room said, in a female voice, "Good morning, Mr. Morton. Don't you look handsome!"

Morton laughed. "Couldn't resist having the programmers do that," he said, and led us through the unpeopled office, divided by semicircular partitions that allowed a small measure of privacy without making employees "feel boxed in."

"This will be the ultimate in smart buildings when it is done. Just the technology in this part of the building alone involves over four hundred new patents," Morton said. "It's completely hypoallergenic. Sensors read each employee's bar code. This tells the room what the employee's temperature, allergies, and Muzak preferences are, and the main computer determines what will be acceptable to the most employees."

"They'll wear this bar code somewhere on their person?" I asked.

"To begin with," he said, flashing a smart badge containing encoded information about him. "Ultimately, we'll just implant a chip in their brains." Then he winked and laughed, and I knew he was joking about the brain chip. With eccentric moguls, you can't be too sure sometimes.

"We're also experimenting with high-oxygen air and hope to install a ventilation system that filters out radioactivity and destroys biological agents," Morton went on, not laughing, and not winking.

"Why?"

"Who knows what the world will be like five, ten, fifty years from now. Even a year from now," he said. "We're going to do everything we can to make this building a refuge. This is all we have to show right now. The rest of the building is still under construction."

Eventually, he said, he hoped to convert the next block to apartment buildings and services for his employees, and do the same thing with each of his plants.

When Morton opened the door to leave, the room said, "Good-bye, Mr. Morton. Come back soon. I'll miss you."

On the way out, Morton stopped in front of the dead doughboy statue and gave us the familiar history of Hock Morton and the Morton Company. People in the lobby began to gather around to watch—tourists, delivery guys, visiting "Morton Families" wearing special buttons. The crowd was respectful and stood back quietly, and though that may have had something to do with the security detail, it seemed to have something to do with Gill Morton too. The man had presence, an aura of power and vision.

"Remember: Courage, tenacity, and responsibility, that's what makes a man, in the past, in the present, and into the future," Morton said. "Look, there's the courage of the common man, the courage that Morton has always supported and honored."

He gestured toward the angel and doughboy.

Behind the statue was a large copper plaque, almost as big as the wall, listing Morton employees who had given their lives in this century's many wars. There were at least a thousand of them. If you stand in that lobby and squint, you can imagine it is 1917, that the clerks and office boys are leaving their jobs to go off to some strange country to shoot Prussians and such. (It was sad, and only served to underscore Alana DeWitt's point about men and war. Still, I couldn't help wondering if women hadn't provoked a war or two. We sure had supported a few. I remembered some old, jerk-time film footage I saw once that showed the streets full of doughboys and old women on corners handing out white flowers, to symbolize cowardice, to any man who had not enlisted.)

There was a small ethical problem in using Gill Morton in the series. We were essentially providing free advertising to the Morton Company at a time when our CEO Jack Jackson was courting Gill Morton to get some of his paid advertising. Call me suspicious, but I figured this was why Jack suggested I use Gill Morton and his archives in our series, to curry favor.

But Phase Two was too good to pass up over piddling ethical things, and when you threw in the Morton archives, it was irresistible. For example, one of the videos Morton's man Duffin had given me was a tape copy of a film that had run in the Morton pavilion at the 1964 World's Fair. The 1964 video would give us a RetroFuture angle, visions of our future from our past, to contrast with current visions. It would work especially well intercut with footage of the Phase Two Workplace of the Future.

Narrated by a bland, soothing male voice, the kind prevalent in educational films and advertising in the fifties and sixties, the 1964 Morton video guided us room by room through the brave new world. There was the kitchen with the perfunctory robot servants (actors in costumes clearly) doing household chores or giving the missus a manicure. The bedrooms had voice-activated lights, automatic pillow fluffers, and for the children, robot nannies to tuck them in and read them stories. The den had a giant wall television and a bar that mixed drinks with the press of a button. They managed to avoid the bathroom completely, so evidently we won't be seeing any space-age toilets or automatic ass wipers.

Still, it was full of surprises. In the workplace of the Retro-Future, computers are really huge and do most of the work, all the secretaries are robots, and, of course, everyone zips around from home to work in rockets. Doctors smoke, of course, and their brand of choice is Morton Bolds. You may recall the slogan for Morton Bolds, "Calm your fears—with a Morton Bold." Who knew courage could be inhaled? (Taken off the market after the tobacco arm of Morton was sold to Smith Tobacco in 1970, Bolds were also the cigarette of choice for Olympic swimmer Loffy Moffat, war hero Widdy Boone, and Father Frank Carpus, who smoked them while delivering his five-minute inspirational message at the end of the *Morton Bold Variety Hour*, which ran until 1956, when Father Carpus was found unconscious in bed with a dead Hollywood starlet, his opium pipe on the bedside table. But you probably know all this.)

In the year 2001, men will drink highballs and smoke cigarettes and women will be pampered by machines. And everyone in the future is white. Who knew? Boy, Yogi Berra was right. The future ain't what it used to be.

CHAPTER FIVE

"When you were a kid, did you think the world would turn out this way?" I asked my cabdriver that evening. The cabbie had already told me that he thought being a man meant being strong, brave, and taking care of his family. The man had been quite cheerful when I got into the car, and so far, we had been talking like two human beings. But for some reason, this question rattled him.

"No, I thought the Palestinians would have a homeland and I'd be a millionaire with a beautiful wife," he said sharply. After that he just glowered as he drove. In one fell swoop I had taken a happy man and turned him into a depressive. Not that that hadn't happened before . . .

When the cab pulled up to my street, my elderly neighbor Mrs. Ramirez was just leaving, going out with her Chihuahua on one of her crime-fighting rounds, no doubt.

"Take me around the corner and down the block toward Eighth Street," I said to the driver. "Drop me there."

As he pulled away, I ducked down to escape the woman's vicious but unreliable gaze. My theory was, Dulcinia Ramirez had an air bubble in one of her cerebral arteries or something, in addition to a huge rough stick up her ass. She looked at me and saw the Devil Incarnate, thought at various times that I was a call girl, a transvestite, a drug dealer, a madam, a child abuser—basically an all-around agent of iniquitous infection. Oh, and she was violent. More than once I'd felt the smack of her mighty oak cane on the top of my head and was unable to defend myself because she's a tiny Catholic lady in her eighties with blue hair and pearls. Pummeling the elderly, even in self-defense, is frowned upon in our society—not to mention an awful hard sell to a jury. Recently, Mrs. R. had given up her cane in favor of her pistol. I'd always believed she needed the cane to walk, but it turned out she'd just used it as a weapon, before she joined the arms race.

The cab dropped me in front of a mom-and-pop bodega, a vanishing breed in the increasingly gentrified East Village, where I bought the evening newspapers, a piece of beige milk fudge from a large glass jar on the counter, and a six-pack of beer.

"You need two *Posts*?" The young guy behind the counter asked. Or that's what I heard. He seemed to have trouble with English.

"You need two *News-Journals*?"

"Uh, no, just one is fine," I said, and wondered if his English was this bad all the time, if he asked customers nonsensical questions all day or just hadn't really grasped the concept of suggestive selling. Had to be hard, coming to a strange country and trying to make a go of it without being fluent in the language.

Walking back from the store, I ate my milk fudge and read the *News-Journal*, which had a small blip on the John Doe I'd seen at the morgue that morning. The only new info on John Doe was that a waitress named Gina at Erin's Coffee House had identified him as an eccentric customer known only as Frenchie.

A lone dead man was a small story to the *News-Journal*. A

bigger story was the update on the bees, a swarm of which had taken a sudden dislike to a bond trader, who was stung twenty-seven times and now calling for the extermination of the bees.

An even bigger story was the one on Jack Jackson on page 5.

"JACK JACKSON —FRIEND OF WOMEN? OR A WOLF IN SHEEP'S CLOTHING?" asked the headline.

Underneath this was an old photo of a much younger Jack Jackson slapping a famous feminist on the ass at the 1972 Democratic Convention and calling her "Honey," according to the caption.

The text mentioned that Jack was the only man invited to speak on the last day of the women's conference, and suggested this was a sellout by women on account of Jack's massive sponsorship, along with other corporate giants, of the festivities. A collection of photos paired with historic quotes, or perhaps misquotes, from Jack followed, such as this one, from the early 1970s: "If God wanted women to be men, he would have made 'em men."

Jack had, I was sure, changed his views since he made that comment. Also his clothes. Another picture showed a drunken, partying Jack at Studio 54. He was dressed in tight black satin bell-bottoms and a yellow shirt unbuttoned to his navel, and he still had hair then, a shaggy brown afro.

In a similar vein and around the same time, Jack had commented on the feminist truism, "If men had babies, they'd give out medals for it."

"If men had babies," Jack had said, "they'd be women."

Lord Otterrill, who owned the *News-Journal*, was no historic friend of women and had once said that women were a lot more sensitive, vindictive, and petty than men. But that didn't stop this overly sensitive sore loser from seizing the vindictive opportunity to poke Jack in the eye with a sharp stick. With a gossipy story, no less! Men are such gossips.

The coast was clear on Tenth Street. Mrs. Ramirez was

nowhere to be seen. Sitting on my stoop was a young man in a baseball cap, bearing the logo of a famous hamburger chain, and dark glasses. When I approached, he said, "Hudson?"

"Yes."

"I need to talk to you. Do you know my friend Dewey? I think you might be in danger."

He took the glasses off. It was the crazy vegetarian.

"What do you want?" I asked.

"My name is Jason, and I need to talk to you."

"You're the Jason who has been calling? How did you get my address?" I asked. "It's unlisted."

"It wasn't easy, but I have ways. Hear me out, all right?"

"You're not gonna run away this time?"

"No. I've checked you out. You're sort of a respectable journalist, and your CEO Jack Jackson is a big supporter of environmental causes."

"Thanks. What's with the hat?"

"I'm incognito," he said, putting the sunglasses back on.

"Oh, I get it. The hamburger logo is to make you look like you're *not* a vegetarian. That's clever."

"I think you might know my friend Dewey," he said.

"And Dewey is?"

"My friend who is in the hospital, in a coma."

"I don't know anyone by that name. This Dewey, is he young? Old?"

"He's in his twenties."

Dewey wasn't the man in the hat or the John Doe then. "Heavy? Thin? Blond? Brunette?"

"Tall, blond, thin. I don't have a photo. He was beaten up yesterday, our offices were burgled, and I think it has to do with that hat-wearing man you met, because I found your name in Dewey's notes."

"My name?"

"Yes. Can we go to your apartment and talk? I don't feel safe out here on the street."

Let a stranger into my apartment. Let me think.

"No," I said. But the next second, Mrs. Ramirez rounded the corner of Avenue C, and I changed my mind. "Aw hell, come on up. But don't try anything funny."

"What would I try with you?" he asked.

I waved him ahead of me into the building and followed him onto the elevator.

"You're old enough to be my aunt or something."

"How old are you?" I asked.

"Twenty-one."

"I'm old enough to be your mother. Christ. Well, all the same, let me warn you. I beat the last person who messed with me with her own comatose granny. That's just for starters."

Not only did I have pepper spray, I had six bottles of beer that could do some damage.

"I'm not going to mess with you. Shit."

No, he was loony, but he was not evil, just young and idealistic, a Sonny Boy in the parlance of my girlfriends and me.

"So my name is in your friend's notes. What do these notes say?"

" 'Asking questions. Hudson.' "

"And you think that's me? We have a Hudson River, a Hudson Street, lots of companies with that name, at least two other reporters named Hudson in this town."

"Yeah, but you're the one who showed up with our address in your hand."

"Hmmm. Good point. This is my apartment. Excuse the mess. The maid's in detox. . . . Why was your friend Dewey beaten up?"

"I don't know. That's what I'm trying to find out. Look, I'm trusting you because I don't know where else to turn."

"How about the police?"

"The police are lackeys of the corporations," Jason said. "They are part of the conspiracy."

I thought, Oh Christ, another fucking paranoid conspiracy theorist. In Special Reports, we hear from a lot of them, obsessives who've been sitting in their mothers' basements for the last thirty-some years thinking about what really happened on the grassy knoll in Dallas, to hunched-over men with wild eyes who want to warn the world about the existence of the "inner earth people" (who were feeling a tad cramped in the bowels of the planet, and would soon be coming aboveground to conquer us surface dwellers). Add to that the small businessmen who think big business is engaged in a conscious conspiracy to drive them under and shut-ins who think the guy next door is a serial killer, and you have an idea why all my calls are screened by my staff to weed out the nutcases, small-timers, and hoaxers.

"Can I see these notes?"

"Before I say anything else, this has to be off-the-record."

"Yeah, okay, sure."

He pulled a folded yellow sheet of paper out of his pocket and handed it to me. It was from a legal pad.

"This was all I found. Whoever broke into our offices took the computers and every scrap of paper they could carry. I found this down the back of the desk."

At the top it said, over and over in a childish scrawl, "bonobos." Down a few inches, he had scribbled, "Asking questions. Hudson." And below that, "Why?"

"What are bonobos?" I asked.

"Chimps."

"Now who are you exactly?"

"I'm with PACA, People Against Cruelty to Animals. So is Dewey."

"And you think Dewey's beating had something to do with his work for PACA?"

"I don't know. I was in South America, like I said. Just got back . . ."

"And the others who presumably work there. They don't know anything?"

"Dewey is secretive," Jason said.

"What kind of work does Dewey do?"

"Animal liberations mainly."

"Let me get this straight. You think that man in a hat didn't stumble into me by accident. You think your friend Dewey, under an assumed name in a hospital, knows me and his beating is connected to the man in the hat and some chimps."

"Right."

"Where is he, Dewey?" I asked.

"In a hospital, under an assumed name. We're moving him soon to a private clinic."

"Of course, an assumed name. Could I see your friend Dewey?"

"Why?" Jason asked, and now he sounded suspicious. "He's in a coma, he can't tell you anything."

I was a tad suspicious myself. Though Jason appeared to be a Sonny Boy, I was beginning to smell a rat, maybe because I'd once been scammed on an animal rights story. If Dewey had my name, maybe it was from that story. Maybe he was the rotten little shit who set me up. Maybe the lost man in the hat wasn't lost at all, but one of their co-conspirators.

"I only have your word that this Dewey exists," I said.

"You don't believe me!"

"I don't have much to go on."

"Why do . . . uh, there's a cat at your window."

Louise Bryant, somehow sensing I was home, had come back from her day at Sally's to cadge a meal. After carefully moving the poison ivy I grew in planters as a form of delayed justice for anyone who broke into my apartment, I opened the window, and Louise darted in and began weaving around my legs and rubbing up against me affectionately, her way of kissing my ass.

"Did Dewey by any chance have Doublemint gum on him when he was found?" I asked.

"It wasn't in his personal effects. Why?"

"I just wondered."

Louise Bryant will be ignored for only so long and then she adopts more emphatic tactics, like taking a clawed swipe at my leg.

"Excuse me, I have to feed my cat. Want a beer?"

"Sure."

Louise Bryant beat me to the kitchen, meowing for her special dinner, Aloof & Fussy cat food sautéed with bok choy, which I had prepared in bulk so I could just micro it. One whiff of steaming animal flesh and Jason the vegetarian was up in arms.

"Do you have to cook meat while I'm here?" he said.

"Unless you want to fight it out with my half-mad cat, and she's meaner than me," I called out to him from the kitchen. "It's for her. But I'm planning to have a big raw steak later."

I let the hot cat meal cool for a moment while I poured Jason a small glass of beer, not wanting him to stay for a full bottle.

"So you're one of those people who only likes cute, domestic animals," he said. "And doesn't give a damn about the . . ."

"Ugly, disease-carrying ones?" I said.

I went into the living room and handed him the glass before sitting down in the armchair across from him.

"Not just them," he said. "Do you eat chicken?"

"Yeah, sometimes. Why?"

"Don't you like chickens? Aren't they cute enough for you?"

"Depends on the chicken," I said.

Funny that he picked the chicken, and not, say, the indefensible cockroach. The night Jack Jackson and I had gone out, Jack had asked me about the last time I *unexpectedly* cried about a story. That's one of the things you find as a newswriter and a reporter—when you follow a story long enough, you can lose your detachment. There were plenty of stories that had sent me from my typewriter to the ladies' room to weep in a stall. Most of these were understandable, deaths of children, Princess Diana, etc.

But the last story that surprised me by moving me to tears . . . it's odd, I guess, but it was the death of Mr. Chicken. Mr. Chicken was this chicken whose legs froze off, and so a doctor made him little prosthetic legs, with square wood platforms for feet. Mr. Chicken adapted, and managed quite well on his little legs, until one night when he died defending his henhouse from some marauding carnivore like a dog or a raccoon. There wasn't much left of Mr. Chicken, except the little legs.

Before his death, the Mr. Chicken story was a "squirrel on water skis," a cute animal with talent and chutzpah doing something unusual—on videotape. It's an "evergreen" piece that can run anytime. But his tragic death defending his hens against a bigger, stronger rival elevated that story. Boy, did Mr. Chicken valiantly refute the stereotype of the chicken. I know I wasn't the only hardened, cynical, ego-driven journalist who had a good nose-blower over that one. RIP Mr. Chicken.

But I didn't tell Jason this. Something about him brought out my contrary side.

"Who has time to care about all the people who live and die in the world except in a global, abstract way, let alone every last lab rat or chicken? Unless it is a special lab rat or chicken," I said.

"That's so Nazi . . ."

"You know, Hitler was a vegetarian who tamed baby deer at his Berchtesgaden retreat. Makes you think, don't it? Hypothetically speaking, I'd give every baby deer in Berchtesgaden and plenty more if it meant Anne Frank, for example, or any other person, didn't have to die. I'd give every Ted Bundy type and maybe a few Al Bundys—and maybe you too on a bad day—to save one baby deer. This is known as the Baby Deer/Bundy formula. In the future, before you jump on me, do the math."

He started to say something to challenge this argument, which is admittedly simplistic, but I shushed him in my best schoolmarm fashion, which I've found is often effective with young men.

"Well, Jason, thanks for the information. I have work to do. If there's nothing else . . ."

"Let me give you my emergency number. It reaches our beeper central. You can leave a message with them. Don't call on a cell phone. Use a pay phone whenever possible if you're leaving a message."

"Why?"

"Other phones aren't safe."

"Oh. Okay. Or, you could just call me if you have some new information, real information."

"You don't care," he sneered. "For some reason, I thought you were a human being beneath that corporate uniform."

"Enough. I am a really busy person right now, okay? I have a story, Man of the Future, FYI, and my job and the jobs of my staff depend on its success."

He swallowed the last of his penurious allotment of beer and left. From my window, I watched to make sure he actually left my building.

He seemed self-righteous enough to be a real animal rights person, but that didn't let him off the hook. I've played my share of pranks, and I've fallen for my share, and one big one involved some rotten animal rights nuts.

So, maybe I was being set up, the way I was set up on a mad cow beef hoax story earlier that year, a story that ran on a day that would later be known downtown as "Meat Is Murder, Dairy Is Rape, Day." On that day, animal rights activists launched an all-night campaign of mischief and vandalism during which those words, Meat Is Murder, etc., were painted on a number of grocery stores, BBQ joints, kosher dairies, and ice cream parlors.

The mad cow *non*story led to my humiliating on-air retraction: "I was completely mistaken when I reported that mad cows from Britain had been brought to this country and insinuated into herds bound for the New American Meatpackers slaughterhouses. I was completely mistaken when I reported that frozen meat from mad cows had been shipped from New American Meatpackers to supermarkets all over the Midwest. The president of New American, Bill Carlan, is not 'an irresponsible megalomaniac insensitive to consumer concerns in pursuit of a bloody butcher's dollar,' as one of our sources called him. ANN and I personally extend our apologies to Mr. Carlan and his many satisfied customers."

We were damned lucky we didn't get sued. It was only because of Jack Jackson's personal intervention that we didn't end up in court, Jack's intervention, plus free advertising time on Jack's all-sports network and my on-air retraction that ran hourly for two days. Somehow, Jack convinced Bill Carlan that a lawsuit would bring New American Meatpackers more bad than good publicity.

But you'd fall for a hoax like that too, I bet, if you had witnesses (who later vanished), shipping documents (faked), vet reports (forged), and a video of black-clad people smuggling the alleged "mad cows" into an existing herd.

And you might rush it to air too, in order to keep Solange and Reb from stealing the story out from under you.

Would those mad cow hoaxers have the nerve to try to scam me a second time? I wondered. It seemed unlikely, but maybe that unlikeliness made a second hoax all the more brilliant. Fool me once, shame on you. Fool me twice, shame on me.

There was only one way to make sure I didn't get scammed a second time: drop the whole thing. Jason had managed to push a couple of my buttons and make me curious. But the truth is, even if Jason's tale was a real story, if Dewey and the man in the hat had taken a drubbing in an effort to liberate some chimps, it wasn't a story for Special Reports. Animal liberation stories, if they ran on ANN at all, were done as quick voice-overs or on-cam readers.

If the John Doe had been connected to it, it would have been a different story. As it stood, my time would be better spent reading up on the next day's interviews and getting ready for my date the following night with Gus, or as my friends referred to him, the Liar. On our seven dates in the past eight months, Gus and I communicated almost exclusively with lies, if we talked at all.

Gus and I had met the previous autumn at a party and art show opening down in SoHo, a group show featuring seven artists, all unusual. I was there with my friend Tamayo, who had just started dating Herve, a guy who painted with his own blood, which limited his output considerably. Unfortunately, the previous night, after he finished the piece for this show, he put it down on the floor to dry and his Doberman ate it. His dog ate his painting. He was still distraught the night of the art show, and while Tamayo consoled him, I wandered off to mingle and see the other paintings and artwork. At the complimentary Skyy martini bar, Gus and I had amazing eye contact over the heads of three other people. (At the time, I thought it was a magic look of recognition between strangers, but later I saw him on TV and realized I recognized him from commercials.)

I made my way to him, but he spoke first, asking me what I thought of the show. After I told him about the dog who ate the painting, Gus told me about his family's salmon cannery and how when he was a kid he had this pet salmon named Harry. Harry was so named because the fish had a freakish tuft of hairlike bristles at the back of its head, like a balding man. According to Gus, this anomaly made Harry stand out, a fish among fish, and saved him from the tin can. Sometimes, Gus said, he'd put Harry in a bucket and take him outside for a walk.

Playing along, I told him my name was Lola and I worked at a Think Tank where the taxpayers paid me obscene amounts of money to think about whatever the hell I wanted. Our motto was "Don't worry your pretty little head about it. Leave the thinking to us!" Gus and I got drunker and just went with the lying game until we ran out of lies. Then we made out for a while in the art gallery office. We had sex on our second date, after I'd checked the various databases to make sure he wasn't a serial killer on the lam and after I saw him act in a commercial on TV.

Obviously, we didn't lie about details—times and places we'd meet, etc. We only lied about important things, like who we were and what our lives were like. Granted, it sounds nuts, but it had its own weird logic. We could say whatever the hell we wanted and not have it mean anything, so the usual mood-killers, the power and control issues, or worse, overfamiliarity, were absent. That's why this thing, this role play, worked for us—keeping the reality and the talking to a minimum.

Gus, an actor, was so much better at this than I was, and I always felt like I needed to have a prepared lie in advance of seeing him. Afterward, I'd need to prepare another lie in case Mike called the following day and asked me what I'd done the night before. Mike tended to get jealous if he heard anything about me and any other man, which was silly, given that Mad Mike was traveling with a circus full of sultry East European women in sequin bodysuits and surely not thinking of me at the moment.

Tonight I was drawing a blank and couldn't come up with even one good lie. Every time I tried to think of a lie, the face of the dead John Doe appeared. Every time I tried to fantasize about Gus, he had the face of the dead John Doe. I couldn't shake it away.

CHAPTER SIX

Curiosity is the number one killer of cats and bumbling quasi-investigative reporters, a lesson I can't seem to learn.

Against my better instincts, I got up early the next morning and took a trip to Erin's Coffee House to talk to the woman who had, according to the *News-Journal*, identified the John Doe.

Most of the crowd was male and older, in their fifties and sixties, white, black, Hispanic, and evidently all blue-collar, a hard way to make a living for so many years. More than a few hats in here. The only other woman in the place was the waitress. An old-timey Irish coffee shop, painted green with paper shamrocks on the walls advertising the specials, it was now owned by Greeks, who had proudly put snapshots of their children and grandchildren up on the wall between the square glass-and-steel dessert case and a shelf bearing two loaves of square bread and a King Edward cigar box overflowing with receipts. In a more jarring juxtaposition, the take-out coffee came in white, minimalist paper cups advertising www.sidewalk.com. The cups were the only thing that ruined the illusion of being frozen in time.

"How's your wife's mumble mumble?" one of the men said

to another, and the other replied, "She has to have it drained again. Her sister's coming down this weekend. You know her, the one who sells tires."

When the waitress came to take my order, I asked if she knew Gina, the waitress identified in the newspaper story about the John Doe.

"Hon, I am Gina. You know what you want?"

"Coffee and a bran muffin and can I ask you some questions about the John Doe?" I said, and gave her my card.

"You want your coffee first? Let me get your coffee," she said, and buzzed off without waiting for me to answer. It was the breakfast rush and she was busy. She was a petite, wiry woman in her fifties with a modest black beehive hairdo. When she came back I noticed most of her few wrinkles pointed upward, which was rather amazing, considering she had worked her butt off as a waitress in Erin's Coffee House for thirty years, raised four kids, and divorced one husband before marrying Ari, the proprietor of this establishment. All of which I learned from her banter with regulars at the lunch counter, before she actually spoke to me.

"Yeah, I knew him," Gina said, pouring me more coffee. "Frenchie came in here once, twice a week. Every Friday, and sometimes on Saturday. It's a shame what happened to him. Life is short."

"Frenchie? What was his real name?"

"I don't know. We just called him Frenchie," she said, and smiled, before excusing herself to take an order. Every few minutes Gina had to run off to take an order, drop off food, and refill coffee cups.

She came back and sat down across from me in the two-person booth.

"Did Frenchie ever tell you what he did here in America?" I asked her.

"He said he was a pensioned teacher."

"What had he taught? Where?"

"He taught somewhere in France. I don't remember him saying where in France. He said he taught all subjects."

"He knew a lot about science," one of the guys at the nearby counter said.

"Yes, he did," Gina said. "And agriculture."

"What specifically did he know about science and agriculture?"

"Specifically? We talked about the Mars rover. And cloning. And bees. How bees could pick up the scent of their queens from miles away sometimes."

"Was he married, divorced? Did he have kids?"

"He said no."

"Did you ever see him with anyone?"

"No. He seemed lonely too. It's a shame," Gina said. "Excuse me."

When she hopped up to pick up an order, a guy at the counter leaned over toward me and said, "With this girl, Charlotte, I saw him. He came in with her sometimes."

"Who is Charlotte?" I asked.

"A girl who comes in here sometimes," the guy at the counter said. "Brown hair, big blue eyes, about five foot, big . . ." He cupped his hands in front of his chest to indicate breasts.

"Do you know her last name?"

"No. Hey! Anyone here know Charlotte's last name?" he hollered.

"Starts with a V," Gina said, sitting back down across from me. "She lives around here somewhere. Come to think of it, I did see her here with Frenchie."

"How can I get in touch with her?"

"I'll keep your card, and next time she comes in I'll ask her to call you," she said.

"Thank you," I said.

"You're welcome. You're the second person from ANN to stop by. I feel quite special. Under sad circumstances, of course. . . ."

"Who else was here from ANN?"

"Solange Stevenson, came by about an hour ago. I'm a big fan of hers. Her books and show got me through my divorce," Gina said. "Is she a friend of yours?"

"A colleague," I said.

"Is she as nice as she seems?"

How I would love to tell her the truth, that a TV persona is like a whalebone corset—take it off and everything goes flying. Not that I didn't have a certain amount of respect for Solange. It's tough to have to go out there in a public way, day in and day out, no matter how shitty you're feeling, and put a smiley face on things, keep that whalebone corset on.

"She's an incredible professional," I said. "Thank you for your help. Please call me if you think of anything else."

"I will," she chirped, and ran off to a waving customer in a booth near the back.

When I went to pay my bill, the guy at the cash register said, in a low voice, "Charlotte, she's an escort, know what I mean?"

"Yes. Who does she work for?"

"I'm not sure. If I see her, I'll ask, and call you," he said.

Were the dead Frenchman and the hooker somehow connected to the missing man in the hat and the paranoid animal rights activist? I wondered. All I had was the Doublemint connection. Or was I drawing connections between things where there weren't any, like I did in the dead dry cleaner case?

In the case of the dead dry cleaner, there was more to go on. One weekend, about a year ago, a man showed up dead during a dry cleaner convention here in New York City, his jacket pockets full of brochures about advanced dry cleaning technology, but his wallet and ID were missing. In the newspaper photos, the dead dry cleaner looked like my dry cleaner, if I squinted a little and imagined my dry cleaner with dark hair instead of gray hair. On a hunch, I pulled my last laundry bill, looked it over, and sure enough, there was something amiss. I'd been charged for a pale orange jacket I did not own. Sure that this was a clue, that finding the orange jacket would lead to the killer or killers, I called June Fairchild at home, asked to see the body, and offered to turn over the laundry receipt.

It turned out my dry cleaner was twenty years older than the victim and alive, well, and safe at church with his wife and grandchildren while I was wasting June Fairchild's day off. The charge for the orange jacket was a mistake.

It wasn't like I didn't have more important things to deal with.

We had an interview that day with a Danish researcher who reported that men had four billion more brain cells than women, though she was mystified as to why, since men didn't use them. If you think about it though, it makes sense, since men have bigger heads and they need something to fill the space, the equivalent of Styrofoam packing peanuts, otherwise their brains would just rattle around inside their skulls. On camera, the Danish lady said it would be interesting to see how men evolved, and whether they put these extra brain cells to some good use. This we could cut with an admittedly sexist female stand-up comic we taped who suggested what this idle part of men's brains might be used for, i.e., controlling the penis, keeping promises, helping with housework, and remembering to put the toilet seat down.

Afterward, we spoke to a group of grade school boys, most of whom thought the man of the future would be some kind of cyborg or superhero, although one little boy very brightly said the man of the future would be "Me!" We also spoke to a scientist who said the man of the future would be Deep Blue, the computer, and an "anthrofuturist" who predicted women and men would evolve beyond the physical to pure intellect. He seemed to think this would be a good thing. A downtown designer gave us his vision of men's fashion in the future. Like most visual artists we'd looked at, his vision was sleek, minimalist, and black with gray and silver accents. Apparently, in the future, we will have no need for color. The clingy clothes had a late beatnik feel to them. Made me wish we could find a designer who predicted a return to something really retro, rococo, men in gold doublets, ornately embroidered velvet capes, powdered wigs, and codpieces, just to jazz things up a bit.

Of course, according to an environmental scientist, whatever we wore, we'd wear it under some sort of transparent, full-body UV-ray-and-air-filtering bubble anyway, which was going to mean the end of kissing under lampposts, or any physical contact in the outdoors.

On the plus side, a scientist who was able to grow human hair in a test tube foresaw the end of toupees.

When the crew went to meet up with the interns to do AOA about the Man of the Future, I went back to the office. AOA stands for Any Old Asshole, known in more polite circles as MOS, or Man on the Street.

"Jack Jackson called for you. He wants you to call him immediately," Liz said as soon as I got in. "And Alana DeWitt called. Or rather, her attorney called. They want to withdraw her interview from the series and they want the raw tapes."

"Why?"

"She didn't like the way the interview went."

"Too damn bad," I said. "She signed a release. Not only that, she approached us about doing the interview after she read about the series in the 'TV Ticker' column of the *Post*. Call her attorney back and tell her so. Did Benny Winter call?"

"Not yet."

"Will you call his office and see if Mandervan has made a decision?"

"Oh, okay," Liz said, as if I was asking her to do something extraordinarily beyond her job description.

"It's very important, Liz," I said. "Help me out, will you?"

"Will you give me a shot at reporting?"

"There are a lot of issues to be considered in this. But I promise you, I will do what I can to give you every feasible opportunity to pursue your goals," I said, very Clintonesque. "But it's a two-way street."

She softened a little. "Want me to somehow mention that I'm blind? That often helps get answers," she said.

"I'll leave it up to you," I said. That was one of the things I liked about Liz, her ability to use her handicap and other people's prejudices about it to her full advantage. Take her two successful lawsuits, which made her wealthy enough to support her mother and three unmarried sisters. Though ANN gossips thought she was only working to find opportunities to sue, the truth was that Liz had a big dream—to be the first blind reporter on a major network. A girl after my own heart, that Liz, if only she wasn't such a bitch and so litigious that I lived in constant fear of her hurting herself and suing the company and me.

"What other calls came in?"

"The only other call was a guy named Gus at the Plaza," she said. "Here's your mail. Only one letter from Balandapur today."

As she turned and felt her way out of my office, I dialed Jack Jackson.

Jack Jackson never bothered with hellos or good-byes.

"Robin, did you see the evening paper yesterday?" he asked.

"Yeah."

Jack laughed. "Pretty funny, isn't it? Did you see the paper today? Some of those feminists are planning to picket my speech! And some of the nutty anti-feminists are threatening to picket the feminists."

Jack sounded oddly excited about this.

"Listen, Gill Morton really, really liked you, and wanted me to bring you out to his estate on Sunday for golf and lunch. I'm planning to warm him up to the idea of advertising on our networks. You free Sunday?"

"Sure," I said.

"Good. Don't forget my cocktail party tonight, up in the penthouse," he said, and hung up.

Before I did anything else, I called Gus.

"Hi, Lola," he said. It was a quirky voice, not particularly deep or well-modulated, but with something rough and sweet that sent the blood rushing from my brain. "How's the Think Tank?"

"Wonderful. We were just about to take our daily champagne break," I said. "How is the jack-of-all-trades biz? What are you this week?"

"A doctor. But I'm thinking of giving it up and going back to the family salmon cannery," he said, sighed deeply, and paused before saying, "Mia Cara at nine tonight."

"Yeah. I'll be there."

"Good," he said.

He sighed again.

"See you then," I said.

"Yeah. I can't wait to see you," he said.

Men were great. Now, why would Alana DeWitt want to get rid of great guys like him, I wondered, or Mike, who despite his admitted Fidocides and occasional bottle-hugging broods—and bottle-hugging broads—was basically a good guy. Or . . . I could go on and on, but I didn't have time. Jack's cocktail party started at five, I had to hang around for minimum an hour, then go home, shower, and change for my date.

While I was on the phone with Gus, another call had come in.

"Was that Benny Winter?" I asked Liz.

"No, but I did speak to his office. Mandervan is still 'considering the proposal.' "

"Good. There's still a chance then. Who called?"

"DeWitt called back. She wants to know if you can meet her at her country place on Sunday to discuss this."

"Can't. I'm going out to Gill Morton's estate with Jack Jackson. Who else called?"

"That loony Jason," Liz said. "He said to tell you, the answer is yes."

"Yes? What was the question?"

"I don't know. He wouldn't say, because of the dubious security of our phone system."

"He's either a paranoid loony or a manipulative scam artist," I said.

Nevertheless, I bit. I called the number he gave me for "beeper central." It rang, it clicked, and then I heard a different ring. An answering machine picked up.

"If you would like to leave a message, please enter your numeric code now," it said. "If you do not have a code, press zero and await further instructions."

I pressed zero and heard another phone ringing, clicking into a different ring, and another, more distant-sounding machine that said, "Please leave your first name, date, and time you called, and a short message."

"Robin calling for Jason. The answer is yes? To what?"

Against my better judgment, I left my beeper number.

• • •

The penthouse elevator was the last manned elevator in the building, scheduled to be fully automated when Ruben, the longtime operator, retired, at age seventy-five. The code, "clover," was simply stated to Ruben, who had received confirming instructions that I was to be taken up to the top floors. Ruben took his job very seriously, had pride in it, and a touch of snootiness toward anyone who did not pilot Jack Jackson's private elevator.

"How many miles you think you've traveled in this thing?" I asked.

"Quite a few," he said, not looking at me. There was not a speck of lint on his beige-and-scarlet elevator operator uniform, complete with gold braid on the shoulders.

"You like your job?" I guessed.

"Yes I do, ma'am."

"What do you like about it?" I asked him.

This seemed to rattle him, but finally he said, "It's a good job and . . . my father did it before me."

"All his life?" I asked.

"All his life," he said.

Then he clammed up.

There were a lot of questions I wanted to ask him. Like, how does one go up and down in a little closed room for forty or fifty years without going stark raving mad? What did you want to grow up to be when you were a little boy? What is that mysterious quality men have that makes women put up with all sorts of crap from them? But I sensed my questions weren't welcome. It was possible this was what he wanted to be when he was a little boy because his father did it. When his father got into the elevator business, it would have been early in the century, when the Otis elevator was the cutting edge of high technology. It had certainly been the hit of the 1893 World's Exposition (that, plus the amazing lightbulb and the first long-distance phone call, from Chicago to New York). It must have been very exciting to go whooshing up the inside of a building in those early days.

He did not speak to me again until we got to the penthouse and he said, "Here we are. Good evening."

"Thank you. Enjoyed that," I said, not knowing what to say. "See you on the ride down."

The elevator opened up into a lobby with a reception desk, surrounded by what I assumed was bulletproof glass. After checking my ID, the security guards buzzed me through a thick steel door.

I'd never been up here before, though the penthouse was legendary, the place where Jack kept a duplex apartment/office. He lived here between marriages and shack-ups, as he was now. He'd recently been ditched by his longtime girlfriend, actress Shonny Cobbs.

We were fifty-some stories above Manhattan, in a huge space with wraparound windows overlooking the steaming, jewel box city—except for one window, which was a transparent map of the world, with little green lights in countries where Jack had holdings, and little red lights where he did not. Suspended from the ceiling was a line of monitors, one for each of Jack's many networks and a few for those of his competitors.

It was a little after five and already the room was full. Jack was over near the bar. The place was crawling with ANN executives, women's conference honchos, moguls, sponsors of the women's conference, and on-air talent from Jack's various networks, stars all of them, except for me and Norma, a cafeteria lady who looked like a younger, toothier Moms Mabley. Jack, surrounded by a bunch of guys in suits, was talking to her, and waved me over.

"This is Norma, Robin," he said. "She's the one who told me about the Flintstones thing. This is Joseph, my head lawyer; Cal, my speechwriter; Larry, my ethicist. Dr. Larry, I should say, guy's got a Ph.D. in philosophy. This here is Robin, the girl I told you about, knows how to urinate standing up."

Norma said hello to me, before she excused herself to go back to work in the cafeteria, or as newsroom wags knew it, the Bad News Café. As she was leaving, their Royal Minuses Reb and Solange came in and headed our way.

Solange was looking very calm and confident, Reb looking around at everyone with suspicion, and blinking rapidly, just one of the tics he'd developed in his years as a war correspondent. His voice was still used on reports, but rarely did he do on-cam stand-ups anymore because the eye tics were too distracting. He'd been chased out of Iraq because Saddam Hussein thought he was sending Morse code messages with his eyes to an unknown traitor within the palace. My Morse was a little rusty, but I was pretty sure the only message Reb was sending was: I'm insane.

That's not a joke. Reb had had a few legendary crack-ups over the years. After he "escaped" from his kidnappers in Beirut, he took to extolling and demonstrating in public the virtues of drinking one's own waste water. It was one thing to do that in front of a bunch of blasé journalists on a bus in Haiti. It was quite another to do that at the Emmy Awards dinner.

Jack and his suits shook hands with Solange and Reb. In Jack's view, Solange smiled at me graciously. Then she turned out of his sight, so only I could see her, and gave me a different look—haughty, imperial. I guessed she was trying to provoke a bad reaction in me that Jack would see. Solange had to be the Queen, all the time. Which was fine with me. Let her be the damned Queen. I was satisfied to be the swearingest princess in all of Christendom. But ever since I became Jack's pet, replacing her, she had unilaterally decided we were at war.

Instead of reacting badly, I took the High Road and smiled graciously back at her.

"Robin, are you okay?" Solange asked with sudden and

[78]

completely fake concern. "You look really tired. I know you've been working really, really hard. Don't let yourself get over-whelmed now. A lot of us are worried about you."

She smiled beneficently while Reb kept glancing silently around the room. Jack was watching Solange and me with interest.

This was her way of saying I looked bad, and hinting to Jack Jackson that I wasn't up to the job he had entrusted to me.

"Have we been working you too hard?" Jack asked me.

"Not at all," I said. "I'm fine, Solange, couldn't be better."

"That's not what I hear. You know my door is always open if you just need to talk, maybe get a little management advice, a referral to a doctor," Solange said.

"Well, I'd love to talk to you sometime," I said, aping her fake niceness. Despite my efforts to Take the High Road, I couldn't help adding, "By the way, I spoke to Susan Brave last week. The baby is sleeping through the night, the new house is great, she and Jack are very happy."

Susan Brave had been Solange's doormat . . . er, producer for many years, until one day, thanks to therapy, Prozac, and suddenly finding some self-esteem, she bolted, leaving Solange for a network job in California, where she fell in love and got married to a fun guy. When Susan resigned, Solange had warned her of the disasters that would befall her if she left Solange and ANN. Few things vexed Solange as much as hearing how happy someone else was, especially Susan. Susan had been the fuckup who made everyone else feel relatively happy and well-adjusted, and it was momentarily discomfiting, having to adjust one's own self-image in relation to her new one. That's human nature, I guess, but Solange just couldn't get over it.

"Do you really think she's happy?" Solange asked. "I hear she's in tremendous denial. I've been deeply concerned about her, but haven't had a chance to call her."

Speaking of denial. Susan didn't take or return Solange's semiregular calls.

"No, they are *really* happy," I said. "Nice, isn't it? Gives you faith in love and all that "

Solange's usual tactic now would be to mention how happy my ex-husband was with his amazing second wife and their baby, but—ha!—she was shooting blanks because I was so over my ex-husband's new family, much to my own surprise.

Instead she said, "It certainly gives me faith. Oh, you know, I almost forgot to ask you, who is the man in the hat you ran into?"

At that point, Jack said, "Lois!" and wandered off to talk to some conference organizer.

"Why? Have you seen him?" I asked.

Solange just smiled and did not answer.

My beeper went off. It was a message from Jason. "Your place, eight-thirtyish," it said.

While I was checking it, Solange and Reb turned and left, without answering my question, to kiss some advertiser asses.

How did she know about the man in the hat? Had she or Reb stumbled upon him through their own sub-rosa investigations? If so, that might mean the dead Frenchman and the missing man who gave me the hat *were* connected.

CHAPTER SEVEN

Lots of theories went through my head as I dressed for my date with Gus, before I remembered that Solange was friendly with Benny Winter, who had supplied her with many big-name guests for her shows over the years. Maybe he told her about the man in the hat. That would also explain why he was so well researched on my career.

Solange was annoying and I resolved to find some High Road way to peacefully coexist with her. Wasn't like I didn't admire her. She and a handful of other women had kicked down the doors for women in broadcasting, and they'd had to be tough bitches to do it, and you had to give them credit blah blah blah. And who was I to criticize her? She was a Power Woman who had broken bread with Power Women all over the planet, Margaret Thatcher, Princess Diana, Hillary, and Janet Reno to name a few.

Checking myself in the mirror, I had to ask myself: Would a Power Woman like Janet Reno, Jeane Kirkpatrick, Golda Meir, or even Solange Stevenson let a man she really didn't know that well feel her up in a deserted corner of the primitive peoples gallery in the Museum of Natural History? Or pretend to be a newlywed in the Oak Room of the Plaza Hotel and let a stranger buy her champagne before they went up to his room? Or put on a white plastic micromini naughty nurse dress, seamed hose, and stilettos, and go out to a cheap motel in New Jersey to watch porn movies with an actor and hump like monkeys? For example.

The risk made it all the better. For some time, I'd been keeping a very low profile, and it would blow me out of the water if the tabloids found out about some of the stuff Gus and I were doing in semipublic places. The *News-Journal* in particular would have a field day, since it was owned by Jack Jackson's archrival, Canadian-British-American media magnate Lord Otterrill. They would slam me, a capriciously promoted ANN exec, to get at him.

But shit, I'm a red-blooded American woman and the moon was just about full in the sky, which turns me into a she-wolf with her nose in the wind, trying to pick up the scent of a like-minded male. I can't get pregnant because of my screwy fallopians, but my ovaries still go through the motions and some part of my brain still sends out a powerful Seek Sperm message during the full moon. In this state, the littlest thing can rile me, a thunderstorm, a smoldering glance from a blue-eyed, one-armed man on a bus, men discussing weaponry, the word "percussion." This was especially true once I turned thirty-five, and nature started to put me through my horny teenage-boy phase. It was bad enough going through it as a mature woman. I couldn't imagine how immature teenage boys handled it, except of course by *handling it*. Bubba, I guessed, got a lot of shucking.

At 8:40, Jason still hadn't showed and I beeped him again and left a message that I was going out, to try me the next day.

When I got off the elevator, I saw Mrs. Ramirez going out with Señor, and I waited a couple of minutes until she was gone. God only knew what she'd say if she saw me dressed like a nurse in a soft porn movie. On the stoop, I looked both ways for her. Her back was to me, and she was heading toward Avenue B, so I headed east toward C to get a cab. It's not the best street to grab a cab—gentrification hadn't firmly taken hold on C as it had on Avenues A and B.

C was quiet. No cars, few people. A piece of blown paper skipped down the middle of the street. The steady traffic on Fourteenth Street, four blocks away, sounded like the rush of a distant river. I walked toward Fourteenth Street, a sure bet for a cab, and heard a low whistling behind me. What the hell was that tune? It was starting to grate on me before I remembered—"Zip-a-Dee-Doo-Dah," from *Song of the South*. I turned back and saw a lone white man walking behind me, whistling.

The whistling man was staring at me intently. It creeped me out, and I wished I had some weaponry on me, something more than my pepper spray. Foolishly, I had been feeling more confident lately and didn't feel the need to be constantly armed anymore. Also, my life was much more hectic, I just didn't feel like schlepping weaponry around all the time. Nor did I have my cell phone.

Approaching me were two other men, men in suits, and I felt safer all of a sudden.

When I looked again the whistling white man was crossing the street, not looking at me. Man, was I paranoid, I thought, just before someone grabbed me and something smacked down on my head. I was unprepared, had no time to go for my pepper spray. Shielding my face with my purse, I wildly kicked and threw punches—a couple of them connected, sending a stinging pain down my knuckles to my elbow—before I fell into a corner where a redbrick wall met a Dumpster.

A very large man in a suit loomed over me, followed by a second man, both their faces shadowed. The large man put his boot on my stomach to keep me from getting up. I slumped to the ground, my purse between my face and the cold concrete, which smelled of spoiled food.

"Don't make me use the gun," the large man said. "Where is Atom?"

"What?" I asked.

A third man, the whistling man, appeared.

"Atom! Do you have Atom!" the large man said.

"You've got the wrong person," I said. "I don't know what . . ."

"Atom!" the man said to me, trying to grab for my purse and knocking it open in the process. I held tight to the purse. A little spray container glinted in the twilight.

"You've mistaken me for someone else," I said. "I'm . . ."

One of them smacked me upside the head again. After that dizzying blow on my head, my vision was so fractured that for a moment, before my eyes refocused, I saw a dozen large thugs, arrayed kaleidoscopically, like the opening shot of *The Lucille Ball Show*. I tried screaming, but I'd bitten my tongue when I got smacked and I choked on the blood in my mouth. All that came out was coughing.

"Hey, what's going on?" a woman shouted from down the street.

In the moment it took the thugs to turn and look, I went for the pepper spray in my purse and sprayed the thug closest to me in the eyes and up his nose.

"Arrrgh," he said, or a reasonable facsimile, grabbing his face.

Using the edge of the Dumpster for support, I raised myself to my knees, and then to my feet, and began to spray another guy.

"Stop, or I'll shoot!" the woman shouted.

"Let's go," the whistling man said. They took off in a thunder of boot beats, without my purse, two of them holding their faces. A moment later I heard a car squealing away.

"Hey, stop!" the woman called.

A dog yapped. When I looked up, I saw Mrs. Ramirez, with

her dog Señor's leash in one hand and a pearl-handled pistol in the other.

"Oh, it's you!" she said, as surprised to see me as I was to see her.

"Thanks for chasing those men away, Mrs. R.," I said, dusting myself off.

"Don't you thank me, you whore!" she said.

In the past, whenever she went off like this, the next step would be to bean me with her cane. Now that she had a firearm, I missed the cane, which she no longer seemed to need. That would be typical of my life, if I escaped fistfighting thugs, only to get shot by my elderly neighbor lady.

"Don't shoot me, Mrs. R.," I said, and then took off running, lamely, with a limp from my fall. Mrs. R's eyes were bad. If she was indeed feeling homicidal, chances were she wouldn't be able to get off a good shot at a moving target. Mrs. R. hasn't had a man since around World War Two, doesn't smoke or drink or have any fun at all beyond judging, misjudging, and slandering her neighbors. Clean living made her mean, but it made her sturdy too. She could really hurt you.

While running away from Mrs. Ramirez toward my building, I saw the black car carrying the whistling white man and his thugs swing around the far corner and come right at me. Though my lungs hurt, I turned around and ran limping in the opposite direction, back toward Mrs. Ramirez, when a large blue sedan pulled up, cutting off the car with the thugs in it.

The car screeched to a stop. The passenger side door swung open.

"Get in," said the black man in the car. "Jason sent me."

Behind me were the thugs. At the other end of the block was my pistol-wielding neighbor. I had to make a snap judgment. I got in the car.

"I'm Blue Baker," the man said as he squealed away from the curb.

The car had bad shocks and was bouncing so much I couldn't keep the seat belt stable enough to put on.

"Robin . . . Hudson," I said.

"I know. I was waiting for you on Tenth Street, almost missed you, then I saw you head up Avenue C."

"Maybe-we-should-call-the-cops-now," I said jerkily, between bumps.

"Can't do that," Blue Baker said, pulling another U-ie just before the approach to the FDR, then tearing down a side street.

"Why-not?"

"Let's lose these assholes, and then I'll fill you in," he said.

Though I couldn't yet wrestle my seat belt together, he was able to manage a car chase while dialing his cell phone with one hand.

"Number seven. Is this secure? Good. I'm bringing her in. She took a couple of blows to the head, should be checked out," he shouted into the phone.

After he hung up, he plugged in an acid jazz CD.

Blue Baker was a large black man, so tall and broad across the shoulders that he had to hunch down over the steering wheel and turn into himself to fit into the car. Aside from the cell phone, a notepad, a bottle of water, a stack of CDs, and a box on the floor (which bore a decal that said "You get through life your way, I'll get through my way"), the car was bare, as if Blue Baker had just acquired the vehicle. It was probably stolen, I thought.

When the car passed under a streetlight, I noticed he had a gun in his lap.

Suddenly, I remembered that I had condoms, lubricant, a toothbrush, and a small vibrator in my purse, because I'd been expecting to see Gus. How is this going to look if I die here? I thought. Like I died in my drug-dealing lover's stolen car while escaping from fistfighting thugs. That's how I think in times of danger, you see. It's a variation of the old "wear clean under-wear in case you're in a car accident." Thank God I *was* wearing clean underwear at least.

We'd lost our pursuers and Blue slowed down.

"Hate car chases," he said.

"Can-we-talk-please?" I said. My heart was beating so fast it affected my speech almost as much as the bumpy chase had.

"Sure," he said. "I'm going to be completely straight with you, Robin. Will you be completely straight with me?"

"Yes. Can-you-explain-why-you-just-put-me-through—"

"Take a breath. Calm down. I probably saved your life. You okay?"

"Yes." I coughed, and Blue gave me the bottle of water. I drank until the taste of blood was gone from my mouth.

"How's your vision?"

"It's okay."

"Reflexes? Memory?"

"I'm fine, I think."

"Well, we'll get you to a doctor. But if you're sure you're okay, I'd like to make a couple of quick stops first. Business stuff."

"You said Jason sent you. Where is Jason?"

"I'm taking you to see him."

"Can't you just take me home, please?"

"You gotta trust me, darlin'," he said.

The intermittent streetlights had a strobe effect on his face as we moved west. His smile was so broad and genuine, his eyes so warm and twinkling, and most of his wrinkles pointed upward. Against my better judgment, I did trust him.

"How do you know Jason?" I asked.

"I'm part of his cell. You might say I help out when I can," he said.

"Cell? A cell of what?"

"It's known just as the Organization. All the cells have

different names, don't always communicate with each other, but are dedicated to the same purpose, preserving the planet. Jason can give you more details."

"How did you know where to find me?"

"Jason said you'd be home at a certain time, and I went and waited for you."

Dewey, he told me, had used him for transportation, contacts, and reefer.

"Dewey was apparently looking into some missing chimps," I said. "You know anything about that?"

"A little. He was on the trail of some bonobos, horniest chimps in the world," Blue said, laughing.

"Excuse me? Bonobos are the horniest chimps in the world?"

"That's what they say. And it's a female-run ape society. Gotta love 'em. Know what I'm sayin', Robin?"

"Yeah," I said, and smiled back at this crazy guy who had saved my life and then risked it in a wild car chase. Not the first time I'd been in a car chase, so I couldn't really hold it against him. "Who coordinates it, this Organization?"

"Central. Only cell leaders talk to Central. Dewey was this cell's leader. Jason is trying some back alleys to get to Central."

"Where is Central?"

"Damned if I know."

"Does this Organization have a leader?"

"It's funded mainly by some eccentric rich guy. I don't even know who it is. We call him Hank. The idea is, we protect the Organization and ourselves by having a pretty loose structure, working independently as cells."

"Oh Jesus. What time is it?" I asked. "Can I make a call on your phone?"

"Who you gonna call?"

"I had a date tonight. I have now officially stood him up."

"Oh. I guess that's okay then. Just be careful what you say."

I called Mia Cara.

"Lola, where are you?" Gus asked.

"Something came up," I said, trying to think of a suitable lie that would get me off the hook for standing him up. I couldn't think of one. "I can't make it tonight."

"Oh. I see," he said, and sounded sincerely deflated. "Want to try again tomorrow night? Say, nine P.M., the Plaza?"

"Yeah, I would. Sorry about this. See you tomorrow," I said, and hung up.

Blue turned right on Eighth Avenue, heading uptown.

"You're about to meet a guy named Fast Tony," Blue said. "Don't say anything about the bonobos. He's not one of us. Young Italian guy, very good-looking, dances in the gay clubs, but he's straight apparently. That's what he says every chance he gets, that he's straight. Likes Times Square, likes the action, or what's left of it since Disney took over."

We stopped on Forty-seventh Street. Fast Tony got in the back of the car. "Hey, Blue. How ya doin'? Still dating your ex-wife?"

"Yeah. Am I a jerk or what?"

"Glad you showed, man, I'm being cruised by all the fags," Fast Tony said, handing Blue something. Blue reached into the box on the floor and pulled out a Baggie, handing it to Fast Tony.

The deal was made in a minute and Fast Tony was out of the car. He was fast.

"I don't like doing deals up here. Tony, he's in, he's out. There are a lot of cops here and they see that and they know it's a deal."

"What is that? Marijuana?" I asked.

"Yeah."

"You're an animal rights activist?" I asked, just to be clear about this. He didn't fit my stereotype.

"That's my hobby," he said, matter-of-factly. "Used to be a sanitation worker, then a sanitation cop. Now I work for myself."

"Are you stoned now?" I asked, because the Henri Paul light just went on in the back of my head.

"No, darlin'. Don't worry. I drive sober. Let me explain a few things along the way. I don't know the whole story, so you'll have to forgive the gaps."

"Okay."

"You have to promise me you won't repeat this to the cops or anyone. The lives of these chimps, if they're still alive, are at stake. Any media or police attention could put them in jeopardy."

"Okay."

"This is what I know. These chimps were missing from Africa somewhere. Dewey had tracked them to this area with the help of a friendly party who knew where the chimps were," he continued.

"What was being done with the chimps?"

"Who the hell knows, darlin'? Medical experiments? But why these chimps? I mean, there are rhesus monkeys running around that island near Florida. Know the one I mean, Robin?"

He was talking about a little island where rhesus monkeys, bred for medical experiments, had overbred and basically taken over the island.

"Yes, I do."

"Why do they need these bonobo chimps, specifically? They got rhesus monkeys for the picking down there in Florida, a lot closer than Africa. Can't figure it out."

"And Dewey?"

"He doesn't know either, or he didn't the last time I spoke to him. I was supposed to see him after his meeting with the friendly party."

"Same friendly party who helped Dewey track the chimps?"

"I think so."

"And you don't know who that is."

"No, darlin'," he said.

"Do you know how I got involved in this bonobo business, Blue?" I asked.

"I know something, a little. I know Dewey was worried about some reporter named Hudson who was asking questions, and worried you'd get too close to the story and jeopardize the chimps."

"What questions? Who was I asking?"

"I don't know. I wasn't around the day Dewey took a beating. I was upstate doing a . . . business deal," he said.

"Does the word 'atom' mean anything to you?"

"No, why?"

"I think that's what those thugs said to me. They wanted to know if I had the atom."

"Maybe Jason will know."

"How did you get into the animal rights thing?" I asked Blue.

"It isn't just about animals, darlin'. It's the whole planet, the environment, the little helpless animals and the big ones, like us. We're all at stake. But I do love the little animals, must admit. Except cockroaches," he said, and laughed. "Dewey and I used to argue about that, if it was okay to kill cockroaches. You know, the female gets impregnated once, and she's pregnant her whole life. So I figure it's an act of mercy to kill her, and an act of justice to kill the male cockroach who done it to her. Know what I'm sayin'? You love me now, doncha?"

I laughed in spite of myself. "I love you, Blue. Why are all the good men married, gay, or dating their ex-wives?" I asked.

We drove to a dark side street off Riverside Drive in the

West Nineties, and pulled into a parking garage driveway next to a brownstone. Blue rolled down his window and punched in some numbers on a code pad. The garage door opened and we drove through. Behind us, the articulated door rolled back down. Blue slid the car into a parking spot and stopped. A tall, thin man hopped into the back of the car.

"Where are we?" I asked.

"It's safe. Don't worry," Blue said.

"Is this her?" the man asked.

"Yeah, she took a thumping from some jerks. She seems okay but better check her out, just to be on the safe side."

"I'm okay. Really," I said. "It wasn't that bad a thumping."

"You gotta trust us," Blue Baker said. "He's a nurse. He'll take you to meet Jason and the doctor there will check you out. You can't go to a regular hospital. They'd call the cops. We can't have the cops involved. Trust me. I gotta go make some more deliveries. But you have our number. If you need me, just call, ask for number seven, and I'll get back to you, all right?"

It took me a moment to answer. I had a slight headache, but was wary of this strange nurse. Sure, go off with some male nurse, wake up the next day with a big scar across my belly and no kidneys. But I did trust Blue, call me crazy, and I had an overpowering need to find out what I had become caught up in.

"Okay," I said.

"You're in good hands with him," he said, winking at the nurse.

He handed the nurse a bag of weed. "For the patients," he said to me. "Look after your karma now, Robin darlin'."

As he drove off, he cranked up Living Color on the car stereo, the garage door opened, and Blue Baker disappeared into the night with the music.

CHAPTER EIGHT

Y ou can call me Horton," the nurse said, leading me through a heavy gray door and up a blue-carpeted staircase. "And if you need to call the emergency number and ask for me, use fourteen."

"What is this place?"

"It's a hospice," he said. "We mainly handle AIDS and cancer patients, but are equipped for all hospital functions except obstetrics."

At the second floor, he opened a door and waved me into a room, decorated like a bedroom but with hospital equipment. A young man with a shaved head was passed out in the bed, while Jason, looking haggard, sat in a chair by the bedside. The room was decorated in soft, soothing colors, and some kind of soothing world music was playing softly.

"Excuse me," Horton said. "I'm going to go get the doctor."

"Is that Dewey?" I asked.

"Yep. Moved him over here last night. He came to briefly today."

For someone who was beaten "within an inch of his life," Dewey looked not too bad. He had a few bruises and a very black eye, a shaved head crisscrossed with stitches, and a broken arm, but looked otherwise okay.

"Did he say anything?"

"He mostly babbled about his auntie, but during a brief coherent moment, he told me to find Dr. Keyes, and said the word or name 'hufnagel' twice."

"Keyes? That sounds familiar. Hufnagel doesn't ring any bells."

"I'm hoping Dewey will regain consciousness again and say more," Jason said. "I hear you took a drubbing tonight."

"A bit of one. You know about this dead Frenchman who washed ashore in Coney Island?"

"No."

"They found Doublemint gum on him, and the man with the hat, he had a half package of Doublemint."

"It's all connected."

"It is?"

"Didn't you get my message?" he asked.

"The one-word message: Yes? That one? Yeah, I got it. What does it mean?"

"Yes, Dewey is part of the Doublemint connection. He had a Doublemint wrapper on him when he was found. Nobody thought it was important at the time."

"So Dewey and the man in the hat may be connected to the dead Frenchman," I said, envisioning the scenario. The man in the hat had a package of gum. He offered the Frenchman, John Doe, and Dewey a piece. John Doe took a piece for later. Dewey chewed his, put the wrapper in his pocket.

The door opened and Horton came in.

"The doctor would like to see you now," Horton said to me, and took me to see a woman, a redhead like me.

"I'm Dr. Nineteen," the redhead said with a smile.

"Robin. I don't have a number."

"Not yet," she said, shining a light in my eyes, making me

touch my nose and perform a variety of other tasks. She insisted on doing an X ray, which showed no damage, before she let me rejoin Jason and Dewey.

By now, it was well after midnight. Jason and I were both exhausted.

"So you'll help us," he said to me.

Fuck.

"Yeah. Don't seem to have a choice. I don't know how I'm going to do it, with everything else I have to do. . . ."

"We all have busy lives," Jason said impatiently.

"Okay, look, I'm going to help you, all right. But when you free those horny, matriarchal chimps, I want the story. I'll keep mum until the chimps are free, but then I want the exclusive."

"Now that it's a story you're interested—"

"I'll help you anyway, but it's only fair you help me out too. I've got a lot on the line right now."

"Okay, you can have the exclusive, but you can't use our real names or provide any details that would help identify us."

"Agreed." We shook hands.

"And do you think you can avoid eating meat and wearing leather when you're around me?"

I hesitated. The contrarian part of me almost blurted out something rude, but then I remembered the High Road thing, and how compromise was the key to all peace.

"Yeah, okay. I'll do my best. Tell me about the Organization. It doesn't sound very organized."

"It's a different kind of order," he said. "Have you heard of the Assassins, from medieval times?"

"A religious sect of hashish-smoking killers or something like that?"

"Well, yeah. We adopted, and adapted, their organization, not their ethos. We don't kill *anything* except in strict self-defense. The Assassins had a secret state that opposed all government and stretched across the Mideast and Central Asia in the twelfth and thirteenth centuries. What made up this state was a network of remote enclaves devoted to gaining knowledge. Information flowed between them via secret agents."

"Do you oppose all government?"

"Not actively. We see it as a necessary evil, but borders just get in our way. Our concern is the entire planet. We want to save our planet."

"Earth?"

He scowled. "Yes, Earth."

"Just checking. That's a rather vague goal, to save the planet. . . ."

"Different cells concentrate on different goals, to save our natural resources, preserve endangered species in their natural habitats, protect indigenous peoples, stop cruelty to animals, fight nuclear proliferation, and so on. Our cell concentrates on animal rights, but occasionally we help out on other things."

"How big is the Organization?"

"I don't know exactly, but everywhere I go on Organization business, I meet a lot of our 'assets,' and we seem to be growing. We are on all continents, in almost every country. We have one ship that I know of, some small planes, some boats."

"And your leader?"

"We call him Hank. I can't say any more about him."

There were a lot more questions for Jason, but he was too tired to answer them. Though Jason wanted to stay with Dewey, just sleep there, there were no spare beds. Horton the nurse insisted he go home, that he, Horton, would stay with Dewey and record everything he might say.

Blue Baker came back and drove us downtown. I was exhausted and so was Jason. We didn't speak until the car dropped me off at my building. Blue sang along to music and cast each of us the occasional sympathetic glance.

"I'll come by and get you tomorrow . . . today," Jason said to me. "Around noon?"

"Yeah, okay," I said.

"We're going to wait down here until you get upstairs," Blue said. "Flick your lights on and off to let me know you got up there okay. You going to be okay? I'm worried those thugs will come back."

"They'd have to get past my gun-toting neighbor Mrs. Ramirez," I said. "And my six locks, plus the poison ivy I keep in my window boxes as a burglary disincentive measure."

"That's my girl," said Blue.

My head hurt a bit and I was dead tired, so tired that all I wanted to do was collapse on my bed in my clothes. But my brain wouldn't stop. It most definitely wasn't a hoax. It most definitely was a real story. The bonobos were real, and the PACA kids were real, and the John Doe, Frenchie, was connected. Where was the man in the hat?

Man, I was getting too old for this stuff, car chases, corpses, and shady characters.

"Asking questions. Hudson," Dewey had written, according to Jason and Blue Baker.

Asking questions. But I hadn't been asking questions, had I? The only people I'd questioned were people I'd spoken to for my Man of the Future series. That might mean someone I interviewed, or pre-interviewed, was involved. Which questions were the offending ones? It was like a game of *Jeopardy!* Here I had all these answers. But I didn't know what the questions were. Here I had the makings of a real scoop, the kind of scoop I'd been waiting my whole career for, a legit investigative story, and I couldn't tell it until it was resolved.

Shit. And Investigative Reports, aka Reb Ryan and Solange Stevenson, were now looking into it. I'd inadvertently led them into it and helped them out. By now, they might know something about the bonobos. Somehow, I had to stop them so they wouldn't jeopardize the bonobos and God knew who else.

If only I'd replaced my dead computer, I'd be able to go on the Internet and look up this guy Hufnagel, see if he was the John Doe. But even then, as Jason said, my phone might not be secure. I needed a safe computer and a safe phone line.

My neighbor Sally had several and she routinely stayed up till 5:00 or 6:00 A.M. working her psychic hot line, as the TV ads for it ran in the wee hours. She liked to take as many of these calls herself as she could (as opposed to switching them over to her far-flung network of psychics all over the tristate area). Instead of calling her, I just went downstairs.

"Sure, use the laptop on the kitchen table," Sally said. "Why?"

"It's work-related. Long story. I'll tell you later," I said.

The kitchen was painted in pastel blue and lit only by dozens of strings of pale pink minilights, tacked up to the walls and falling in erratic swoops from the ceiling. Sally is a practicing witch and her apartment smelled vaguely of sick-sweet pagan herbs and aromatic balms, which always made me think of dead pharaohs and virgin sacrifices.

"How do you like my hair?" she asked.

Formerly bald, with a Scorpion tattoo up the back of her skull, Sally had grown her brown hair out to appease her last boyfriend, and it was almost Beatle length now.

"Looks great, Sal," I said, sitting down in front of her laptop. There was astrological software up on the screen, and from the file list it appeared she'd been doing compatibility charts between her and various dead celebrities, something she often did in the wake of a bitter breakup.

"It's been a slow night. Just switch out of that program to my on-line server. It's the little lightning icon," Sally said. "I'll make some tea. How are you doing? I haven't seen you in a while."

"Busier than a one-armed paperhanger with a persistent itch," I said.

"You heard about me and Mad Jimmy."

"You broke up, right?"

"Yeah, he got arrested again and I couldn't take any more."

"Codependent no more, Sal. I'm proud of you."

"I never should have gotten mixed up with him. I mean, he's an Aries sun and Gemini moon, with a Leo rising!"

She said this as if it was supposed to mean something to me, the same way an old Czech friend of mine explained another friend's behavior with the all-encompassing, "That's the way he is. He's Moravian," or the way people still explain another by saying, "What do you expect? He's a *man*, she's a *woman*."

"And?" I said to Sally.

"And I'm a Pisces sun and moon with Scorpio rising!" she said emphatically.

I did understand a bit about the double Pisces thing, having had it explained to me at length by Sally. Evidently, Pisces is a condition that should be put on a medic alert bracelet so, in case of an accident, emergency room personnel know that "I feel *extra* pain so give me *extra* drugs, please!"

My cat, Louise Bryant, emerged from the bedroom, yawning and stretching.

"I gotta make some changes. Maybe monogamy isn't the way for me right now," Sally said. "Maybe I'll try cautious nonmonogamy, like you. I'm a polytheist, so it makes a kind of sense to be more poly in my love life too."

"It isn't all it's cracked up to be," I said. "What's your log-in and password?"

"Bigwitch and Athena," she said. "You're disillusioned with nonmonogamy?"

"I dunno. What else works for people like me, who are always on the go? But it's got its flaws like any dating system,"

I said. "This isn't logging me on, Sal. I'm getting an error message: incorrect password."

"Oh right. I changed my password. Log-in is still Bigwitch, password is now . . . oh dear, I've forgotten. But I wrote it down somewhere."

She began shifting around the papers on the table, looking for the new password.

"You still see Mike?" she asked, as she picked up one scrap of paper, discarded it, and picked up another.

"Yeah, he was just here. But that's not going too well. He's looking for monogamy, I think, with someone else."

"Aw, it's too bad he didn't go for monogamy with *you* when you wanted it, after that wild Halloween when we all almost got killed," Sally said. "And the guy who lies? Do you still see him?"

"Gus? Yeah, now and then."

"And you say I'm crazy," she said. "You know nothing about this guy."

"Wrong, I know a lot. I know he has money, because he always stays in nice hotels. I know he's an actor. I know he has imagination, wit, and intelligence because of the quality of his lies, and I know he's got sensitivity and a masterful sexual technique. What else do I need to know? Everything else is superficial bullshit. Have you found that password?"

"No. Wait, try this: Atlas."

I typed it and got another error message.

"Don't you get tired of lying?" Sally asked.

"I don't see him that often and we don't talk that much. It's just a more advanced version of role-play. And it's nice, because we can say whatever we want without it being taken seriously or being held against us later. Yet, in this weird way, it feels more honest than any other so-called relationship I've been in, Sally. It probably is nuts, you're right," I said.

"But you and Mike lie, too, or withhold the truth at least,

with your 'don't ask, don't tell' policy. Oh, here's the password, Pangod, one word. Of course. Because I had that dream about the god Pan. You were in it actually," she said.

"I was?" I said as I typed. I didn't hear what else Sally said. This time, the password worked, and I tuned Sal out.

The first thing I wanted to check was the name Hufnagel, a more common name than you might think out there in cyberspace; 482 documents came up in the Net search. More information would be needed to narrow the search and I didn't have more. Next, I went to the European wire services to see what they were reporting about the Coney Island corpse. The guy was French, so French police and Interpol were probably looking into it and the Europeans might have a few little stories on him.

But no.

They had big stories, all recent, having run in the last few hours.

Frenchie, the John Doe, had been identified by French police, using fingerprints and the tattoo, as Luc Bondir, a biochemist. A French national, he was believed killed when his illegal drug lab burned down in the mid-1980s. The charred remains of a man with nine fingers were found in the smoldering ruins and identified as Bondir at that time. Bondir had originally lost his finger after running afoul of the criminal gang that distributed the LSD and methamphetamine Bondir produced. The case was closed, until Luc Bondir's body washed ashore on Coney Island fifteen years later.

It made me think of something my friend Louis Levin had once said about time travel. Time travel wasn't possible and never would be, because if it was, for sure some asshole in the future would use the technology to dispose of a body, and we'd have unexplained, anachronistic bodies falling out of the sky. Or some do-gooder would travel back, kill Hitler in his crib, and send the body into another time. Or drunken frat boys or bachelor partyers with access to the technology would use it for a variation on the old gag of getting the groom drunk, stripping him naked, painting him green, and dropping him on the steps of city hall in a neighboring town . . . in a neighboring century.

Fuck, I thought. Scientist dead for fifteen years suddenly washes ashore in Coney Island. It wouldn't be long until this story broke here in the new world.

Sally's psychic hot line rang, and she went into the bedroom to take the call, followed by Louise Bryant.

Bonobos were next. There was quite a lot on these, the horniest chimps in the world, starting with an article by Natalie Angier in the *New York Times*. According to Angier, the female domination in bonobo society is so benevolent it hardly counts as domination. It is more of a partnership in many ways. Females rule, but everything is shared equally, regardless of rank. They were . . . Commies. Horny Commie chimps.

Another old news story reported had been a controversy at a zoo upstate when it opened a bonobo exhibit and drew a big outcry from parents, and not just from the churchies— there were plenty of former hippie parents with "Make Love, Not War" T-shirts in the attic who did not want their young children watching a bestial, shrieking chimp orgy. Insert your own Congress joke here. They closed down the exhibit after that.

There was a world band that called itself the Bonobos too, and a book, *Bonobo: The Forgotten Ape*, by Frans De Waal. At the bottom of one of the sites was a hyperlink to something called the Diogenes Project—to Save the Bonobos.

This, it turned out, was a group headquartered in Kinshasa in the Congo, and headed by Dr. Karen Keyes. There was a phone number. It would be late morning in Kinshasa, I figured, and there might be someone in the office.

"Sally?" I called out. She was in her bedroom now, talking on one of her psychic hot line phones.

"Yes?"

"Can I make a long-distance call on one of these phones?"

"Yes, the pink one covered in little blue starfish," she called back.

The distant, tinny phone in Kinshasa rang four times, and a machine picked up.

"This is Dr. Karen Keyes at the Diogenes Project. I am in New York for a women's conference and will not be back in Kinshasa until August."

Keyes was here for the Women's Conference. What a coincidence.

It was 4:00 A.M. and I was fully exhausted. Tracking Keyes down in New York City would have to wait until I got some sleep.

Sally let me borrow her cell phone so I could make some calls the next day. "I need a secure line," I told her.

"Keep it as long as you need it," she said. We hugged, and as she pulled away from me, her face darkened.

"Oh my God, you're in trouble, I can feel it," she said.

"Yeah, but I can't talk about it."

"I can throw a tarot for you . . ."

"No no, not necessary."

"Take good care," she warned ominously. I hated when she did that.

After thanking her and retrieving the reluctant Louise Bryant, I went back to my place, made a list of "to dos" for the next day, and collapsed into a dreamless sleep.

CHAPTER NINE

The next morning I was awakened abruptly by my phone ringing and my machine answering. It was Mike, so I reached past my snoring cat to the nightstand and picked up the phone.

"Robin. I'm glad you're home, Girl."

"Hi, Mike . . ."

"I called last night. Did you get my message?"

"No . . . I guess I forgot to listen to my messages. Um, what day is it?"

"Saturday. Girl, I need to talk about . . . I've been agonizing over this . . . so can we talk now?"

My fears are true, I thought. He was having an affair with Veronkya the trapeze artist, she was demanding a commitment, and she wanted it today, the day she was to fly without a net. If not Veronkya, then one of the other double-jointed East European women in sequin bodysuits in that circus, maybe the lion tamer—he talked about her a lot too—or the lady who did flips while standing on two galloping horses.

I was still in a state of postsleep amnesia, aware of little more than that it was Saturday, my bedsheets smelled warm and good and clean, and I didn't have to go to work. But now it was all coming back to me. There were bigger things to worry about than losing a boyfriend.

"Are you there?" he asked.

"I'm here. Mike, I'm going through a really hard time right now. You have no idea."

"Me too. But I just had to talk to you about this."

"Mike, whatever it is, can you just sit on it a few days, think about it a bit longer? *Because I really can't deal with it right now.*"

"You're always too busy, Robin . . ."

"It's not that. I can't really explain on this phone, Mike."

"Give it a try."

"Let me call you back," I said. I called him on Sally's cell phone and said, "There's been a murder."

It's remarkable how many conversations I've had that began that way.

"Oh Jesus, Girl!"

"Don't get pissed off. I didn't kill him. I'm involved because of a quirk of fate and I'm in a very awkward position. That's on top of the pressures of this series, and the gossip . . ."

"The gossip?"

"You do not want to know. It's so bogus."

"That stuff about you and Jack Jackson?"

"How did you know?"

"I hear things. I used to work there, you know."

"So you know the pressures I am under. And I know you're under pressure too, so maybe we should wait until we are both . . ."

"Another murder. Jesus, Girl. How do you manage to . . ."

"It has nothing to do with me. It just happened. And I have to deal with it now. Don't say anything to anyone. It's a very delicate situation."

"So that's where you were last night? Caught up in this murder?"

"Yeah," I said, relieved not to have to lie to him, which I'd had to do once before when he called me after a previous date with Gus.

"It's time for you to get a gun."

"I have that Enfield rifle you gave me."

"You need a smaller, more efficient weapon you can take on to the street. No time to get you a carry permit, but I know a guy . . ."

"Mike, I know where to buy a gun illegally," I said, annoyed that he was treating me like some helpless waif who didn't know her way around town. And if I hadn't known I could have gone to Mrs. Ramirez and asked for the name of her arms dealer. But I'd managed this far without a firearm, especially an illegal firearm.

"Then get one," he said.

"Mike, you want absentminded, clumsy me out there with a loaded weapon? I'd probably end up shooting myself. I've been trying to figure out a way to use a squirt gun, honey water, and bees . . . but I think the gun would leak in my purse."

He sighed with, I thought, irritation. "Promise me you'll take care of yourself, Girl."

"I have so far, Mike," I said. "Hey, tonight's Veronkya's big night, isn't it? The trapeze deal, without a net?"

"Yeah."

"Well, tell her to . . . I suppose break a leg isn't appropriate in her branch of show business, is it? Hmmm. Tell her good luck."

"I will," he said, and I got that nostalgic vibe off him again. It's hard to describe this nostalgic thing. It was a sad distance in his voice I was sure I recognized from other breakups. Though the words "I am going to miss you" weren't being overtly said, I was sure I heard them there, below the surface talk.

"Be careful, okay? *Okay?*" Mike said.

"Okay. You too," I said, wondering when it was exactly that we stopped saying "I love you" at the end of our phone calls, and which one of us had stopped saying it first.

Maybe if he had a few days to think about it, he'd change his mind, I thought. In the past, we'd both come close to dumping each other for other people when we were caught up in outside infatuations who demanded commitment, but something stopped us, and reason returned. The one time he had suggested monogamy to me he did it because a friend of his had hit on me at a party. What Mike wanted at that time was for me to be monogamous while he was away in Russia doing a PBS special on mail-order brides. Mike was motivated by jealousy, and I knew I'd feel compelled to keep my word on it, but he might not, so I declined his generous offer. Sure enough, he wasn't in Moscow two weeks before a story appeared in the ANN company rumor file about my erstwhile boyfriend being chased naked down a Moscow street by a psycho lover.

It's that old double-standard bullshit, you know. He gets to go off on the Crusades, wenching all the way, while I sit at home watching the rust grow on my chastity belt. Mike was a hound and was unlikely to change. Despite this, somehow I had thought it would maybe work out for Mike and me, eventually. As Nora Ephron said, every cynic is secretly a hopeless romantic. Emphasis on the hopeless.

Maybe it was like Wallace Mandervan had said in an article the previous year: Forget the Orgasm pill, the only way everyone is going to be happy is if you invent a pill that lowers our expectations. But then, the species doesn't evolve, though it would no doubt improve everyone's love lives.

Of course, Mandervan also said that the burden of evolution falls on the young, and I was not all that young anymore.

It was a lousy time to get dumped. That nostalgic vibe I got off Mike made me think it was really serious this time. That's the thing about nonmonogamy, though. When they wanna go, you have to let them go, without a scene, without emotional torture, without retribution, with your good wishes—what they used to call being a gentleman, more commonly known now as having class.

Men. If they weren't trying to dump me, fuck me, beat me up, get information from me, they were running into me on streets and giving me hats and drawing me into murder cases. Why on earth did I ever think I could do a positive report about men? What was I thinking when I suggested this to Jack? But I wasn't thinking. I was drinking.

On to other things. I crawled out of bed, still in my clothes from the night before, stripped down to my underwear, made coffee, and turned on the news, which I listened to with half an ear as I tried to figure out what to do. Had to find the man in the hat. I remembered seeing something on *Kojak*, in which Kojak traced a revolutionary bomb-making group through a designer purse bought at Bloomie's. I could take the hat to Harben Hats. . . .

Mike had the hat. I called him back, but he was gone already, so all I could do was leave a message, asking him to courier the hat back to me as soon as possible, that it was important, though I had no idea if it was important or not. For all I knew, there were ten thousand hats like that.

Somehow, I had to thwart Reb and Solange's investigation, which was going to be tricky. If I told them the truth, they wouldn't believe me. They'd think I was trying to scam them. Also, there was no guarantee if they did believe me that they would stop pursuing the story. The lives of others were of little concern to someone like Reb Ryan, whose ethic was pure journalist—the story, the truth, at any cost. Hell, the man had put lots of people into danger, from cameramen to civilians to whole countries, in pursuit of stories.

They didn't know what my connection was. Solange presumably knew about the man in the hat because she had spoken with Benny Winter and he'd told her. She had no idea it was somehow connected to the Man of the Future series, to questions I was asking.

Someone had the bonobos, someone I had asked questions . . . Jesus. That could be anyone from a cabbie to Jack Jackson. Chances were, though, it was someone I'd formally interviewed, or pre-interviewed in depth.

Whatever this Atom thing was, we needed to find it, and use it to get the bonobos back.

It would have been nice to be able to pick up the phone and get advice from friends and mentors about this. Even if I hadn't promised to keep it quiet, I would have had a hard time finding someone to discuss it with, since most of my friends were away at the moment. My building super, Phil, who was as close as a man can get to being a saint without giving up drinking, women, and bawdy music-hall songs, was off in India volunteering for the Leprosy Eradication Project. Tamayo Scheinman was unreachable. Claire Thibodeaux was traveling with the President in Africa and not due back in Washington for days. Bob McGravy was in Eastern Europe. You couldn't have a conversation with Susan Brave-Ruper without being interrupted twenty or so times by her baby, and in any event, she'd tell her husband and he was a gossip.

I was on my own.

While I waited for Jason to come by at noon, as we'd arranged the evening before, I made some calls on Sally's cell phone. The escort Charlotte hadn't called me, so I dialed up one of the call-girl sources to see if she could track down possible Charlottes and beep me with the info.

Next I called the women's conference, but the office wouldn't tell me which hotel Dr. Karen Keyes was staying in.

"According to the schedule, she's hosting a fund-raising tea at a restaurant called the Sad Marquis this afternoon, two P.M. It's a hundred dollars a head. You might be able to speak with her there," said the chirpy woman in the conference office.

Had to get a weapon. Though Mike was a big believer in guns, I'm not good with guns and felt I was better served with some odd, seemingly innocuous weapon. That gave me the element of surprise. The pepper spray wouldn't surprise the thugs if they came back, and it was too small in any event. The honey water and squirt gun idea still appealed to me, though it was more a delayed justice weapon, like the poison ivy in my window boxes. The honey water might not attract any bees at the time it was applied, but it might later. That wasn't going to be effective under the present circumstances.

Just about anything can be turned into a weapon if it falls into my hands, and I blame this on my father, a weekend inventor, who taught me how to spot the hidden menace in things, then died before he had a chance to teach me how to thwart it. I did pick up a few tips about how to turn a menace to one's own advantage though. A potato peeler, a glue gun, an Epilady hair removal system, an eyelash curler, all were weaponry.

The problem was finding a really *effective* weapon. Finally, I opted for a combination of a camera flash attachment, to stun and blind, and pepper spray, to hurt.

Promptly at noon someone buzzed.

"It's Jason," I heard, and I let him into the building. But when I got the knock at my door and looked through the peephole, I saw instead a woman in full makeup with short dark hair—à la Louise Brooks—in a long-sleeved, pink and yellow dress.

"Who is it?" I sang, sticking my eye to the peephole.

"Jason," said the woman.

It was his voice.

I opened the door.

"What the hell?" I said.

"I'm in deep disguise," he said.

"Come on in. You look great. But don't you get tired of wearing makeup and high heels and playing to men's sexual objectification fantasies?"

He ignored this.

"You're going out dressed like that?" he said.

I was in a simple summer dress.

"I'd dress like a man, but I can't pull it off with these boobs," I said.

"Well, I'm not going out with you recognizable like that. Do you have a wig?"

"No."

"Scarf? Hat? Where's your closet?"

"In here," I said, taking him into the bedroom. "Are you gay?" I asked, as he plowed through my wardrobe.

"Your generation just loves to label, doesn't it? No, I'm not. Here, this scarf will work. And this hat."

By the time he was finished, my hair was wrapped in a scarf and covered with a big hat. I was taller than he was, and had bigger feet, and I noted with some distress that he had succeeded in making me look like a man—in drag.

"What did Dewey say?" I asked.

"He said that he met with two men involved in the bonobo project. They wanted out of the project, they hated the people they were working for. One of them was a guy named Hufnagel. He found Dewey via the Internet. The other was a guy named Bondir, nickname Frenchie."

"Bondir is dead. He's the guy who washed ashore in Coney Island. The French police say he died fifteen years ago. We'd better go. Let me get my weaponry."

"I have a gun," Jason said.

"Where?"

"Holster strapped to my inner thigh."

"Would you use it?"

"If I had to," he said without hesitation. "In strict self-defense."

"All the same, I'm going to bring my pepper spray. And my camera flash attachment," I said.

"Where are we going?"

"A fund-raiser at the Sad Marquis."

Where better for women's righters to meet than the Sad Marquis, across from the World of Beauty Multicultural Unisex Salon on West Twenty-third Street. The Sad Marquis is a tongue-in-cheek, S&M-theme eatery where you can get grilled chicken over field greens, raspberry mousse in a chocolate shoe, and for a few extra bucks they'll spank a man at your table. I kid you not. According to a bit I heard on the news, it had been doing a booming business with women at the conference, and not only because of the discount coupon enclosed in their registration packet.

I'd been by the Sad Marquis before, and seen the news coverage on it when it opened, but I'd never been inside. The windows were blackened, to heighten the "taboo" of it, though this wasn't real S&M, but a watered-down version for the tourist trade. As far as theme restaurants go though, this one beat the heck out of Planet Hollywood, no pun intended. The place was painted black with the occasional splash of red here and there. All the wait staff were in black leather, of course, and a hostess in a leather cat suit led us to our table, which was next to one of several cages around the dining area, each holding a giddy feminist. Other giddy women took pictures.

A handsome young man wearing nothing but a leather G-string approached us.

"Hello, my name is Anton, and I'm not worthy to serve you," he said, and went into a recitation of the drink specials. A plate of hors d'oeuvres, vegetarian or mixed, was included with the price of our admission.

"Mixed, please," I ordered, more to vex Jason than anything else.

"Vegetarian," Jason said in a whispered falsetto. "You promised, no meat around me."

"Vegetarian," I corrected to the waiter.

"Thank you," Jason said.

"Just for the record, are there any members of the animal kingdom you don't like? Other than omnivorous people?"

"I wouldn't even kill a fly," he said.

"You don't kill flies? You just . . . let them hang around?"

"We keep nothing around that they can eat."

"So . . . they eat out. They're someone else's problem. Like mine. I have to kill your share of flies too."

"You are a bloodthirsty woman. . . ."

"What about snakes? If you confronted a cobra and had to either kill it or be killed . . ."

"Well, in self-defense. But when was the last time you had to defend yourself against a cow, for example?"

"There's a cow in Ohio who tracks, captures, and eats chickens," I said.

"So?"

"Neither here nor there. Just thought of it."

"I'm beginning to wonder if you and I are on the same side," Jason said.

"Me too," I said.

As Edgar Rice Burroughs said, it is remarkable how quickly friendships are formed in the midst of a common jeopardy. But I could sympathize. It's a tough job being a pharisee in a world full of publicans and sinners—the work is never done.

One of the event organizers said a quick hello and dropped an information packet on our table before running off to the next one. In it was a glossy pamphlet about the Diogenes Project and some press clips.

The already dim lights went down and a spotlight went up over a podium in front of a screen. A short, dark-haired woman decked out in Prada walked up and blew into the mike. I recognized her. It was Belle Hondo, a maverick globo-feminist who wears makeup and had chastised some of her hard-core feminist sisters the years before in a big Op-Ed piece for "spending too much time and energy obsessing over Barbie's unnatural figure while there are millions of poor women in the third world being treated like soulless chattel."

"Can you hear me?" she asked.

"Yes," the audience said.

"I'm glad to see so many women here today," Hondo said. "We've all heard the stories of how feminism is dead, how we no longer have clear leadership or purpose, how feminists today are like the carpetbaggers after the Civil War."

There was some light booing, and a voice in the back said, "We're not dead, we're just resting."

Hondo continued. "We haven't won the war, but we've won most of the big battles. The country is tired of fighting and wants to get on with Reconstruction now."

Only a third of the women at the conference called themselves feminists, she pointed out, and every feminist seemed to define the word feminist differently. But while card-carrying feminism was in decline, Western women continued to gain power and prosper overall.

"What we have lacked is a guiding vision to lead us forward. Dr. Karen Keyes has a vision, a bonobo utopia. I think you too will be inspired by the example of these remarkable animals and by Dr. Keyes," she said, and then gave a précis of Dr. Karen Keyes's career—a doctor of zoology *and* anthropology, who had devoted her life, like Jane Goodall, to observing and preserving African chimps in their own environment, specializing in the bonobos for the last ten.

"Please join me in a warm welcome for Dr. Karen Keyes."

A tall, pretty woman with short, curly blond hair, freakishly large blue eyes, and the face of a cherub stepped up to the podium.

"Thank you for coming," she said, and cut right to the chase. "Bonobos are a female-dominated chimp society centered largely in the jungles of the country formerly known as Zaire. Their DNA differs from ours by just one percent. They are our closest primate cousins. And they are the horniest chimps in the world."

When the hoots and hollers quieted down, Keyes went on about the threats facing the bonobos and their diminished numbers—"less than twenty thousand of them left in Africa, and we're losing scores every day. And now I'd like to introduce them." Then the spotlight went down and the film began.

Horniest chimps in the world might seem like a hard claim to quantify, but it was a well-deserved accolade for these noble beasts. According to the film, these chimps have sex an average of eight times a day, hetero, homo, and mono, to resolve conflict, to obtain food, and just plain for fun, and we saw plenty of it in brilliant color on the screen. When aroused, the bonobos' genitalia became very red and pronounced. They made a lot of noise.

This was the new vision of feminism, female rule maintained with a lot of noisy sex? Come to think of it, it was a pretty winning recruitment pitch. It beat the hell out of "a woman without a man was like a fish without a bicycle," or the anti-sex feminists' dictum that all heterosexual sex was a form of rape.

The bonobos were the last large mammal to be discovered, we heard, in 1929. They have longer legs than other chimps and often walk erect. They part their hair in the middle.

"Bonobos French-kiss, they grin, they laugh, and are a bunch of happy, peace-loving chimps," said Keyes's voice on the film.

After the film ended, Keyes took a few questions.

"How do the male bonobos like this arrangement?" someone asked.

"The bonobo males are interesting," Dr. Keyes said. "They don't mind being dominated by females because the females have sex with them. A lot. And they have peace within their community. It's the external threats we have to worry about— civil wars, poachers, encroaching civilization, deforestation, pollution, hungry people who hunt them for food. All these things threaten the bonobo population, and other chimps. A few zoos have small bonobo populations but we want to preserve them in their natural environment."

After Keyes exhorted the crowd to give generously, she stepped down from the podium and was surrounded by interested women. Jason and I waited for a moment for the crowd to thin and then approached her.

"Dr. Keyes," I said. "I'm Robin Hudson. This is . . . Jason."

"I'm in disguise," he whispered.

She was not at all surprised by this. "Ms. Hudson," she said. "I've been quite anxious to talk to you but your staff wouldn't put my calls through. Let me finish up here, then perhaps we can go somewhere to talk."

Right after she left, Jason said, "Excuse me, I have to go to the . . . ladies' room."

While he went off and Keyes courted rich women, I hung at the bar. Suddenly, I felt a terrible chill run up my spine and was moved to look toward the door. That's when I saw De-Witt, standing near the door, scanning the room with narrowed eyes. Her eyes caught mine for a second, but she didn't recognize me in my Tallulah Bankhead getup, which, I thought then, was probably a good thing, since she'd tear a strip out of my hide for not returning her interview tapes. I looked away, and when I looked again, she was gone.

CHAPTER TEN

When Keyes returned, the three of us slipped away in the limo the conference had provided for her.

"I'm heading over to the Jackson Hotel and Convention Center," she said. "Where should I drop you?"

"I'm heading toward east Midtown, the All News Network," I said.

"Have you heard from my friend Dewey?" she asked.

"Sort of," I said.

"Where is he? What do you know?"

"He was beaten after meeting with a man or men who knew where the bonobos are. . . ." Jason began.

"Is he still alive?"

"Yes. He's in a coma, slips in and out of consciousness, Mostly out," Jason said.

"One of the men Dewey allegedly met, a Frenchman named Luc Bondir, is dead now. Another is missing. I am pretty perplexed about what is going on, so I can't tell you much more than that," I said. "Why did you call me originally?"

"Dewey had contacted me just before I left Kinshasa to come to New York and told me you'd been asking questions. He wanted to know if you had contacted me."

"Do you know what questions I was asking and who I asked?"

"I'm pretty sure Dewey heard this from one of the scientists he'd made contact with. I don't know anything more about it. Dewey was kind of secretive, a lone ranger."

Jason nodded when she said this. He started taking notes.

"And what's the deal with the missing bonobos?" I asked.

About two years earlier, she said, a dozen bonobos disappeared, six male, six female. The bonobos move around a lot, the females in particular are peripatetic, so there was a chance they had migrated, or been slaughtered by poachers. But then she began to hear rumors that they had been abducted and smuggled out of Zaire. Subsequent investigation led her to believe they were somewhere in the New York area. That's when she contacted Dewey.

"How?" I asked.

"I got his name from a mutual friend, made contact through an Organization website, and then we exchanged encoded and anonymized E-mail," she said. "He said he'd look into it. I didn't hear from him again until I received an encoded E-mail saying he was hot on the trail of the chimps and had been contacted by a scientist working with them. He suggested I might want to attend the women's conference in New York, where he would contact me. As I said, I heard from him the last time just before I left for New York last week, when he asked if I'd spoken with you or been contacted by you. I was waiting for Dewey to contact me. When he didn't, I got worried and remembered you. I called you."

"I see," I said. "Help me out with this. Why would someone steal a dozen bonobos? I mean, first of all, why would someone want a dozen horny chimps around all the time? Nothing personal."

"I don't know why," she said. "They're adorable, so at first I thought they might be part of the illegal pet trade."

"Or some weird bestial porn or something."

"But Dewey said no. They were being used in some experiment."

"Well, why wouldn't someone just steal the ones at the San Diego or Cincinnati zoo, instead of going all the way to Africa?"

"These are endangered animals. They are well-guarded in San Diego, and if they disappeared, the media there would make a big stink about it, I'm sure."

"It had to be expensive to smuggle out those bonobos. Why not just buy some lab monkeys?" I asked.

"I don't know, I just don't know," she said, tearing up. "And the thing is, these were 'my' bonobos. I knew them, they knew me. They let me observe them. They recognized me and smiled when they saw me. I gave them names. Want to see some pictures?"

She pulled out a packet of photographs of bonobo chimps in the lush Congo jungle, pointing out the ones who were missing by name. It was because she had given them all names, Binky, Popover, Ralph, Madonna ("she's a classic diva, this one," she said), and so on, that made me tear up too.

"So you see, I want to publicize the Diogenes Project, but not the missing bonobos. We don't want whoever has them to panic in the face of a media frenzy and kill them. We want to find them."

"I understand," I said. "I noticed Alana DeWitt was at the fund-raiser. Do you know her?"

"Yes, she's one of our biggest contributors," Keyes said. "The female domination appeals to her."

"I bet it does."

"She's not crazy about the sexual aspect," Keyes said.

"No, she's anti-sex. I interviewed her last week, coincidentally. Does she know about the missing bonobos?"

"Yes, I told her, in confidence. I know you'll fall in love with the bonobos too."

"I already have," I said. "Have you heard about the female monkey who took over her community in the Tokyo Zoo? She's not a bonobo."

"Well, word is spreading. Or monkeys are evolving," she said, and laughed through her tears. "We have observed more and more dominant females in other chimpanzee communities that have traditionally been run by chest-thumper males. Perhaps the apes are evolving a little faster than we are."

Whenever people use lower animal behavior as a parallel to human behavior, you have to look at the animals and wonder when was the last time one of them wrote a symphony, baked a pie, or built a stereo cabinet? When do they get any work done if they have sex eight times a day? Would they still have so much sex if they had bills to pay, or if they had other entertainment options, like television or video games? Or cigarettes? In lab tests, primates choose cigarettes over sex most of the time.

I put these questions to her, and she laughed again.

"The male-dominated chest thumpers aren't building pyramids or writing epic poems either. They're too busy fighting and killing each other," she said. "Though there are chimps and gorillas who paint, and their artwork has been exhibited."

"Do you think they would have so much sex if they were able to talk to each other?" Jason asked, looking up from his notebook. When his eyes met her eyes, he blushed and looked back down slightly.

"Sexual interaction seems to replace other forms of communication for them," he continued.

"They communicate with sounds, gestures, smells, and with sex itself. . . . They love to make funny faces. And they laugh," Keyes said.

"I thought man was the only animal that really laughed," I said.

"Nature is full of surprises," she said.

It was a lovely vision, her bonobo utopia.

I hated to cast a shadow over it. "You know, your life could very well be in danger. You should maybe lie low," I said.

"But I have to be high-profile here. I need to raise money to save my babies," she said. "I'm planning on using reverse psychology. Go about my business at the conference, happy-go-lucky, as if nothing is wrong. Not be alone if I can help it. Keep talking about how many of my endangered bonobos have vanished or been killed by civil war and environmental destruction. That way, it looks to the guilty parties like I am aware of the missing bonobos but blame other forces for it. See?"

"Yes," I said. "That'll work, hopefully."

We exchanged all pertinent numbers when she dropped Jason and me off at the Jackson Broadcasting Building.

"You like her," I sang to Jason.

"Shut up," he said.

"Nothing wrong with that," I said. "She's older than you, not as old as me, but still . . ."

"Don't say anything to her about it!"

"I won't."

After I cleared Jason through security, signed in as Theda Bara, I led him the long way to the Special Reports offices, avoiding the newsroom where my style of dress was sure to draw comments. My friend Louis Levin was on the sked as the supervising producer, and Louis would be sure to stop me, and talk to Jason, and maybe get suspicious. This was bad because, even though Louis was my friend, he also ran the rumor file, Radio Free Babylon, which floated around our companywide computer system.

"Don't move any furniture in there," I said, waving Jason into Special Reports. "Do you want some coffee or something?"

"Do you have herbal tea?" he asked.

"I think so. There's the kitchenette. Help yourself. I'll be in that office there, cuing up some tapes."

Jason came into my office with a cup of herbal tea for me,

a thoughtful gesture, though I'd just as soon drink a cup of boiled peat moss.

"Let's go over the suspects again," Jason said.

"Alana DeWitt, she has bucks, she's insane, and she's nasty. But according to Keyes she's a bonobo supporter. Dr. Budd Nukker. Know him?"

"No."

"He's definitely into weird science, but geared toward longevity. I've heard of monkey glands being used before as youth potion, and sheep placentas and stuff. But these days, he hardly leaves his treadmill. Then we have Gill Morton. He has labs and they probably do or have done animal testing on their cleaning products."

"Yes, they do," Jason verified. "He has a pharmaceutical company."

"Why would he have to employ a bunch of black sheep scientists? He has teams of legit scientists working for him."

"Right, I see your point. So, what else do we have to do?" Jason asked.

"Mislead the Investigative Reports Unit. They've been sniffing around the Luc Bondir story. We start with them, then we mislead the rest of the news media, too, somehow. Once they get wind of this 'man dead for fifteen years' business, they're sure to be on it like flies on manure."

"I can help with that," Jason said.

"How?"

"Send someone to them with a cooked-up story, lead them astray."

"Investigative are gung ho on tobacco stories. Maybe you can lead them to believe Luc Bondir is connected to the tobacco industry."

"Or the Cali Cartel," Jason offered.

"Too dangerous. We don't want to get them killed. Tobacco is safer."

"I can do that. I know some anti-tobacco people who can get me some legit-looking information," Jason said.

"Let Solange and Reb harass tobacco lobbyists, keep them all out of worse trouble. Two birds, one stone," I said, probably a bad choice of words with an animal rights nut. "Breast implants are good too—Solange has gone after them a lot. But be careful. Reb Ryan used to work in U.S. Army intelligence before he went into news, it's hard to slip anything by him. Unless you're wearing that dress and all tarted up the way you are. He's a raging heterosexual. He'd probably think you were a woman and fancy you."

"We'll do tobacco with them, maybe use breast implants on a couple of other media outlets."

"Misinformation is nothing new to you, huh? Have you done that before?" I asked, suspicious.

"Sometimes, to cover our tracks on an operation. Had to lead some mercenaries astray in South America recently, because they had a contract out on me. . . ."

"Were you people behind that mad cow beef hoax last year?"

"*No!*"

"You swear?"

"I swear. That was cruel. I know those guys though. . . ."

"The guys behind the mad cow beef hoax?"

"Yeah. They're not with the Organization. Why?"

"I'm the reporter who put that story on the air. It just about killed my career."

"Oh. That explains a lot. Like, why you hate animal rights people."

"I don't hate you. So you know those assholes behind that hoax, huh? You know where to find them?"

"Yeah. Why?"

"I might need you to do me a favor if and when this bonobo business is resolved."

"Did that hoax get you to stop eating beef?"

"No, I still eat it once in a while. I just don't eat ground beef," I said.

"Why?"

"Two things, one involving a run-in I had with mobsters. Long story. That put me off burgers for a couple of months and then . . ."

"Then?"

"Well, have you noticed how few homeless there are in the city these days? Where did they go? Did they all suddenly get self-esteem, jobs, and apartments? Until I have answers, it seems wise to avoid all ground meat products. Call me paranoid . . ."

"I wouldn't call that paranoid," Jason said.

"No, *you* wouldn't. Were you always a vegetarian animal lover?"

"I used to eat meat."

"What made you stop?"

"In high school, I was dating a vegetarian and she got me into it. . . ."

"Oh yeah. That's how my Uncle Fred became a Mormon."

"I met Dewey because of a girl too."

Dewey and Jason had met freshman year at college because they were in love with the same girl, Marcia, who worked with PETA on campus. Jason joined PETA to get close to her. Dewey, it turned out, had done the same thing. Neither of them got Marcia, but Dewey and Jason became fast friends.

"You've done a lot on account of girls."

"I bet you've done a lot on account of boys," he said.

"Touché," I said. "Would you eat meat if it didn't involve killing an animal?"

"How—"

"Nanotechnology. It's amazing. One day they might send little tiny machines into your arteries to Roto-Rooter out the fat blocks, and microscopic machines could also be used to assemble beef molecules, for example, from raw materials like carbon and whatever, and then assemble the beef molecules into whole steaks."

"It's playing God," Jason said.

"What about cloning? It seems like that would be a boon to endangered species. . . ."

"We're against all genetic engineering."

"What about the scientists who are trying to find a way to put the gene that makes a snake lose its skin into fur-bearing mammals. See? No more trapping? People could just follow the animals around picking up their molted pelts, and everyone could wear fur in winter without guilt."

"Monster making, playing God," Jason said.

The phone rang. It was Belinda, one of my call-girl connections. She knew a Charlotte who fit my description, a woman who worked with the Sterling Escort Service. When I called, Charlotte was out on a job. The dispatcher didn't want to take my number and was suspicious of my attempts to book her later that evening. This was a job for a man.

"Jason, I need you to do me a favor," I said.

"I can't believe I'm doing this," Jason said as we looked for a cab to take us to the Plaza Hotel to meet a hooker named Charlotte. I picked the Plaza because I had a date with Gus there later and this way, perhaps, I could make my date.

"What's the big deal, Jason?"

"I just hired a hooker. That's not a big deal with you?"

"Jason, I want to talk to this woman. She wouldn't talk to me, so I had to use you. It's not like you're going to have sex with her," I said.

Ironically, the cabbie who took us over to the Plaza Hotel thought we were hookers. "You going to meet a john?" he said.

I'm old enough that I would probably be flattered by the idea that I could make a living on my back, if I wasn't a feminist.

Our eyes met briefly in the rearview mirror and then I looked away. Discretion being the better part of valor and all that, I didn't answer, while Jason giggled nervously.

"Didn't I see you on Channel Thirty-five?" the cabbie asked, looking at me. Channel 35 is a leased-access cable channel that shows escort agency commercials and sex-oriented programming like Al Goldstein's *Midnight Blue* talk show. (In addition to lots of porn, the superhumanly unsexy Goldstein does annual London theater reviews, in which he offers such erudite and memorable criticisms as "That actress was so ugly I wouldn't fuck her with *your* dick!")

"I'm a journalist, and my girlfriend here is a model," I said, gesturing to Jason.

"Oh sure," the cabbie said.

The cab smelled vaguely of previous occupants and their sins—a trace of Giorgio, a vague hint of vomit, and someone had broken a city bylaw by puffing on a cigar in this cab sometime in the last twenty-four hours. I swear I'm not making this up: My sense of smell is heightened when I'm ovulating—if not my sense of smell, then certainly my imagination. I rolled down a window and smelled the outside city for a while.

When we stopped at the hotel, the cabbie turned around and looked me up and down. "I was right! I recognize you. I've seen you on Channel Thirty-five, in one of those escort commercials, old commercial too, from the eighties."

"Have it your own way," I said.

When we got out of the cab, we looked both ways to make sure there were no thugs around. Jason, his hand on his thigh, followed me into the Plaza. I paid for the room, leaving one card-key at the desk for Charlotte, and we went upstairs to wait.

"You seem very natural in women's clothes, Jason, if you

don't mind me saying so," I said, parking my tired old bones on one of the double beds, while Jason staked out the other.

"Lots of practice. For my gender studies thesis in college, I dressed as a woman once a week and wrote about how differently people treated me, good and bad."

"Yeah, what did you find?"

"There are advantages and disadvantages," he said. "People are quicker to help you, especially men, but men look at you differently. Like you're prey. People expect more and less from you. You're not expected to be as strong, but you're expected to be gentler, nicer. You get talked down to a lot too. What surprised me was how much more patronizing or rude other women were toward me when I was dressed as a woman. And how few people, men or women, could tell I was a man."

"You're small-boned and have fine features, it works for you. But you're starting to get a five o'clock shadow."

There was a knock on the door. Charlotte was punctual. Jason and I looked at each other.

"I'll get it," I said.

When I opened the door and the woman saw me, she said, "I must have made a mistake."

"No mistake," I said, yanking her into the room.

"Oh wait," she said, looking first at me then at Jason in drag. "I don't do lesbian stuff."

"You're not here for sex," I said. "My name is Robin Hudson. I want to talk to you about Luc Bondir. You may know him as Frenchie. . . ."

"No way. I don't want to be mixed up in this," she said, turning to go. I blocked her way.

Jason had his gun out. Charlotte whipped out a gun of her own.

"Put the guns away," I said. "Look, Charlotte, we won't involve you in this. Just answer some questions. Lives are at stake."

"You wearing a wire?"

"No."

"Prove it. Strip down to your underwear. Do it, or I'm not talking."

Jason and I looked at each other.

"We'd better do it," I said.

When we were down to our underthings and panty hose, Charlotte picked up our clothes and threw them into a corner.

"You're a guy," she said to Jason, and, indeed, in his underwear he made a distinctly male impression.

"Yeah."

"Whatever. Cool. Is there a key for that minibar?" she asked.

"Yeah. Here. Help yourself," I said.

"Frenchie was a client," she said, opening a mini bottle of vodka and downing it straight. "I saw him once a week at least, when he came into the city for the weekend. He sometimes spent the whole night with me, so I knew he had some bucks."

"Who did he work for?"

"I don't know. Some asshole he had to work for, for some reason. I think it had to do with immigration. That's all I knew. By the time he got to talking about his problems, I was drunk, I wasn't listening too close."

"What problems?" I asked.

"You know, he talked about his problems a lot, but not real specifically. He was a real depressive, Frenchie. I know he was a scientist, and for some reason he couldn't go back to France. He hated his boss. He had limited freedom, had to work almost all the time."

"When did you see him last?"

"Sunday night. He was with his buddy Huf. We were going to get a girl for Huf, but Huf was agitated, just wanted to walk around, said he'd meet Frenchie in the morning."

"Huf?"

"Frenchie called him Huf, or Harris sometimes."

Hufnagel.

"What did Huf look like?"

"Tall guy, older, brown hair, wore a hat. Clung to that hat like it was made of gold."

"I bet that's the man in the hat," I said. "Was he a scientist too?"

"I don't know. I guess so. He worked with Frenchie."

"Anything different about Frenchie that night?" Jason interjected.

"Well, he had great drugs."

"What kind of drugs?"

"This stuff you inhale. Not like coke. You don't snort it. You just smell it for a few minutes. It was kind of like ecstasy. I mean, it made you feel good, but it wasn't heavy like X. It crept up on you. Wish I could get more. It made things so pleasant. Will this be cash or credit card?" she asked.

I handed her my Visa, wondering how I was going to expense three hundred dollars an hour for a hooker.

"You look familiar," she said to me. "Did we used to work together?"

"Where have you worked?" I asked.

"Platinum Escorts, Very Best Escorts, A-One Escorts. . . ."

"No."

"I coulda sworn," she said.

Just before she walked out the door, she turned to me and said, "You know, I think Frenchie called that drug something like Adam."

"Atom?"

"Adam, like, Adam and Eve."

CHAPTER ELEVEN

As soon as she shut the door, Jason and I looked at each other and said, at the same time, "Adam!"

"A drug. An illicit drug. Made from bonobo ape glands or something," I theorized.

"No, it would have to be some kind of secretion, otherwise they'd have to keep replenishing the supply of bonobos," Jason said.

"You have access to a computer?" I asked Jason as we dressed. I did not put the scarf and hat back on.

"A safe one? Yeah."

"And the Internet?"

"Of course."

"Find out what you can about Harris Hufnagel, print it out, and I'll beep you later so we can meet and go over it."

"Where are you going?"

"I have a date," I said. "Where will you go?"

"The hospice. I can use a computer there, and I'll be close to Dewey."

"Okay. Beep me if it's *urgent*," I said.

Before I went downstairs to the Oak Room to meet Gus, I

brushed my hair, touched up my makeup, and psyched myself out of work mode and into sex mode. It was hard; I was a *tad* distracted. But—carpe diem—who knew when Gus would be back this way again. Successful men didn't have to sacrifice sexual release for work, even if they were married and in the middle of a crisis. Why should I?

Just thinking about him gave me a dangerous ache, the kind you have to suppress when you're nonmonogamous and having a casual relationship, so you don't get your heart broken. Suppress, and channel those feelings into pure lust. Gus was just a "chapter in the memoirs" for me, as I was for him, that was understood. You don't expect it to last forever, you just see it as a great experience to be had with a great person, set entirely in a fictional present, until that theoretical True Love comes along.

I was running a bit late, and Gus was already waiting for me in the Oak Room. He looked nice, dressed up in a nice suit as befits a newlywed, his brown hair neatly combed in an earnest, Sunday school way. He was such a boy in so many ways, though he was only a few years younger than me. It was endearing.

There was a bottle of champagne in an ice bucket by the table and two glasses. When Gus saw me coming, he stood, pulled out my chair, and gave me the Look.

"Is this your bride?" The waiter beamed, pouring the champagne.

"Yes, this is Lola," said Gus. We kissed, and I sat down.

"I've heard all about you," the waiter said. "It's very romantic, meeting on a mountain-climbing expedition in Peru."

"Uh, yes, isn't it?"

"And him carrying you down the mountain to a hospital after you succumbed to altitude sickness."

"Oh yeah, he's my hero!" I said. The lies weren't disconcerting, but the waiter's demeanor was. Almost everyone in New York had become surprisingly friendly, even trusting, and I still wasn't used to it.

"Enjoy your stay at the Plaza. And I hope your mother is better soon," the waiter said. "It's amazing she can still play the piano."

"What's wrong with my mother?" I asked Gus after the waiter was out of earshot. The truth is, my mother is a schizophrenic whose key delusion is that she is an heir to the British throne, but she manages quite well when she's taking her medication. She doesn't play piano. In any event, I had never told Gus this because it was the truth.

"She got her arm caught in a combine on the wheat farm she runs," he said. "Now she has a hook for a hand. Naturally, this has affected her playing the piano every Saturday night at the over-sixties single dance, but last week she played the dance for the first time since losing her arm."

"How?"

"She taught herself to play the left-handed parts with her foot. Those extraordinarily long toes of hers came in handy. She plays with her right hand and her left foot."

"Good for Mom! And how is your family?"

"My mom's over her late husband's death, and the salesmen are starting to call again," he said.

According to Gus, when he was a kid, his divorced, working mother was too tired to go out and meet men at the end of the day, so she devised a plan to lure men to the house. She filled out coupons asking for information about various products, enthusiastically checking the box that said "Yes, I want a salesman to call." It was quite brilliant, really. She brought hardworking men with jobs to her. When they thought they were manipulating her, she was really manipulating them, sizing them up, picking up clues about their characters, if they were any good at their jobs, how they interacted with Gus and his younger brother, what their ambitions were. Promising candidates were invited back to try to close the deal, though she rarely bought anything they were selling. This way, she weeded out the "nerds, losers, married men, assholes, and child molesters," Gus said. Among the perks were the product demonstrations. Vacuum cleaner salesmen cleaned her living room for her, cookware salesmen made her and the kids dinner, blender salesmen made the kids milk shakes.

According to Gus, this was how she found Gus's late-stepdad, an encyclopedia-salesman-turned-cannery-owner.

"Did she ever date a Morton Man?" I asked.

"Yeah, after the aluminum siding salesman and before the insurance agent," he said. He picked up the champagne glass and looked at me through the bubbles. "Hey, to us. To our life together, the house by the seashore and all our little redheaded children to come."

We clinked glasses lightly, and looked into each other's eyes. He has very soulful eyes, dark and sweet. All I wanted to do was get naked and rub up against him. This was nice. Being with Gus made me calm and energized at the same time, if you know what I mean. It was like being at the eye of a hurricane. This is how, um, mature I had become. I could look at Gus and say, Yeah, I could fall in love with you, but it doesn't seem a wise course of action in this case. And then I could keep myself from falling in love with him through an elaborate tissue of funny lies.

"We can have the rest of the champagne sent upstairs, right?" I said.

My beeper went off. It was from Jason. "Come here. Seven is on his way to get you," the message said. Seven, I recalled, was Blue Baker.

"Damn. I have to go," I said.

"Damn," Gus said. "Why?"

I struggled to think of a worthy lie to tell him and came

up empty, so I just told him the truth. He'd never believe it anyway.

"Between you and me, someone has kidnapped a dozen of the horniest chimps on earth, for medical experimentation, and I've stumbled into it. There's been a murder and last night I got accosted by fistfighting thugs and ended up being rescued by a mobile pot dealer who belongs to a shadowy organization that is plotting to save the planet."

"Oh. You really have to go?"

"Yeah. Sorry."

"Will you come by my room later?"

"I don't know how long I'll be and I have to be up early tomorrow to go golfing with some eccentric moguls. How long will you be in town?"

"I don't know. I have an audi— I mean, I have to see a patient on Monday afternoon here. Brain surgery. After that, I'm not sure."

"I'll come by tomorrow evening sometime then, okay?"

"Yeah, okay. If you really have to go . . ."

"I do. Trust me."

"Want me to walk you out?"

"No, please don't," I said. "Finish the champagne."

Before I went out to the front of the Plaza to wait for Blue, I put the scarf, hat, and sunglasses on while Gus looked on, puzzled.

"Sunglasses after dark?" he said.

"Disguise," I said. "Not pretension."

He stood and gave me a big swoop of a kiss. God, I hated to leave him.

"Blue, this better be important, because I just left a really great guy in the Oak Room," I said, bending down the sides of my big hat to hop into a late-model gray Caddy.

"If he's worth anything, he'll wait for you," Blue said.

"Unfortunately, men have to wait and wait and wait for me," I said. "I am too fucking busy. And when I do have a man around he gives me trouble most of the time. What is it with you guys anyway?"

"Men are trouble, women are trouble, people are trouble. That's life, darlin'."

"I guess."

"I have one quick stop to make not far from the hospice. It's on the way. This chick's cranky. She runs a darkroom for a news wire service."

"Do we have time?"

"It'll take five minutes."

On West Seventy-ninth, a young, short white woman jumped into the back and glanced at us quickly.

"Jesus, what took you so long," she said to Blue.

"Had to look after my karma, darlin'," he said, not bothering to introduce us. "Long time."

"Yeah, how you doing, Blue? Still dating your ex-wife?" the woman asked him.

"Yeah, am I a jerk or what?" he said, handing her a little bag of weed. "How's it goin'?"

"Shit, I've been working seventeen hours a day. It's even worse than usual," she said.

"Why?"

"Because of all these fucking feminists in town. It's worse than when the pope was here during the high holidays and I spent Yom Kippur at work eating like a pig and swearing like a sailor."

"They didn't give you Yom Kippur off?"

"Hell, no. You don't know how it is? Ever since *Newsday* laid off all those people, the market is glutted. I wanna keep this job, I kiss ass."

"It sucks. Fewer people control more of the money. People are worked like dogs," Blue sympathized.

"Nothing against the pope," the woman said to me. "Just in case you're Catholic. I'm a Jew, I don't think he's God's anointed whatever on earth, but he was a partisan during World War Two, against the Nazis, and I give him credit."

"And he has said some nice things, good things, gentle, loving shit lately," Blue said. "Know what I mean? I don't mind the pope. I'd like to get stoned with the pope. But he doesn't do this. I bet Jesus would do this. He could party. He liked to hang out with sinners and took a bad rap from those . . . what were they called?"

"Pharisees," I said.

"I shouldn't do this tonight," the woman said. "My boss wants me back in at four-thirty A.M. I told him I couldn't come in on such short turnaround. I'm only human, you know? And he says I have to do it. And all I wanna do tonight is go home and blow a fifty-dollar dube."

"I hear ya, darlin'," Blue said.

"I'd almost given up on you, Blue," she said. "I was gonna go to the river to get some pot."

"You have to be careful down there. They're busting a lot there now. Cops pose as pot sellers and then bust you."

"I always go to a cool guy, X, got dreads down to his ankles. If he's not there, I don't buy. Hey, thanks, Blue."

She was out the car.

When we got to the hospice, Blue dropped me off and said he'd be back later to pick me up.

Jason was sitting in Dewey's room working on a laptop. He was no longer in drag, but he still had traces of makeup around his face.

"What did Dewey say?" I asked. Dewey was again unconscious in the bed.

"Not much. But I have learned some things. I retrieved an encoded E-mail from Central. Dewey had requested a boat and some commandos for a liberation sometime next week. He needed saboteurs and primate specialists and had requested some people he'd worked with before. But Central hadn't heard back about the particulars. Dewey was supposed to get a map at his meeting with the scientists the day he was beaten up, and learn the identity of the evildoer or doers behind the bonobo abduction. When Dewey came to, briefly, I asked him about the map. He said he had it. But the map was not in Dewey's personal effects."

"Damn."

"The boat's on its way though. It'll be here for a week. We have it at our disposal."

"And Hufnagel?"

"Here," he said, and handed me a computer printout. "There's a photo on the Internet. Let me find the website."

There were only a few small blips about Hufnagel. One of the stories was from his hometown newspaper, the *Greason* (Idaho) *Globe*, which reported that Hufnagel had disappeared shortly after an investigation was begun into the financial affairs of his lab. Investigators said he had gambling debts and appeared to have siphoned off large amounts of money earmarked for research to help pay his debts. He was divorced and had lost his only child, a son, in a plane crash.

Among the other press mentions of Hufnagel was a short paragraph in an old *Time* magazine from the late 1980s, in an article about advances in fertility drugs, hormonal therapy, and pheromonal research. The things you learn from reading. For example, did you know that for many years, the most popular fertility drug, Pergonal, was made from the urine of postmenopausal nuns? Why postmenopausal Italian nuns? Because the urine of childless, postmenopausal women is rich in the chemicals needed to produce the drug, convents are rich in childless, postmenopausal women, and the maker of the drug, Serono, was originally Italian-owned. But evidently the demand for the drug far outpaced the urine output of Italian nuns (I had a cartoonish image of nuns lined up like laying chickens in coops, being continually force-fed water in order to produce for their evil pharmaceutical masters), and new drugs had been developed to take up the slack.

Hufnagel's work had focused on hormones and pheromones, how nature regulated them, how they could be manipulated. He'd done work with insects, livestock, and primates, including bonobo chimps in captivity at a midwestern zoo.

"Look at this," Jason said, handing me the laptop.

It was a picture of Harris Hufnagel.

"It's the man in the hat," I said. "Okay, we know Hufnagel and Bondir were both scientists, and they met with Dewey the day he was beaten up. . . ."

Dewey stirred, groaned, and without opening his eyes, mumbled repeatedly, "The hat, the hat," before snoring loudly and falling back into a deep sleep.

"Where's the hat?" Jason asked.

"My sort of boyfriend has it. Actually, it should be on its way back to me. Probably won't get it until Monday."

Jason sighed and looked over at his friend Dewey. Poor kid, I was almost starting to feel for him.

"You okay?" I asked.

"It's hard to see Dewey like this," he said. "He's my best friend. What if he has brain damage? What if he doesn't come out of the coma again?"

"I'm sure he'll be okay," I said. "What do the doctors say?"

"They think he'll have minimal damage, but they won't really know until he fully regains consciousness. People come out of comas sometimes with different personalities, speaking with strange accents, with memory loss."

"I'm sure he'll be fine. I hope he doesn't come out of it as a meat eater."

"Tell me again the people you've interviewed and the questions you've asked? Maybe there's something we've overlooked."

Just like a man, I thought. As Wallace Mandervan said in his book, *Men Made Easy*, "Swallow your feelings and get back to business."

"You saw the DeWitt interview, and the Morton interview, Nukker . . . I asked them to describe their vision of the man of the future . . . what it means to be a man. . . ."

"But Dewey was beaten before you began the interviews."

"In pre-interviews I asked similar things. The role of men in relation to women, to children, what makes a man manly. You know, there was also a guy who grows human hair in a test tube. Did I mention him to you?"

"That's a horror movie waiting to happen," Jason said.

I smiled because I had thought the exact same thing, in those very words.

"What if the hair escapes and spreads?" he went on.

"Like kudzu. Before you know it, the whole eastern seaboard is wearing a toupee. People would have to comb their lawns."

"Scary. See what I mean about monster science? But I don't see why the test-tube-hair man would need bonobos," Jason said.

"Nor the fashion designer, the at-home fathers, or the Anthrofuturist who thinks Deep Blue the computer is the Man of the Future."

"So we have three likely culprits, DeWitt, Nukker, and Morton. . . ."

"Morton seems awfully nice and normal, relatively speaking. I'm golfing with Morton tomorrow on his estate."

"Why?"

"My boss is trying to sell him a whole lot of advertising time."

"Capitalism," he sneered.

"What's the alternative?" I asked. I was tired, and starting to lose patience a little. "You want us all to go back to living in the woods, foraging for nuts and berries? That was no Disney World of happy people and woodland creatures. If mankind didn't fiddle with nature, we'd all still be living in caves."

"I'm not against technology, just the misuse of it. If we put as much into developing solar energy as we put into fossil fuels, we wouldn't have to go to war with tin-pot dictators over oil. We have a world full of useless crap Madison Avenue convinces us we have to have, and we're destroying the planet to get it."

"Let's not argue," I said. "I'm tired. Is there anything else we need to do tonight?"

"No. I'll beep Blue and have him come get you," he said.

I was dog-tired when I got home. After I fed Louise Bryant, I dropped onto my bed and wished—for a moment—for a simpler life, like the one in the old Morton ads, where I was a mom and a wife in a crisp pink apron with a big strong man to look after me. I looked up at the photo of my friend Susan Brave and her husband and baby on my wall and wondered why I couldn't do that—find one guy, settle down, have a child, work part-time. Technically, I can't have kids biologically without expensive and difficult in vitro, due to my screwy fallopians, but there's always adoption. But for some reason I have not been able to make those sacrifices. My dad did. He always wanted to work for NASA, but he gave that dream up, became a math teacher and weekend inventor to support my mom and me. He made sacrifices.

Why couldn't I? Seemed like it would make life a whole lot easier and more pleasant, having someone big and strong to look after me, instead of me having to look after so many people.

How was I going to work on my series, play the executive game with Jack, save the bonobos, and get laid? The responsibility was crushing, and an old panic stirred to life within me, a panic I hadn't felt since just after Jack gave me my big break, when I seriously thought about chucking it all, getting into my Soyuz rescue vehicle and jetting outta news. I had even drafted a Plan B and a Plan C, for escape or in case of failure. Plan B: Take my savings and my 401(k) and buy a diner or some roadside attraction, like the world's biggest ball of string or a vegetable simulacra museum. Just live a goofy, loose-flowing life in a shack by the side of an interstate, hosting the curious, selling souvenirs, writing my memoirs, and maybe tending a little garden out back. Only have to do one thing at a time, instead of two or three. Plan C: Take a leave of absence to go off with my absent super Phil and his friend Helen Fitkis to Calcutta to work on the Leprosy Eradication Project. Every month, during my period, when I'm feeling like the Good Jesus and lamenting that my life has no humanitarian purpose, I feel the urge to pack it all in and run off to Calcutta to help the lepers. But as Phil pointed out, first bad postmenstrual day and I'd end up telling the lepers all *my* problems, and, you know, the lepers have enough problems of their own.

Anyway, I have a curse on my head. I could be living the pastoral life a zillion miles away from everyone but a few slow-witted chickens and a cow, and a dead body would probably drop on me out of the sky.

I couldn't quit now. If I did, they'd just close down the unit, fire everyone. They were depending on me. The staff was depending on me, Jack Jackson was depending on me, and maybe the bonobos were depending on me too.

CHAPTER TWELVE

Jack's car, an impressive stretch limousine, picked me up at 9:00 A.M. that Sunday, and took me to an East Side heliport, where Jack and a helicopter were waiting.

When we were all in, Jack handed me a set of miked headsets.

"So we can talk on the way out," he shouted over the sound of the chopper blades. "You ever been in a chopper before?"

"No," I said. "I never got news chopper assignments."

"It's fun, not as secure a feeling as a plane. Much freer," he said as the helicopter lifted off the pad.

"Will I be able to get back to the city if I need to leave early?" I asked Jack. "I am waiting for someone to beep me about my series. Might be a good lead."

Jason was working his animal rights connections to find out what he could about Dewey's bonobo mission, and I'd asked him to beep me if he found out anything. But I couldn't tell Jack all this. I wanted to tell this father-figure everything about the man in the hat and the bonobos and the dead French scientist, Luc Bondir. But again, I'd been sworn to silence, and Jack, for all his good points, had a big mouth.

"Yeah, no problem. The chopper can take you back any-time," he said, and his leg rubbed lightly against mine before he pulled it away.

It seemed like an accident, but I couldn't help wondering if the gossip was partly right, if Jack was attracted to me, if I was being recruited to be his concubine or something. As Louis Levin had said to me when I was complaining about the gossip, Jack and I were both nuts, both unattached, and both hetero-sexual, so it wasn't completely off the wall.

Jack was certainly good-looking. He could have bought himself new hair, but he didn't—he stayed bald, "no plugs, no rugs." It worked for him. It heightened the Daddy Warbucks, Yul Brynner, kinglike thing he had going with that shiny pate. Even if he didn't have 4 billion dollars and a worldwide media empire, which can compensate for a lot of flaws, he would have been an attractive man. But to me, he was Our Fearless Leader, and I couldn't quite get far enough past my awe to lust after him. I didn't get a vibe from him that he was lusting for me either, but then I'm often wrong about these things. Often, I think men are attracted to me who aren't at all, and I miss all the cues from men who are until they practically declare themselves to me in a public place.

For example: "Gill Morton really, really liked you," Jack said. "I think he's sweet on ya."

"On me? Seriously?" I didn't get that vibe from Morton when we met.

"Yeah, he went on and on about you when he and I spoke."

Gill Morton—by all accounts a square, old-fashioned, fam-ily values kind of guy—being attracted to me? What a laugh that was. Obviously he had projected some illusion of a woman on me and didn't see the real me at all. This often happens to television personalities. People see you on TV and construct a fantasy about who you are. Hey, I do it all the time myself with my favorite television personalities. Normally, when this happens, I just open my mouth and let my real personality come out, thoroughly shattering any illusion my misbegotten suitor has about me. But with Gill Morton, it would be tough. I didn't want to offend him and jeopardize my series or Jack's business, but I didn't want to lead him on either.

Damn. Why am I so irresistible?

"Too bad about Mandervan," he said. "I heard he turned you down. But at least someone on our team is getting the exclusive."

"What? Who?"

"You hadn't heard. Oh. Solange Stevenson is getting an exclusive with Mandervan as soon as his new book comes out, which should be next spring. Quite a coup. Lot of strange stories going around about Wally Mandervan. You heard that he collects his own hair and toenail clippings?"

"Yeah."

"You heard the rumor that he's trying to clone himself?"

"Yeah, that's a good one," I said, and mustered a smile, thinking, that lousy story-stealer Solange hadn't shown any interest in Mandervan until I went after him.

"Speaking of Solange . . . you get along with her well," Jack said.

"I do? I mean, how do you know that?"

"I watched you two talk at the cocktail party," he said.

What conversation was he watching, I wondered. Not the one where Solange and I were politely skewering each other.

"Well, too bad about you not getting Wally, but you know, a door closes, a window opens. Gill Morton really likes you. You might just be the ingredient we need to get our hands on some of his advertising money."

"He's pretty successful, Gill Morton," I said. "Is he doing well these days?"

"Better than ever. Has more money than I do. But my building is taller," Jack said. "And I have more power, because media is ultimately more powerful than cleaning products and hardware and whatever. You got a pen and paper with you?"

"Yeah."

"Take some notes. I have some questions," he said, and began with, "You been watching the coverage of the women's conference?"

"I've been kind of busy with other things," I said.

"Interesting stuff. Some of those Third World women at the conference have incredible stories, bride burnings, dowries, arranged marriages, clitoridectomies. How stupid is that? Cutting off the clitoris so women can't enjoy sex. It's cruel to the women, and to men too. Women not enjoying sex causes a lot of problems for men. You know, I should mention that in my speech. Write that down, will you, Robin?"

I did.

"Still, I think nature made men to want a variety of sexual experiences. Shonny says women feel the same way, but suppress it," he said, referring to his ex-girlfriend, and he suddenly teared up and looked out the window. Actress Shonny Cobbs had been Jack's "girl" for three years when she abruptly split from him and took off to Asia to make a movie.

"Do you think women are monogamous and men polygamous?" he asked.

"Depends on the woman, I think," I said. I was feeling a *tad* uncomfortable, being a mouthpiece for my entire gender, though Jack had a way, through his own outspokenness, of making me feel all right about speaking my mind. "I'd say women are polygamous, but men are more polygamous, and freer to exercise it than women."

"Yeah, that's what Shonny says too," Jack said. "So how come women seem to find it easier to control than men? Is it all that, uh, social conditioning?"

"Partly that. But studies now show that a woman's brain has to be engaged in the sexual act for it to be satisfying for her, but blood actually rushes from a man's brain when he's aroused. Maybe that contributes to the differences in behavior. There's a lot I don't understand about men."

"There's a lot I don't understand about women. I get mixed up about their signals. I'm expected to just understand things without them being spoken. Why can't women just say what they really mean? Isn't your gender the one that believes in expressing feelings?"

"Men do that too, though," I said. "Send mixed signals, don't say what they really mean."

"Well, what about double standards? Women complain about double standards, but they're guilty of perpetrating them. How come women expect men to be understanding of PMS, but if a man says anything about women's hormones they jump all over him?"

"Women's hormones were used to freeze women out of jobs for a long time. You know, some men say women are in the grip of their hormones a week a month. . . ."

Some men. Jack himself had said this publicly in the early 1970s. To be precise, what Jack said at that time was that he thought those primitive cultures that put their women in huts at the edge of the village during their "time of month" were on to something. (And, hey, I can see his point. If I was a woman menstruating in the wilderness a thousand miles from the nearest Midol or Tampax dispenser, and I had a chance to go away for a few days, I'd have my bags packed and by the door when the happy day arrived every month. Let me see . . . stay home and deal with a husband, kids, backbreaking menial labor, and cramps . . . or go to a hut at the edge of the village to chill out for a few days with nothing to do but rest and drink a tea made from the bark of some intoxicating root? Tough choice.)

"And the feminist response to that," I went on, "is that men are in the grip of their hormones three hundred and sixty-five days a year, which often impairs their judgment. But we still let them handle sensitive and demanding jobs."

"I've got a point, though, about double standards, and—" Jack said, interrupting himself to say, "There it is, the Morton estate. See it? All that beachfront property in Southampton. The guy has it good."

Below us, the Atlantic glittered, deep blue in the bright morning sun.

"Anything you want me to say to Morton?"

"If you want to really get on Morton's good side, ask him about the island he won in a poker game," Jack said, and you could tell he wished he had his own island.

"He has his own island?" Mandervan had his own island too. Islands were the latest status symbol among the very rich, the very famous, and especially the very eccentric.

"Yep, he does. But my building is taller than his building. Did I mention that? Morton's island is called Bald Scot Island. Ask him to tell you why. He loves that story. Oh, and better not bring up his wife. He was widowed a couple of years ago. He's kind of sensitive about it, though he's looking for a new bride." He winked at me when he said that.

"So there really is an old boys' network. All you moguls know each other."

"Not all of us, but you run into the same rich guys, and rich gals, at a lot of functions. Gill belongs to my club."

Jack's club had been exclusively male by charter, until a few years back, when it succumbed to pressure and started admitting women. Of course the entry requirements—military service, Ivy League school, and a healthy financial endowment—eliminated most women, and the few who joined were not in the Inner Circle. I must have made a face at the mention of Jack's club, because Jack said, "You don't like a club that's mostly men, do you? We got women reporters in the locker room, women going in to use men's rooms because the lines for the ladies' rooms are too long, there is nowhere a man can go just to be with other men without being accused of shutting out women and denying them opportunities. . . . What do you gals think we do at these clubs?"

"Homosexual sex," I said, and then realized that this wasn't just my pal Jack, a guy I could rib this way. This was the man who owned the company.

But he laughed. "What else?"

"Cook up schemes to keep women and people of color down and take all our money."

"Well, I can't say definitively that those things don't go on at my club, but I've never seen 'em," he said.

We hovered over Morton's estate for a moment like a hummingbird, and then descended onto a helipad. Gill Morton was waiting for us with a bunch of big, beefy men.

They all had guns.

"Good to see you, Jack. Nice to see you again, Miss Hudson," Morton said, and he smiled at me.

"And you, Gill," Jack said.

"Change of plans," Gill said in his dubbed voice. "Pipe burst and the golf course flooded. So I thought we could go hunting for lunch. You hunt, Robin? Or would you rather wait at the house?"

"I'll come with you," I said. Hell, I'm a journalist, I told myself, and even if I don't like what I see, I can't avert my eyes from it. Union rules.

"Most women can't handle it," Morton said.

"I can," I said, keeping the sarcasm out of my voice. After all the corpses I've seen, I thought, what's a little hunting?

"You know how to use a rifle? It's got a decent kick to it."

"Yeah, I have an Enfield at home," I said.

"Come on then."

As we tramped off into the woods, I thought to ask, "What are we hunting?"

"Doves!" was Morton's enthusiastic reply.

A queasy look quickly crossed Jack's face and then it was gone. We hung back from the group a bit.

"Don't shoot any doves," Jack said to me.

"I don't intend to. I hate this. What are we gonna do after lunch? Stomp bunnies? Kick Buddhists?"

"You might have to eat a dove for lunch, to be sociable," Jack said. "You should have told him you were a vegetarian."

"Come on, you lag-behinds," Morton called. We followed him and his men to the edge of a clearing, where dozens of white doves were held in big cages. At the side of each cage was a small (jockey-size) man in the same outdoorsmen gear.

"Ready," Gill said, and he and his men all raised their shotguns to their shoulders, aimed at the sky. Jack did, too, so I followed suit, keeping my safety on.

"Release the first doves," Gill commanded, and the jockey-sized men opened the cages, released the doves into the air. Before I could ask about it, guns were firing and doves were falling.

When the shooting stopped, Morton said, "Retrieve those," to the two jockey-sized men.

"You think you hit anything?" Morton asked me and Jack.

"Could be," Jack said, while I shook my head.

"Most of them flew toward the woods," said one of Morton's men.

"Let's spread out, cover more territory, get some of the stragglers," Morton said.

While the men spread out, I dawdled. I found myself a nice lichen-covered log at the foot of a tree and sat down and waited. Where is the sport in a bunch of men tracking helpless doves and then shooting them with high-powered guns? What was Morton trying to do? Impress me with his masculine hunting skills? It made me kind of ill and I put my head between my knees and breathed in the moist, green air. A line of ants crawled around my boots. Hunting was one of those things that seriously tested my theory that women are just as good as men and as bad as men. Somehow, I just couldn't see even the toughest, most macho women I knew choosing to stalk small woodland animals with shotguns in their spare time.

Gunshots echoed around me. More doves to the slaughter. Dove hunting, I knew, was big among certain sections of the upper classes, particularly down in the genteel south.

As I turned my head, suddenly, there was a whistle and a thunk right by my left ear. I looked behind me. A bullet had lodged in the tree. People were running and soon I was surrounded by big men. One of them examined the bullet.

"Who shot that bullet?" Morton demanded angrily. His face grew all red, so red that it showed up through his blond brush cut, making it seem orange.

"Not one of ours," a guy who looked like Dobie Gillis said to Morton.

"Well, go find out what happened. Whoever shot it might still be out there. Bud, Gary, get the local cops out here, ask them to take the bullet for testing."

"Yes sir."

"You okay, Robin?" Jack asked.

"Yes, are you okay?" Gill asked.

"Yeah. I'm fine." Traveling under a curse, but fine other than that. I looked in the direction of the shot and saw nobody. Someone was trying to kill me and it scared the shit out of me, but fear was something successful men didn't show, I'd noticed. I wasn't about to either.

"We'd better get out of here," Morton said. "In case the shooter is still hanging around. I'm very sorry. . . ."

"It's not your fault," I said.

"Probably one of the neighbors, shooting at targets, shot

went wild. People next door are hobby shooters," Gill said. "We're going to get it all checked out for you."

I was still shaking, and trying not to show it, when we got to the house, a sprawling two-story yellow-and-brown-brick monstrosity. As soon as we walked in a woman's voice said, "Hello, Gill. Welcome home!"

There was no woman there. Gill Morton was using the same smart-card technology in his house as he had in the Work-place of the Future, so his house talked to him.

Morton chuckled and Jack chuckled, too, but it just made me feel sad for poor widowed Gill Morton.

"The voice is computer-generated," he said. "I can re-program it to say anything I want. Follow me."

While the "help" prepared the doves, Jack, Gill, and I re-paired to his den to discuss business and eat goat cheese cana-pés. Well, I didn't discuss much business. Taking my cue from Jack, only speaking when spoken to, I sat back and observed. But I politely drank some brandy-spiked tea and ate the goat cheese canapés, though normally I have a firm rule about not eating anything that comes from a goat.

Jack didn't kiss ass, he approached Gill as the equal he was, as a guy who had something to offer Gill—worldwide advertis-ing for the price of domestic, and with great demographics. Gill listened with interest, pointing out potential pitfalls in advertising on Jack's network, and it reminded me of a shop-ping expedition I went on with an Indian exchange student in college. The salesman tried to sell her a carpet, she pointed out its flaws to him and tried to bring the price down. Jack and Gill were playing a similar game. It was very cordial, though I suspected that had I not been there, the dialogue would have been rougher and more manly, more David Mamet or Martin Scorsese than Miss Manners.

"We'd get better numbers on the broadcast networks," Gill said.

"Ostensibly," Jack said. "But they are confined to domestic coverage. You're a worldwide company. Overall, you get greater global numbers with us. And let me tell you, we have very high demographics among women overseas. Women are still your biggest customers, Gill. Have you been watching the coverage of the women's conference? You know, India has a huge middle class, which is rapidly growing, and a lot of disposable income, and they love ANN."

"And what do you think, Robin?" Gill asked, and he leaned over toward me so our knees touched. I was sure it wasn't a mistake. He liked me.

"I think you can't do better than to advertise on our networks, because you reach people of influence all over the planet," I said. Was I the Company Girl or what? I didn't even pull my knee away.

"I may just listen to you," Morton said. "It was your request for our archive materials that got me thinking about our next ad campaign. We're gonna update those old twenty-first-century ads from the fifties and sixties. We're gonna show a new vision of the future. Want to see the sketches? Just got them couriered out last night."

"Sure," Jack said.

Gill leaned over to a flat panel on an end table and pressed a button. "Roger, bring in that portfolio the messenger brought last night. It's in my bedroom."

So puffed up was I by Morton's praise, I almost forgot he was a polluter who kept and killed doves. Oh, how we come to love our flatterers. Jack's interest in me wasn't as flattering, because he has these whims and elevates people to his confidence fairly often—one of the cafeteria ladies, a video editor named Valerie, a philosophy Ph.D. Jack sat next to on a commercial flight and now introduced as his "official ethicist," all these folks were part of Jack's loose-knit, wide-ranging "feedback network." But Gill Morton was different, and suddenly I wasn't a mid-level manager going nowhere fast. I was consultant to moguls. When I talked, moguls listened, and all because I got drunk one night with Jack Jackson.

"Have you seen these?" Gill asked, handing me a different portfolio of print materials while we waited for the new portfolio. "This was the magazine campaign we ran in 1959, post-*Sputnik*."

More RetroFuture stuff. If the Madison Avenue seer behind this campaign was to be believed, in the year 2001 Dad and Son would wax the family rocket with Morton Gleamwax, while Mom, Sis, and a team of robots prepared Space-Age Tuna Casserole on a Morton "atomic" range from a recipe provided by the Morton Family Test Kitchens. I'm not sure what made it "space-age." The canned tuna, macaroni, Morton creamy cheese soup, or canned peas?

"In the year 2001, you and your family may take a vacation to Mars!" said the caption in an ad that had run in *Life* magazine.

And there's Dad, in his hat and tie, piloting the family rocket, while Mom, in dress and gloves, hands out sandwiches in individual Mortonware sandwich packs to the kids, a freckle-faced boy in a striped shirt with a cowlick and an angelic girl in a dress, bow in her hair. Mortonware, you may recall, was the company's short-lived attempt to take on Tupperware in 1957, halted after a chemical in the plastic was found to cause nerve disorders in small children, though no mention of this was made in the documentation.

A young man brought in another portfolio and Gill moved closer to me and opened it.

"These are the sketches for the new campaign," he said.

"IN THE YEAR 2025" said the heading. Essentially, the sketches showed the same things as the 1959 ads, but more high-tech and with different clothes. The family was still on its way to Mars, for example, but the rocket had a more streamlined shape and a more complicated-looking control panel, the clothes were distinctly Trekkie, and the Mortonware was missing. Mom and Sis still made dinner but Space-Age Tuna Casserole was out, and a recipe for Chicken of the Future, a healthy stir-fry using Morton-brand olive oil, was in. Women and their robots still were responsible for running the home.

I mentioned this and Morton said, "Well, we want people to be cleaner in the future. We want to promote housecleaning. A couple of years ago, the *New York Times* did a story about how housework has fallen off nationwide."

"My point is, men do more of those tasks now. You only show women involved in those tasks in your proposed ads."

"Good point!" Morton said as if it hadn't occurred to him.

Sometimes men aren't too bright. It made me wonder about them anew, and made me wonder how many ideas that ostensibly came from men throughout the years had originated with women, who never got due credit.

We were interrupted then by another of Gill's men, who came in and said, "The neighbors say they weren't shooting today. But one of the gardeners says he saw a late-model car, black or dark blue, driving away on the access road. We were unable to track it, but we alerted the local police."

It must have been those thugs, I thought. How did they know I was going to be out here? Who had I told?

"You know who it was, Gill?" Jack asked.

"No, no idea. Wouldn't count out the neighbors though. We're involved in a property dispute and they might not want to admit a shooting mistake while we're in litigation. The car must have been driving by. Did the gardener say if he saw the car stopped, or saw its occupant?"

"He didn't," said Gill's man.

"All right. Keep an eye on the neighbors. Thanks."

The butler called us for lunch then, and as we were led to

a table in the sunroom, Gill said, "Have your advertising guys call my advertising guys, Jack. I think we can do business."

The butler poured us wine and served another appetizer made with some kind of goat excretion. The combination of winey goat cheese and being shot at made me queasy.

When a dead dove was placed in front of me, I lost it.

"Where's the jo . . . bathroom?" I asked.

"Around the corner and down the hall . . ."

"Excuse me," I managed to mumble, flying from the table, down the hallway, to the john, where I just barely missed the toilet and threw up all over the pink marble floor. I managed to get my head to the bowl for the second wave of goat cheese canapés and brandy-spiked tea. I sounded like a laryngitic whale in labor—they had to be able hear me in the sunroom. A third wave came, and I felt the first tremors of a fourth, but it subsided.

Using the very soft pink toilet paper, I mopped up the floor before splashing cold water on my face and rinsing my mouth out a few dozen times with the Scope in the medicine chest. I had to flush the toilet repeatedly, waiting each time for the tank to fill. When I was done, I stood there for a moment to get my composure, go out and face the men who had been listening to me puke and flush for the last fifteen, twenty minutes. I knew they had heard me because I could hear them. I stood there and listened for a moment. The tone of their conversation had changed somewhat.

"So this girl isn't your girlfriend, is she, Jack?" Morton asked.

"No, no. Can't do that, she works for me."

"Not like the good old days, eh, Jack. The pussy I got on the job in the old days. These days they sue. Might as well hire ugly women now."

Jack didn't answer, but started coughing, a diplomatic

avoidance cough, I figured, a good excuse not to respond to Morton.

"Of course, ugly women sue too. Look what happened to Wally, and while his divorce was going on," Morton said.

He was talking about Wallace Mandervan, who had been sued for sexual harassment by a woman employee who claimed she could identify his distinctive penis. The woman lost, but not before Mandervan submitted to a court-ordered physical exam to see if he did indeed have an eleven-inch Bubba. He did not, not even close, though he had claimed to for many years. On the upside, he won the case. On the downside, his self-aggrandizement leaked out to the media. Not long after, his bitterly fought divorce came through, and Mandervan disappeared from public view.

"You seen him lately? Mandervan?" I heard Jack say.

"The cocksucker is a recluse. Finishing his book out on his island. I'll be anxious to read it, see what he says is going to happen."

"I hear he's really gone off the deep end."

"Yeah, you hear a lot of things. Is that girl okay? She's been gone a long time."

"Maybe we should check on her."

They were talking about me.

It was a difficult moment, but I had to go back out and face them.

"You okay? You missed a great dove," Jack said when I came back.

Mortified, I sat quietly after that. Morton entertained us with more amusing legends about his life, and I was grateful to have the time to get my stomach settled before we got back on the chopper.

CHAPTER THIRTEEN

It was early evening when we got away. On the way back, the chopper ride was not nearly so enjoyable.

"What a character," Jack said.

"Yeah."

"You going to throw up again?"

"No," I said. The bravado I had had before with Jack was gone, now that I had completely embarrassed myself in front of my patron. "Sorry about that."

"Aw, it could have been worse," Jack said. "You could have barfed at the table. Of course, that, uh, would have saved me having to eat a dove."

I managed a weak smile.

"Gill got a good laugh out of it. No harm done. Did I ever tell you about the time I threw up on Lord Otterrill at a cricket match in London?" Jack said.

I managed a bigger smile. That's the kind of guy Jack was. He'd tell one of his own embarrassing stories to put you at ease about your own embarrassment.

"Thanks, Jack. Sorry I forgot to ask Gill about Bald Scot Island."

"It's not that great a story. He won the island off a Scottish lord or laird or whatever in a poker game. A bald Scottish lord. You had a rough day, the hunting, then that stray shot fired . . ."

"And the puking."

"Oh yeah, the puking," Jack said, and laughed. "You like Gill?"

"He's okay."

"He seems to like you . . . a lot."

"He's too retro for me," I said. "And he hunts."

"Yeah, I didn't think he was your type. You got a boyfriend?"

"Kind of," I said.

"Good!" Jack said, and seemed genuinely delighted. "Everyone should have someone."

At that, he caught his breath and turned to the window. He was thinking about Shonny, I presumed.

When he turned back to me he asked, "What does it take to make a woman want to stick around these days?"

"I dunno, Jack. What does it take to make a man want to stick around?"

Neither of us had the answer. We both fell silent. Jack looked back out the window. I did the same.

Jack had two limos waiting for us at heliport, one for him and one for me. On the limo ride from the heliport, I had the driver stop at ANN, so I could pick up some tapes, and then wait for me at my place so I could change for my date with Gus. Romance was the last thing I was in the mood for, but I'd blown him off twice, and the next week was shaping up to be crazy with work, so this was my only chance to make good with him. If all went according to plan, we could have sex in about a half hour, and I could come home and do a little work before I went to bed, unless Jason beeped me.

When I got back in the limo to go to the Plaza, I scoped

out the street to make sure we weren't being watched or followed. I'm sure the limo driver thought I was a complete loon, though he was classy and betrayed nothing, wouldn't even answer my questions about men with anything more than, "I am really not in a position to comment on that."

"You're a man," I said.

"Yes," he said, the only straight answer I got out of him. I understood. He worked for Jackson Broadcasting and didn't want to say anything provocative, anything that might land him in hot water and jeopardize his job.

As soon as I knocked on Gus's door at the Plaza, as soon as my knuckles touched door wood, Gus opened it.

"I'm so glad to see you," he said, in a tone of voice he'd never used before, touching and sad. Then he hugged me and kissed me. He'd been drinking a bit and was unshaven.

"I'm glad to see you too."

"Come on in. Can I get you something from the minibar?"

"Water?"

"Bubbles or no bubbles?"

"No bubbles please," I said.

"How have you been?"

"Oh, you know, working at the think tank . . . it's tiring. Between the fistfighting thugs, the eccentric moguls, and the missing bonobo chimps . . ."

"Heh. That's funny," he said with absolutely no enthusiasm, and didn't parry back. He handed me a glass of water and slumped down on the bed.

"How are you?" I prompted.

"My audition tomorrow was canceled. I heard from my agent this morning," he said.

"A patient, you mean?" I asked, prodding him back into the game.

"Oh right, a . . . patient, second patient this week, fourth this month."

The way he looked at me, I knew he wanted to talk awhile first, which was going to totally upset my schedule.

"Sorry to hear that," I said.

"I lost two parts this month to the same asshole. Stash Tumley. Pumped-up pretty boy. Casting director didn't think I was good-looking enough. . . ."

"You're great-looking," I said.

"Hollywood doesn't think so. . . . It's not just Hollywood. The part last week was for a Boston chamber of commerce commercial, a national ad. The casting director was such a dick. . . . What am I going to do?"

Damn, he was getting *real* on me now. Okay, I hadn't been lying either when I told him about the fistfighting thugs and the bonobos, but he didn't know that. I put a little effort into it at least, making my voice sound like I was lying. But no, he wanted to talk and be truthful and ruin everything.

So I reached over, brushed my lips softly against his face and put my hand on his crotch, and I could tell he appreciated that, but he didn't stop talking. Man, had I moved into some parallel universe where men I wanted to have sex with only wanted to talk to me?

"Maybe I should just go back to Canada and get a job in my family's salmon cannery, like my brother."

"You're from Canada? Really?"

"Really. I wasn't lying about that."

"You don't have an accent."

"I lost it so I could work as an actor in the U.S."

"Your family has a salmon cannery. Really? You weren't lying about that?"

"No, I wasn't lying about the cannery. The family has several canneries and some real estate."

"Harry the hairy pet salmon?"

"True."

"Your late stepfather being an encyclopedia salesman who bought a cannery, then another . . ."

"It's true," he admitted. "I only started lying because you thought I was lying and I was trying to play along. Oh Jesus, I am such a loser, just like my late stepfather always said. I'm going to spend my life in salmon. And I'm probably lucky to be able to do that. . . ."

"You're not a loser," I said.

"How do you know?"

"I . . . I just know," I said.

Well, hot, primal sex was definitely out now. At this point, it was looking more and more like sympathy sex. I had to get that ball rolling, too, take the initiative as they say. His mind was elsewhere, mine was elsewhere. The sex had all the fire and passion of a sneeze. When it was over, he had another drink and went completely silent and sullen.

Now, if this guy was my boyfriend, I'd make a little effort to get to the bottom of it, draw him out, cheer him up. But he had broken the rules. We were liars, in this for the fun and games, and he'd spoiled it by telling the truth and being all depressing and real. He was forcing me to feel for him and worry about him when I had, oh, one or two other things to worry about and surely didn't need any more emotional complexity right now.

"Want to hear a good joke?" I asked, and then couldn't think of one. My beeper went off. It was Jason, and the message said simply, "Beep me. Hat important."

"Thanks anyway," Gus said. "Can you stay the night?"

"I really wish I could," I said. "I'm sorry. I have a lot to do tonight, and I have to be up early tomorrow. . . ."

"Who beeped you?"

"This loony animal rights activist who is working with me on the case of the missing bonobos," I said.

"You know, you can stop lying now," he said. His voice had turned suddenly cold. "You can talk to me like a real human being."

"Oh, okay," I said. "We'll try that, next time I see you. I gotta go make a call. Keep the faith, okay? Try to have a laugh tonight or something. It's always darkest before the dawn. . . ."

And so forth. How I wanted to be a goddamned ray of sunshine, but I just couldn't pull it off tonight.

For some reason, I felt really guilty about Gus, not just because I'd deserted him in a time of need, but like I was cheating on my Irish boyfriend, Mike, which was silly. We were both free people and Mike had certainly hinted he wanted to be even freer, of me at least. After all, Mike was traveling with a circus full of sultry East European women in sequin bodysuits and surely not thinking of me at the moment.

Yet I felt bad because I was sure that, despite everything, if Mike knew about me and Gus, it would hurt his feelings. Mike got jealous sometimes, but I was not allowed to. I mean, I remember picking up my laundry from the wash-dry-fold place on Avenue C, and the guys there were really friendly with me. Mike got miffed. Afterward I said, "They're just being nice."

"Yeah, because you let them wash your panties," he said, and was in a lousy mood all day after that.

But I was not allowed to get upset when, e.g., I read in the rumor file six months ago that former ANN cameraman Michael O'Reilly had been chased naked through the streets of Moscow by a hysterical lover. Let me rephrase that. I was allowed to be upset that poor Mike had been subjected to such humiliation by some psycho woman. I was not allowed to be angry with him, even though this came not long after he had discussed monogamy.

My guilt about seeing Gus had never lasted too long before. I always rebelled against it. When it was just sex, it seemed okay. But now that Gus had opened up, now that there was intimacy involved, I felt kind of shitty about it, about Mike's obliviousness, about leaving Gus instead of spending the night.

What a shit I was. Why wasn't I more nurturing and all that, the way women are supposed to be? I felt for him, a lot, and I felt guilty for leaving but I had problems of my own, you know? Missing bonobos, dead scientists, thugs, not to mention a major series I was supposed to be writing now so I could start editing on Monday. I needed his problems too? He was supposed to use me sexually, and here he was, trying to establish intimacy. The reason this fling worked was because of a simple understanding: No intimacy! Gus had wanted it that way. I guess I did too, if only to keep me from falling in love with him, which would have been oh so easy, and oh so dangerous because he was, after all, an actor, and younger than me, and out of town most of the time.

In an alcove near the Plaza gift shops, I found a bank of pay phones and beeped Jason, sending the message, "Going home now. Why is hat important?"

Before I left the hotel, I bought the tabloid newspapers at the gift shop, as I hadn't had time to read them that day. They hadn't yet heard the rest of the story about Luc Bondir, Frenchie, you know, being officially dead for fifteen years, having faked his own death by killing someone else in a drug lab explosion.

When I got home, there was a message from Mike on my answering machine. Veronkya had successfully made her no-net leap and it was a huge triumph. And the Harben hat was winging its way toward me.

I beeped Jason again with the message: "Hat here tomorrow."

A few minutes later, he beeped back: "In meeting. Talk to you tomorrow."

One of the tapes I'd brought home earlier was of the De-

Witt interview and before I went to bed I watched it, hoping to pick up a clue. Friend of bonobos, my ass. Alana DeWitt had no feeling for anyone other than herself and her women followers who thought exactly like her. The rest of us were meaningless to her except in that she could use us.

"Women compromise themselves, their 'selves,' constantly to get along with men. We should have been running the world long before now," Alana DeWitt said in the interview, and cited a study that showed a correlation between high estrogen and high IQ in women. She read a quote from Elizabeth Gould Davis—"Maleness remains a recessive genetic trait like color blindness and hemophilia, with which it is linked. The suspicion that maleness is abnormal and the Y chromosome is an accidental mutation boding no good for the race is strongly supported by the . . . discovery by geneticists that congenital killers and criminals are possessed of not one but two Y chromosomes, bearing a double dose, as it were, of genetically undesirable maleness."

No doubt about it—something wasn't right with Alana DeWitt. But the tapes were inconclusive. They proved she was a man hater who looked forward to the elimination of men and that's all. If there were other answers there, I was oblivious. Didn't have enough information to pick up on them.

The thugs, though, were men, as were the man in the hat, Hufnagel, and Luc Bondir, the dead Frenchman, and DeWitt had a stated policy of hiring only women. Of course, she might secretly bend that rule for her own nefarious purposes. And then kill them when she was done with them. I could see it in her personality.

"Men are rapidly becoming unnecessary, and not a minute too soon in my view. The Man of the Future will be extinct," DeWitt said on tape, and paused to take a sip of water and let some of the color drain from her face. "The best of them have limited control over themselves sexually, the worst commit the rapes, make the wars, commit the vast majority of crimes and murders."

"You're not suggesting we should take active steps to get rid of men?" I had said to her at the time.

Her face reddened again.

"Of course not!" she said, and breathed deeply a few times to calm herself down.

I was not convinced.

"Ultimately, men will be extinct," she said. She anticipated the obvious question, how will we reproduce without men, by adding, "We'll reproduce through sperm banks, cloning. One day scientists might be able to splice genetic material from two women together and create a whole new female human being."

And the advantages of this?

"There are so many advantages. No more wars. No more rapes. Women would have higher self-esteem. No longer would women be subject to body fascists, to the brutality or condescension of the patriarchy," she said.

Later in the interview, she quoted the cartoonist Nicole Hollander, "What would the world be like without men? A lot of fat, happy women and no war."

I listened to her tell the joke about the estrogen bomb again. According to Charlotte the escort, Adam was some drug that made women happy. What was its effect on men?

Speaking of the news media, NY 1 had picked up the story the European wires had been running for the last couple of days, that Luc Bondir, the John Doe found in Coney Island, had been listed as dead for fifteen years in his native France. He was a biochemist, it reported, and authorities were now trying to figure out what he had been doing in this country. All the news jackals would be barking after this one by the morning. How long before they all trooped to Erin's Coffee

House or tracked down Charlotte the escort? Jason and Blue had promised to plant some false info to mislead them, but I had no idea what they planned to do.

Fuck. What was I doing? I owed the sponsors, the network, and my staff, a Man of the Future series, and I was spending most of my time running around with animal rights nuts trying to find some bonobo chimps. Sure, there might be a big story in it, but it was risky, and we might never find them.

If I hadn't stopped for that man, Hufnagel, the night of my meeting with Benny Winter, I'd be free of the Econuts and the chimps. I'd be working on my series instead of trying to help save the planet. Why did I ever stop for that man in the hat, I thought? Why? Because of the "dead people in the doorways," who will forever haunt me. Back in the early 1990s, I took a friend's seven-year-old daughter around New York City—*Secret Garden* matinee, high tea at the Pierre Hotel, long walk downtown—from the glittering facades of Fifth Avenue to the charming bohemianism of Greenwich Village. Afterward, her parents asked her how she enjoyed her first visit to Gotham. "It was nice," she said. "Except for the dead people in the doorways." What she was referring to were the many mud-colored homeless people, passed out on steps and stoops, which I, and most New Yorkers, had become inured to and didn't even see. She thought they were dead, and that vivid image would always be with her, that New York was a fairy-tale city littered with corpses. Ever since then, I've had a harder time walking away from someone genuinely in need, often to my own detriment.

When will I learn, I thought, as I began to type up a script for the first part of the series. I worked until 3:00 A.M. on it. I had to be up at 7:00.

CHAPTER FOURTEEN

Monday morning I was hit over the head with a cold sock of mundane reality. Mondays always began with the weekly unit heads meeting, chaired by ANN president George Dunbar, who has never liked me. Only a doctor's slip could get you out of the meeting. Being on good behavior, I got to the meeting early, which gave Dunbar time to tell me he was "watching me" in this suspicious, pseudo-principalesque tone he always takes.

"There's no point having an Investigative Reports Unit and a Special Reports Unit," he said to me, as if he was personally offended that the unit was still alive, as if I was keeping it going just to thwart him and maliciously suck money out of the network. "You may have Jack Jackson fooled, for now," he said. "But you and I know better, don't we?"

Good one. Try to activate my human fear of being a fraud, the least of my fears at the moment. But even if I was a fraud, so what? Half the guys in that room were bigger frauds than I was. At worst, my promotion was a kind of feminist victory. As Bella Abzug said, we'll have equality when a female schlemiel can get promoted as easily as a male schlemiel.

That's my kind of feminism.

"Thanks for your concern," I said to him. "If you'll excuse me, I have to get back to work. As you always say, time is money."

Before I went to the morning interview, I asked Litigious Liz to get me DeWitt's conference schedule for the next week, "discreetly," and I called Mike out in San Francisco, waking him up.

"I'm glad you called, Girl," he said. "Are you ready to talk? . . ."

"Mike, is that hat going to arrive today?"

"Uh, yeah. I think so."

"Do you have a tracking number?"

"Yeah, hold on," he said. "Okay, here it is."

After I wrote it down, he said, "Can we talk for a moment?"

"Jeez, Mike, this is really a bad time. I've got people coming over. Did I congratulate Veronkya on her amazing feat? If not, please give her my best, etc. I hope you're well, too, not too tired . . ."

"Robin, give me five minutes, will you?"

Liz buzzed in. "Gus on line two. He says it's important."

"Another call," I said to Mike. "Hold on."

Click.

"Hello?"

"Robin, this is Gus. Look, I feel like I let you down. You ran out of here last night. It's been so hard to get together. I've been down this road before, if you don't want to see me anymore, tell me, don't play these games. . . ."

"Gus, I do want to see you again. You've misunderstood. I have another call. Can I call you later? Are you still in town?"

"Yes . . ."

"Great. I'll call you."

I clicked back to Mike.

"Hi, Mike."

"Hi, Robin," he said, and sighed, a sigh heavy with disappointment. Speaking of letting people down, I was letting men down left and right.

"Robin," he said. "I'm thinking it might be time to settle down a bit, that this playing the field thing, it isn't working for me anymore. It's easy to say that you can avoid being hurt, and hurting others, if you keep it nonexclusive and light-hearted, but it doesn't work that way for very long. Pain is part of the game. It's unavoidable. When Veronkya took that leap it confirmed everything I've been feeling. . . ."

Here it comes. The big dump. No! I thought. I won't let this happen. I won't let him do it. A few more days with that crazy trapeze artist and he'd change his mind, I knew he would. He always did.

"Mike, I have to go do an interview. I'll call you when things settle down, okay? I apologize, but the problems of three little people don't amount to a hill of beans, etc., you know? Gotta go," I said, and hung up on him.

I called the courier service to find out when they delivered on my street. When they got back to me, they said the delivery guy usually delivered there around noon, and then took lunch. I had an afternoon interview though, and budget figures to crunch and turn in. I'd have to run home between my interviews to check for the hat.

First, I had to shoot a Daddy and Me class, all work-at-home fathers whose wives worked outside the home, and their toddlers. We had just enough time to do it and get me back by lunch. The dads were pretty manly for Mr. Moms (a term they, to a man, despised, by the way) and enjoyed telling dumb guy stories about their ignorance when they took over the child care, and the innovative ways of nurturing they came up with, from games to trick your kids into helping you with the housework to "make watercolors with seltzer instead of tap water. The kids love the bubbles."

Though there were two million of them in the U.S. alone, some of the fathers felt isolated, especially in suburbs where most of the at-home parents were women.

"This is the wave of the future," said the Daddy and Me leader. "*American Demographics* magazine foresees one in three two-parent households could have a dad at home in the year 2000."

When the crew dropped me off at home at lunchtime, I looked to make sure there were no fistfighting thugs about, or Mrs. Ramirez, and went quickly inside. There was a delivery sticker on my mailbox, noting that the parcel had been left with the super, who was actually just the temporary super, filling in until Phil came back from India. I knocked on the temporary super's apartment. There was no answer, so I wrote a note and left it for him.

How long would I have to wait? I wondered. This was going to blow my sked out of the water. I had an afternoon interview with a sociologist who specialized in male leisure activities, and budget numbers to crunch and turn in.

Well, I thought, that's why God made flunkies . . . er, employees. To dump your work onto. Using the cell phone I'd borrowed from Sally, I called ANN and began delegating. Though the company bean counters would disagree, the budget numbers weren't a priority—that job I could delegate to Shauna the associate producer, who despite having no self-esteem had good math skills. She didn't have the proper security clearance for even seeing those figures, but what the fuck. Rules are for robots, as my friend Tamayo likes to say. When I asked Liz to reschedule the afternoon interview, Liz begged me to let her do it. Right, send a blind girl to do a TV interview, a litigious blind girl, I thought, who wasn't insured for fieldwork. On the other hand, it was an interview she could handle, low on visuals, and it would save me a lot of time later.

One of the key differences between men and women, Wallace Mandervan had written in his book *Men Made Easy*, is that men will bend rules and take risks to get things done.

"Okay. Do the interview," I said to Liz.

Next I beeped Jason, with the message: "Waiting for hat at home."

Within fifteen minutes, he was downstairs, in drag, buzzing me.

The first thing he said when he got upstairs was "Did the hat arrive yet?"

"Yeah, the super picked it up, but he's not home. . . ."

"Old guy on the first floor?" Jason asked. "Big potbelly, wears an undershirt?"

"Yeah."

"He came in behind me," Jason said. "Tried to pinch my ass."

"Well, Let's go get the hat then. But on the way down, watch out for the blue-haired old lady with the Chihuahua. She's armed and dangerous, and I'd hate to get into a shootout with the old broad."

"Okay," he said, and had the nerve to look at me like I was the loony one.

"Did Dewey say anything today?"

"He's out like a light. Stirred a bit and snorted, but didn't come to."

"What about the meeting you had last night?"

"I met with an advance man for the boat and crew arriving this week for the liberation. He knows nothing. He was supposed to get the lowdown from Dewey. So it looks like we're flying by the seat of our pants on this operation."

We knocked for about five minutes before Nico finally came to the door. He'd had a few belts of booze already this morning, enough to make my eyes water as he stood in the doorway of his deliberately unlit apartment. Jason and I both stepped back safely away from his depressing aura of stale liquor, spoiled food, and lonely old manhood.

"A parcel for you? Yeah, sure, it came," Nico said. "I gave it to you a little while ago, on the stoop. Don't you remember?"

"Not to me."

"Yes, I did."

"No, Nico, you didn't."

"Hey, whatcha trying to pull on me? I know I gave it to you? Are you trying to get me fired? Mrs. Ramirez was there. She saw you too. You and she argued. Don't fuck with me, girls," he said, slamming the door in our faces.

"Gave it to you?" Jason said. "But how . . ."

"Sssh. I'm thinking," I said.

Now it all added up, the cabbie, the deli guy asking if I wanted two of the same newspapers, Mr. O'Brien thinking he'd seen me on Eighth Street when I wasn't there.

I had a doppelgänger, and in my own neighborhood.

"Maybe we should talk to this Mrs. Ramirez," Jason said.

"First, let's try my neighbor Mr. O'Brien," I said. "Back upstairs."

When we knocked, "Mrs. O'Brien" shouted through the door, "Who is it?"

"Robin Hudson."

She removed the board from behind the door and opened it. A steamy gust of spicy cooking blew out at us.

"Yes?" she said. The little Filipino lady was wearing a dark black wig. Little silver hairs poked out from underneath it.

"Is Mr. O'Brien here?" I asked.

"I don't know where he is."

"Do you know when he'll be home?"

"No, I don't. Why do you want him?"

"I just want to ask him a question about a woman he saw . . ."

"What woman? One of his—" She used a foreign word I'd never heard before, but from the way she hissed it out I took it to mean "whore."

"Nothing like that. A woman who looks like me," I said. "He mistook her for me once."

"Oh. I don't know anything about that," she said. "But if you see him, you tell him to come home."

She shut the door just as I said, "Okay."

"Mrs. Ramirez?" Jason suggested.

"Unless I can think of some quick alternative," I said. I couldn't.

"Okay. Keep your gun handy, and make sure you don't let on you're a man in women's clothing," I said. "She's a religious nut, has a bubble in one of her brain veins."

For all the years I'd lived in the building, I'd gone out of my way to avoid Mrs. Ramirez's door, a difficult task at times because my friend Sally lived on the same floor. Now I was poised in front, gone to meet the devil herself. There was noise coming from inside, people talking in Spanish, a tinny sound like a television or a radio.

"Cover me," I said to Jason.

I knocked. Inside, her Chihuahua Señor started yapping, and you could hear her sliding the metal plate away from her peephole.

"What do you want?" She shrieked through the door.

"I need to speak to you, Mrs. Ramirez," I said as sweetly as possible.

"What?"

"*I need to speak to you.*"

"You need to what?"

"*Turn your hearing aid up! I need to speak to you,*" I shouted, and doors started to open, partway, up and down the hall. Sally must have been out or she would have been there like a shot, trying to find out what was going on.

We heard Mrs. Ramirez unbolt several locks and then her door opened slightly. Thanks to heavy brocade curtains, her apartment was also kept very dark, the only strong light coming from a fringed red lamp and the portable television.

"I've got a gun," she said, while Señor barked.

"I know you do," I said. "I just have a quick question. Did you see Nico give me, well, someone who looks like me, a parcel just a while ago?"

"Did I . . ." She looked confused. She said something in Spanish to Señor, who immediately shut up, and then said to me, "Someone who looks like you?"

"Yes, Mrs. Ramirez. It wasn't me."

"It wasn't you?"

"I was at work at that time. It wasn't me."

"You're not the drug-running whore?"

"No. I'm a TV newswoman," I said, something I'd been trying to convince her of for years, but she'd never listen. "See, this is my NYPD press pass."

This time, she looked at it, moving it back and forth in front of her until her eyes were able to focus on it.

"Oh," she said.

"Who is the drug-running whore?"

"I don't know her name. She's a redhead, used to live on Eighth Street until she moved into this building . . . but she didn't move into this building . . . that's you."

Now she moved back and forth until I came into focus for her.

"Do you know where on Eighth Street she lives, the building, or even the cross streets?"

"I don't remember. It's a redbrick building, around Avenue C, or maybe D. Does she still live there?"

"Chances are," I said. "What did she say when you saw her today? What did she do?"

"She was looking at the buzzer, and Nico came out, said

he had a package for her. Nico went in to get it. Then she saw me and started screaming at me to leave her alone. She swore at me."

"Nico gave her the parcel and what did she do?"

"She left, swearing at me. Said she was going to beat my . . . a word that rhymes with grass . . . one of these days. She ran away. She's afraid of me," she said, and she said it with some pride.

"Thank you, Mrs. Ramirez. I appreciate it," I said.

It would have been nice to hear an apology from Dulcinia Ramirez for all the grief she'd put me through over the years, but under the circumstances, I was satisfied when she said, "You're welcome."

"Would you girls like to come in and have a cup of tea?" she asked in a sweet, almost frail voice. Gone was the shrill, knifelike voice of hate I had known so well. "I have cookies, too, from the Italian bakery."

"Some other time, Mrs. Ramirez. Thanks a lot."

"Are you going to look for her?"

"Yes, Mrs. Ramirez."

"I'll come with you. Maybe I'll remember the building," she said.

Despite my protests, she insisted, and she was the only realistic lead we had. There we were, the four of us, a clumsy redhead, a little old lady and her Chihuahua, and an animal rights freak in drag, a semi-armed posse walking down Avenue C, looking this way and that for thugs and ne'er-do-wells. Go ahead, make our day. It was weird, too, because Mrs. R. had a rep. People walking toward us would catch sight of her and cross the street quickly to avoid her.

As we walked, she told us some of the secrets she knew, or thought she knew, about the neighborhood, this place used to be a crack house, that one harbored a known wife beater, now in jail, there was a nest of anarchists in that building, and so forth. Despite her penchant for busting other people, and particularly public urinaters, I noticed she didn't bother to scoop up after Señor.

Unfortunately, Mrs. Ramirez couldn't remember the building where my doppelgänger lived. Of all the things for her to blank out on. We walked Eighth Street between Avenues C and D three times with no success, stopping strangers to ask, "Do you know someone who looks like me, lives around here?"

"It might be that building," Mrs. Ramirez said, and then quickly changed her mind. "No, it's not that one."

Mrs. Ramirez was getting tired and confused. Very quietly she said, "I want to go home." Jason offered, in falsetto, to walk her home while I stayed to try my luck with strangers. I gave him my keys, and we agreed to meet back at my apartment. I felt exposed, alone, as Mrs. Ramirez walked away with Jason.

But finally I hit pay dirt.

"Oh yeah, I know who you're talking about," one man on Eighth Street said to me. "I don't know what building she lives in. But I've seen her. Go to the deli. If you want to learn the secrets of a Manhattan street, ask the guys who deliver for the nearest twenty-four-hour deli."

"A woman who looks like you?" the deli delivery guy said, in halting English. "You mean Miss Tee, Miss Trix?"

"Possibly," I said. "Do you know where she lives?"

"Oh yes."

"Will you take me there?" I asked.

The delivery guy looked at the man behind the counter, who shrugged.

"Okay, no problem," the delivery guy said.

We walked around the corner and east on Eighth Street toward Avenue D, and I asked the delivery guy where he was from ("Gaza"), why he came to America ("Opportunity"), and what he hoped to accomplish here ("Become a businessman—

I want to have ten Americans working for me someday"). His family was still back in Gaza, but he hoped one day to bring them all over. What a lot of responsibility on his shoulders, I thought, and in a country strange to him.

When he pointed out the apartment building where Miss Trix allegedly lived, I tipped him twenty bucks.

"Thank you, miss," he said, bowing his head slightly.

"No, thank *you*," I said. "Hey, you know the apartment number?"

"Three C."

It was a dilapidated little brick building with a windshaft, almost an alley, separating it from the burned-out shell of a squatter building next door. In the seventies and eighties, this was where junkies came to get heroin. They'd huddle in this alley, waiting for a bucket to come down from a window, put their money in the bucket, and wait for the drugs to come back down. Even during the day, I hadn't liked coming to this part of the neighborhood. It was so sad, all the wasted people walking around like ghosts, being victimized by human animals who lay in wait on every stoop. It had been cleaned up but gentrification hadn't hit yet, not the way it had in the rest of the East Village.

With more than a little trepidation, I buzzed 3C and waited. There was no answer. I buzzed again. When there was still no answer, I buzzed the super. An old woman in a stained housedress and orthopedic hose came to the door and did a double take.

"No, I'm not Miss Trix or whatever her name is. I'm looking for her. Are you the super?"

"Super's wife. He's out somewhere," she said. She had a piece of dried, cheesy macaroni stuck to her floral slippers. "You're taller than Miss Trix."

"Well, that's the least of our differences. Can you help me out? I've been trying to buzz her, but there is no answer."

"She's up there. I saw her go in. She might be passed out."

"Can you take me up there so I can knock on her door?" I smiled my sweetest smile.

"No, I can't do that."

"I'll give you twenty bucks."

"Let me see it."

"See. Twenty bucks."

After holding it up to the light to make sure it looked real, she said, "Hmm. Okay," and motioned for me to follow her in and up a dilapidated stairwell that smelled of urine and bad meat. On the wall, a gang member had written some sort of garish red message in hieroglyphics.

On the second floor, a grungy-looking man was passed out in front of an apartment door, and the super's wife kicked him lightly.

"Nick, wake up and go in to your woman," she said. He didn't budge, so she kicked him a little harder, to make sure he was alive, and banged on his door.

"Cara, Nick's passed out in the hall again," she said, before proceeding up the stairs. Behind us, a door opened and someone dragged Nick's body in feet first.

"We want a better class of people in here," the super's wife said, idly scratching her ass through her flowered shift.

"Who is this Miss Trix?"

"Not a better class of person. Just got out of jail. You don't know her?"

"No."

"Ten years ago, busted for selling bad heroin, using deaf-mute orphans from Guatemala or somewhere as her mules and lookouts. If they didn't work, they starved, or she beat them. I guess she's paid her debt to society and all, but someone should kick some niceness into her," the super's wife said.

"Uh-huh," I said.

"This is it," she said, and banged on the door. "Miss Trix? Miss Trix? Open up please."

More banging was required before the door opened a crack. Only the super's wife was visible to her.

"You have a visitor," the super's wife said.

The door swung open.

"You!" Miss Trix said, and tried to close the door, but I threw my full weight against it and pushed it back open.

"Hey, I don't want trouble," the super's wife said.

"Me either," I said. "Let's just keep this door open, shall we?"

I walked in, while the super's wife waited outside.

"What do you want?" Miss Trix asked.

Though Miss Trix was astonishingly good-looking, she didn't look anything like me, aside from the hair and the pale complexion. Not only that, but I'd seen her before on the street, noticing her only because natural carrot-redheads aren't that common in my neighborhood. It had never occurred to me that she was my doppelgänger. I didn't see it at all. She looked nothing like Rita Hayworth.

"I don't want to make trouble," I said. "But if I have to, I will. And I can . . ."

"You've already made trouble!" she said. "Someone grabbed me off the street late last night, thought I was you. . . ."

"Who grabbed you?"

"Do I know? All I know is, they called me by your name, and they threw a bag over my head and tried to push me into a car. I just barely got away."

"How did you get away if you had a sack over your head?"

"I learned how to fight back in the last place I lived," she said.

"What did the people who grabbed you say?"

"They asked me for Adam. I said I didn't know an Adam. And that's not the first time. I went to your building today to give you a piece of my mind about it."

"I have to go," said the super's wife behind us. "You okay, Miss Trix?"

"Yes," she said sharply.

"I'll leave the door open," said the super's wife, shuffling off in her floral slippers.

"What else did they say?"

"That's it. That's when I escaped. And last week, some woman accused me of sleeping with her boyfriend. . . ."

"Who?"

"Some blond in the village."

"I have no idea who any of these people are," I said. "I'm here for a package addressed to me that my super gave you."

"Nobody gave me anything," she said.

"My neighbors saw it," I said. "It may be connected to a murder case. Unless you want to go back to prison . . ."

"What's in it for me?"

"Aside from not going back to prison? What do you want? Money?" I riffled through my wallet and handed her all the cash I had, eighty-seven dollars.

"I want two hundred."

"Can I write you a check?"

"I don't take checks," she snarled. "What size shoe do you wear?"

"Nine."

"I'll take your shoes."

"My shoes?"

"Give me your shoes and the eighty-seven dollars, and I'll give you the box."

After I gave her my pale pink pumps, she went into a back room and came back with a box.

"I want your clothes," she said.

"Excuse me?"

"I'll give you the box if you give me your clothes," she said.

"What will I wear?"

"You can have my clothes." Her clothes were garish green and orange, and very dirty.

"Shit," I said. What was it with people making me strip lately? With the door wide open, we stripped down to our underwear and switched clothes. Though I was taller than she, we were roughly the same size.

"Stay out of my life," she said as I left.

"Likewise I'm sure."

These clothes smelled. I needed a shower, I thought, as I rounded the corner on to Avenue C and headed north toward Tenth Street.

CHAPTER FIFTEEN

While I changed out of the ugly doppelgänger clothes, which were itchy and probably full of mites or something, Jason sat in my living room and examined the hat.

"I feel something inside it," he said.

"Wait for me," I said, throwing on a blue and green sundress and going out to the living room.

Jason handed me the hat. The lining was silk. When I ran my hand inside it, I felt something, too, a piece of card or something, inside the lining. You had to be looking for it to feel it there. Using a letter opener, I ripped away the stitching, and a folded paper square fell out.

Jason picked it up and unfolded it. It was actually two sheets of paper, a hand-drawn map and a chemical formula of some kind, with the words "Last Manly Man Project" at the top. There were drawings of three separate molecules, and below that was one large molecule, with a lot of mathematical-looking text beneath.

The map was tricky. It was a very detailed drawing of an underground lab complex, showing the ventilation and water hookups, with obvious arrows pointing to the place where the bonobos were held. The only locator was a larger arrow that pointed south, with the word "Montauk."

"It's somewhere north of Montauk, Long Island," I said. "That doesn't narrow it down much."

"Does this mean anything to you?" Jason said, handing me the chemical formula.

I tried to make sense out of the chemical jargon, words like androstenone, copulin, "effect reversals through molecular recombination," "transducing cilia," "nucleotide-gated channels," and so forth. Greek to me. A brainiac was required. Now, to find the right egghead, someone who could be trusted to decipher the formula without stealing it or blabbing about it to the media. Probably, some of this stuff was available on the Internet, or the library could pull some stuff from its many and sundry databases, but that might leave a trail that Investigative Reports or the bad guys might somehow be able to follow. We would need a safe computer and a photocopier.

Sally had both. She wasn't home, but I had the spare keys to her apartment, so we could use one of her computers. For now, all we could do was look up some of the words in the chemical formula and try to figure out what they were. Thank Sally's gods and goddesses, she hadn't changed her password again. After I logged Jason on-line, I put in a few calls to the smartest mad scientists I knew and waited for them to call me back.

"I found something. 'Androstenone is a male pheromone. Pheromones are molecules, often odorless, detected by the veromonasal gland in the nose,' " Jason read off the screen. " 'The veromonasal gland is known as the second nose, the subconscious nose. It picks up messages the "thinking nose," which smells smells, misses. It was long thought dormant in humans, but recent studies show it may be more active than previously thought.' Hmmm. You know how the menstrual cycles of women who live or work closely together start to align?"

"Yeah," I said. "Happened in every office I've worked in."

"That alignment is believed to be initiated by an airborne pheromone. Chemicals extracted from male and female underarm sweat and later applied under a woman's nose could beneficially alter the timing of her menstrual periods."

"Does it say more about androstenone? Or this other one, Osmone two?" I asked.

"Maybe the next article will," Jason said.

An hour later, we had read about copulin, Osmone 1, and sundry other airborne chemicals. Androstenone, we learned, is a male-delivered pheromone that repels women when they are infertile and attracts them when fertile. Copulin was female-delivered, and incited testosterone development in men. Osmone 1 was a steroid with tranquilizing effects, being experimented with in aromatherapy. There was nothing on Osmone 2.

"The androstenone molecule in this diagram," Jason said, pointing to the computer screen, "is different from the one in this diagram. See? There's an extra line here. . . ."

"The copulin molecule is different too," I said.

"Like it has been altered somehow. Well, we know Adam one is an airborne chemical, possibly odorless, that can work on the veromonasal gland to alter behavior," Jason said. "Other than that, it's Greek to me. Maybe it's a love potion."

"Or an estrogen bomb," I said.

"A what?" Jason asked.

"Something Alana DeWitt mentioned."

The pink phone covered in little blue starfish rang. I answered it. It was Dr. Budd Nukker, the Extropian biochemist who wanted to live forever. He said he could see me for fifteen minutes before dinner at 7:00. It was now 6:00 P.M.

" 'There's been some interesting new research involving gene splicing and molecular recombination,' " Jason read. " 'There are already colognes containing pheromones on the market.' "

"I've heard of colognes with pheromones in them. They advertise them on the *Howard Stern* show."

"According to this, independent studies of those colognes showed them to be ineffective. The pheromonal concentration is too low. If they work at all, it's the power of suggestion, the placebo effect. If they actually worked and someone tried to market them, the FDA would move in to regulate them as mood-altering substances."

"So, as long as they don't work, it's okay to sell them."

"According to this, yes," he said.

It was pretty scary, the idea that some odorless or near odorless particle could be released in the air and somehow alter or influence behavior. How invasive is that? You can close your eyes to things you can't see, but it is hard to close your nose to things you don't want to inhale, given the primal urge to *breathe* every few seconds. Already, there was an environmental group targeting perfume the way it had targeted cigarette smoke. But how to counter something you can't smell, something that operates on you subconsciously?

"Can't market it legally. So it's for the illegal drug market?" Jason said.

"Or someone with a political agenda."

"Blue Baker is coming by with some info. He travels all over the city and Long Island, so this map might make sense to him. He's going to drop me off, but you should stay with him. He'll take you to see Dr. Nukker."

"Where are you going?"

"I have another meeting with the liberation specialist."

"Once we find out where this place is, what's our next move?"

"Case the place, then plan the liberation," Jason said. "In a nutshell."

Jason's beeper went off.

"It's Blue. He's almost here. We should wait downstairs."

We waited for Blue in the foyer of my apartment building. A black and silver car drove up, and the driver turned its interior light on and off quickly.

"That's Blue," Jason said.

We ran out to the car. Jason hopped in the back and I hopped in the front with Blue.

"Hello, ladies," Blue said, and laughed. "Dewey's talking again. I just left him. Nurse made some notes."

"Thanks," Jason said. "Drop me off at the Bog, okay?"

The Bog was an ecofriendly bar and music joint near the Chelsea Piers.

"Then Robin needs to go see a man," Jason went on. "And we have a map we want you to look at."

"Sure. Keep an eye out, make sure we're not being followed," Blue said, checking his rearview mirror. He had some kind of acid jazz playing low on the CD system.

"What has Dewey said so far?" Jason asked.

"He had one coherent burst. Apparently, he went to meet with these two scientists . . ."

"Hufnagel and Bondir," I said.

"Right. That was the day he got beaten up. He told them he was going to meet you next at some restaurant, to find out what you knew. . . ."

"How did he know where . . . wait," I said. "I remember now. Someone called my office to find out where my dinner meeting was. I assumed it was Benny Winter. . . ."

"Must have been Dewey. Getting back to the story, one of the scientists was supposed to give Dewey the information on where the bonobos were. But they'd been followed, and they were jumped . . ."

"By the thugs," I said.

"I assume they're the same thugs."

"Did Dewey say who these scientists worked for?"

"He doesn't remember getting that information. He's had some memory loss."

"Anything else?"

"Yes. He kept saying 'hat' and 'women.' Mean anything to you?"

"The hat, yeah," Jason said. "The map and the formula were in the hat."

"You have the map?" Blue said.

"We both have copies," I said.

When we stopped at a red light, Blue looked at the map.

"It doesn't ring any bells. I got a cousin who's a building inspector. Maybe he can make some sense outta that map. Oh, I looked after that other matter."

"What matter?" I asked.

"Steering your friends in Investigative Reports astray," Jason said.

"Yeah? Cool. What did you do?"

"Doctored up a couple of old reports from my sanitation cop days, changed dates, made the officers' names unreadable. One of them was a report on illegal dumping of lab waste— threw in a couple mentions of nicotine by-products . . ."

"That was my idea," Jason said.

"Yeah. The other is a report on a dead lab monkey we found in the Brooklyn dunes a few years back. So I took these reports and faxed them to the numbers you gave me, Jason. Speaking of monkeys and so on, you hear about those gorillas in equatorial Guinea?"

"Which ones?" Jason asked.

"Stormed a village to free a baby gorilla captured by a hunter. They succeeded."

"Yeah, you heard about the elephant in India that was working on a road crew, moving logs? He escaped into the forest, took two female elephants with him."

"Two females! My man!" Blue said.

"Did you hear about the guy in East Africa?" I said. "Went around shooting gorillas with tranquilizer darts and dressing them in clown clothes."

"Those gorillas must have been pissed when they woke up," Blue said.

"It's mean to do that to gorillas," Jason said. "But I can think of some people I'd like to do that to."

Blue pulled up in front of the Bog, a white plaster building, two stories, that stood out in a block of one-story buildings and parking lots.

"You'll be okay?" Blue said. "All tarted up like that, Jason, you be careful."

"Yeah, yeah. Beep me when you know something," Jason said, and hopped out of the car. We waited until he went inside before we drove off.

"Jason won't let me use my cell phone for Organization business," Blue said. "Says the phones aren't safe . . ."

"Use this one. It belongs to my neighbor. I'm sure it's safe," I said.

Blue dialed. "Malcolm, is your daddy home? It's Uncle Blue, baby. What? Where? Okay. You take care of yourself."

"Well?"

"We have to go to Queens. It's his bowling night," Blue said.

"We can head over there after Budd Nukker," I said.

Having Nukker look over the formula required him stepping off his treadmill and away from his heart and lung monitors. He did so, but each moment away from his life-lengthening activities made him visibly more anxious, bringing him a moment closer to the "possibility" of eventual death.

"Androstenone is reported to make women sexually receptive. Copulin incites testosterone development in men," Nukker said.

"Makes them horny?"

"Theoretically. Makes them more aggressive in general. This has been reengineered though. I don't know why, or what the effect would be. Perhaps to make it easier for men to absorb it."

"What about this one, Osmone Two?"

"Well, Osmone One is an airborne tranquilizer," Nukker said. "I've never heard of Osmone Two, but clearly it is some sort of adaptation of One."

"Could it affect men and women differently? The way pheromones do?"

"Possibly. All the studies I've seen show women are far more sensitive to these things."

"How so?"

"Well, women are a thousand times more sensitive than men to musk molecules. Women tend to respond more strongly to aromatherapy, and women's menstrual cycles are often aligned by pheromonal signals."

"I've heard that. So this could be an airborne tranquilizer that operates on women only?"

"Could be," he said. He was starting to sweat profusely and glanced at his treadmill. "I would have to run it through the computer, perhaps conduct lab tests to know more. That could take months."

"Thanks anyway," I said, not wanting to leave the formula with him, though he'd probably be too busy staying alive to rip it off. It had been risky showing it to him, but he was the only one of the eggheads to respond to my call.

"It confirms what Jason and I found," I said to Blue after I left Nukker. "Adam is some sort of odorless, virtually undetectable, airborne substance designed to subconsciously alter the behavior of men and women."

"No shit. Who do you think is behind it?"

"I was leaning toward Alana DeWitt. But why would Alana

DeWitt want to make men more aggressive? Unless it is part of some long-range scheme to make men kill each other off while women sat by contentedly. She's mad enough to do it, but she doesn't seem patient enough to wait out the resulting wars. On the other hand, this would probably be faster than waiting for the Y chromosome to devolve."

"Huh?" Blue said.

I brought him up to speed on Alana DeWitt's theory of male extinction.

We turned into the parking lot of a small mall in Bayside, Queens, dominated by a bowling alley with a vertical 1950s-drive-in-style cutout sign shaped like a large bowling pin that said "BowlMuch Lanes" in big black and red letters. The sun was finally setting, and the red neon outline of the bowling pin lit up as we were walking through the parking lot.

Inside, we were hit by bright lights and loud noises, balls rolling, pins falling down, and sixties rock on the sound system. It was league bowling, and people were in matching shirts. Blue found his cousin Ernie and pulled him aside to the bar, which was bright red and yellow. Everything in this place was 1950s Technicolor.

"Hiya, Blue," Ernie said. "Still dating your ex-wife?"

"Yeah, am I a jerk or what? Hey, take a look at this map. Any way you can find out where this building is from this information? All we know is that it's on an island somewhere north of Montauk."

"Is it important?"

"Yeah."

"Let me ask Jackie. The plumbing specs might make some sense to him. Jackie," Ernie called to another big black guy. "Come take a look at this."

Before it was over, Ernie's whole team was huddled over

the map, discussing the possibilities. One of the bowlers knew a plumber out on Long Island who worked near Montauk. He went to call him. Others on the team left to bowl their turns.

"See you Labor Day, for the picnic," Ernie said to Blue.

"Yeah, thanks, Ernie."

"You wanna beer or something, Robin?" Blue asked, reaching into a bowl of peanuts at the bar.

"Maybe a soda, a Coca-Cola."

"Give us a coupla Cokes," he said to the bartender, and popped more peanuts into his mouth. "You bowl, Robin?"

"Once in a while, on a lark. My average is about sixty-six, as I recall. You?"

Blue shook his head. "Tell me about this story you've been working on, the one that got you involved in this bonobo business," he said.

"Man of the Future. How men might evolve, a lot of different visions of it. I've been trying to nail down something eternal about masculinity, beyond anatomy, of course. What do you think it means to be a man, Blue?"

Blue took a drink of his Coke, then wiped his mouth with his hand. "In twenty-five words or less?"

"Or more."

"When my pop died a few years ago, my oldest sister, Ruby, found some letters he'd written as a kid to his ma, when he was away at this boarding school for poor boys, run by some church in Massachusetts. In one of the letters, he wrote that he was in the hospital. 'Don't worry, Ma, it's nothing serious,' he wrote. 'Just a touch of polio.' "

"Wow."

"That just sums it up for me, my pop far from home, trying to better himself, getting polio, having to be strong, and yet sensitive to his ma's feelings. That's a man. He was only ten at the time."

"He recovered from the polio though?"

"Yeah, but it stunted the toes on one foot and left him with a limp. Your dad alive?"

I shook my head. "I was only ten when he died. He was a math teacher and a weekend inventor. He died while trying to make the world safer for his womenfolk and everyone else."

"How?"

"He was campaigning to get a streetlight on a bad corner. While he was measuring the street to get its specifications for his safety report, a truck barreled around the corner and mowed him down. You know how they say someone has to die before they'll put a streetlight at a bad corner? My dad was the guy who died. Shortly after, a traffic light was put up. When I was little, I liked to imagine my father was in the traffic light, a benign authority telling me when to stop, to go, or to slow down and use caution."

"I understand," Blue said.

The bowler who knew the Long Island plumber returned.

"I found Les. It's his poker night. He plays at the Surfside Bar in Coney Island. He's expecting you."

"Thanks, bro," Blue said. We paid for our Cokes and left.

"You think men will be stronger *and* more sensitive in the future, Blue?" I asked.

"I think so, I hope so. There are some bad young 'uns out there, but the good ones seem a lot better than the good ones in my day. Jason and Dewey are good guys. You like Jason?"

"Yeah, he's okay," I said. "Young and idealistic. A firebrand."

"Yeah, and Dewey is too. But it's nice to know there are still kids who care, you know what I'm sayin'? Our generation, they're facing 'reality,' or what passes for it. You know things aren't the way they should be, but you go along to get along. You want to save the spotted owl, but you know how those loggers feel, being put out of their jobs. They got mouths to feed. Some of 'em, all they've known is logging. What are they going to do?"

"It's hard for men. Their self-esteem seems so much more tied up in their work than women's is, generally speaking."

"That's a fact, even in these modern times. Dewey and Jason, they aren't practical, God bless 'em."

"So how come a guy of your generation is involved?"

"Bottom line, I think they're right, those kids. Not practical. But right in the long run. Some people make practical choices, some take the high road, no matter the cost. Me, I gotta look after my karma. I was a bad guy when I was young. Mean. Had a lot to prove."

"You were a bad guy, Blue? I have a hard time believing that."

"I used to cheat on my wife, lie about everything, I was selfish. . . ."

"Well, that's human stuff a lot of people go through. It's not like you killed someone. . . ."

"Yeah, I did. Killed some men in Nam," Blue said, and his dark skin took on a different kind of darkness, the kind that comes from within. For a moment, he glowered over the dashboard, the streetlights strobing his face.

"I didn't want to kill. I did it because my country told me to. That's when I stopped believing in countries, know what I'm sayin', Robin? There's just planet Earth, the Organism, a part of the Big Organism, no borders, no real estate. How can anyone own a piece of the planet? I've never understood that. Who gave them the right to buy it, or sell it?"

"That's what happened to change you from bad to good? Nam?"

"It happened later, after I got back. Long story. Like a miracle. I got high with an angel, and I got nice."

"A real angel?"

"Who knows? 'Be not forgetful to entertain strangers, for thereby some have entertained angels, unawares,'" he said. "Hebrews."

When we got to Coney Island, Blue parked near the armed services recruiting center just off Surf Avenue and we walked down to the boardwalk. It was around ten, and the lights were all on in Coney Island. All the rides and amusements were lit up and moving to their tinny carnival music. There were sailors on leave and girls in polka-dot dresses with beehive hairdos. If you squinted a little, it seemed like it was 1952, the Dodgers were still at Ebbets Field and Chevrolet still ruled the road. But then two punked-out lovers walked by, followed by a couple of yuppie dads in Dockers pushing yuppie puppies in strollers. I heard the Ramones blaring from the sound system of one of the open-front bars on the boardwalk, and I was caught in this lovely anachronistic warp.

We walked down the boardwalk toward the Surfside Bar. Tucked into a long line of concessions, the front was wide open and facing the ocean. We walked in and looked around, until we saw a table of guys playing cards at the back.

"One of you guys Les?" Blue asked.

"Yeah, I am," said a short white guy with a monkish fringe of hair and dark-rimmed glasses. "Excuse me, guys, I gotta go talk to these people. Can you get me another beer and some French fries?"

"Thanks for helping us out," I said.

"No problem. Larry and Ernie vouched for you. Let's sit down at this table. You need a beer?"

"No thanks," I said.

I unfolded the map and put it on the table between us, and Les took a long hard look at it.

"I didn't do this job," he said. "But I might know who did. Can I keep this?"

"Well . . ." I said.

"How about this? Here's my card. Fax a copy of this to me tomorrow, and I'll make some calls."

"Thank you," I said.

"Les, your fries," called one of the cardplayers.

After he left them, Blue said, "Don't expect there's much more we can do tonight. And Jason hasn't beeped. Come on, I'll take you home. You in a hurry?"

"Not a terrible hurry."

We wound our way through the anachronistic, somewhat seedy midway, and Blue stopped at a shooting gallery and shot off a few rounds at little metal targets that moved back and forth along a wire. He was a good shot, and won me a tiny gold Buddha.

"That's good karma," he said to me.

When I got home, my cat was at the window, and the message light was blinking. Liz had called to say the interview went well—I'd forgotten to call the office and check up on her. Gus had called to say he was moving to the Metro Grand Hotel and would be in town for a few more days, could we please get together to talk, to really talk. He asked that I call him, but I couldn't deal with it right now, though I felt bad. He was confused by my blowing him off without a logical explanation and he was falling into an old trap, where you think you like someone more than they like you just because they seem to be cooling to you. No matter what I told him, he wouldn't believe me: Hey, Gus, I'm hot on the trail of a biological weapon at the moment, can we talk later?

I crawled into bed with the hat, a beautiful hat despite its now torn lining. Boy, the world had changed. When I was a kid, you would see a steady stream of men in hats walking down the street on a Saturday afternoon, even more on Sunday, as men always wore hats to church in my town, which they removed before they entered. Now you see men in hats and it either seems old-fashioned or a retro affectation. Funny, too, that hats, which protect the head and serve a practical purpose, went out of style and ties survived. Between the two, wouldn't you vote for the hat over the paisley noose? Men got screwed on that one.

I fell asleep holding the hat and dreamed of Jesus, one of those Jesus dreams like I used to have as a kid, after my dad died, Jesus as cartoon superhero, swooping down out of the sky to kick the shit out of the bad guys, with lots of *thunks!* and *pows!* Adam West–Batman style. In this dream, Superhero Jesus rescues me, Jason, and the bonobos, and we all hold hands and fly through the sky to some safe, warm, dry place. Jesus is wearing the hat.

CHAPTER SIXTEEN

The next morning at the office, I faxed the map to Les the plumbing contractor, pounded out a script for the second part of the series, and delegated all other authority to my staff. Liz got another interview. Shauna got one, too. Karim the agoraphobic tape editor was assigned the promo. The interns were assigned to help the others.

This presented a problem, because there wasn't one of my employees I trusted. Word that they were doing these challenging assignments could cause quite a ripple around the network. Not only would this give newsroom gossips something to fictionalize about, but it might tip Reb and Solange off that my energies were being focused elsewhere.

To prevent this, I convened a staff meeting in our conference area and spun my abdication of responsibilities this way: You, my loyal employees are being given increased opportunities on account of your excellent work. There are risks involved in these new responsibilities. The newsroom naysayers are watching you, ready to pull you down before you even get started. Don't give them any ammunition. Work quietly and discreetly until the series airs, showing me, the newsroom naysayers, and all other doubters what you can do.

Now, my employees were professionally and emotionally invested in the quality of the product. Their butts were on the line.

Jack had called, and that was one task I couldn't delegate. I called him back immediately.

"Robin, I was readin', uh, an article by this woman Suzy Hibben. You know her?"

"Not personally. But I know of her. She's spent most of her adult life running all over the country telling other women to stay home and serve their husbands and children."

"She's here at the women's conference with a bunch of her college girl followers."

"Yeah, her college followers have a group called the Mrs. Degree," I said.

"That's clever. She says here that women have always secretly run the world, as the power behind the throne. . . ."

"Those women who have been secretly running the world, they sure have been doing a lousy job," I shot back. "What was up with the Inquisition? Or World War Two? Or Watergate? Or the Vietnam War? Or all that postwar wife-beating? What were women thinking?"

"Touched a nerve, huh? You havin' a bad day, Robin? You sound aggravated."

"Oh. No. It's just one of those days, Jack. Hectic, you know? Women have influence and always have, sure. But not enough. That secret-power-of-women crapola is a myth they feed women to keep them from clamoring for more real power."

"You have more power than you think, in my opinion," Jack said.

"Yeah, probably so, and we have just as much of our own crapola," I said.

He laughed and hung up without saying good-bye.

Les the plumbing contractor had left a message to call him back, but he wasn't in when I returned the call. While I waited for him to get back to his office, I read through the papers. All the tabloids were reporting the Luc Bondir "dead for fifteen years" story. All the papers hinted at a connection between Bondir and illicit nicotine experiments. Blue and Jason had been effective in their ruse to mislead the media so far.

"I think I've found the place for you," Les said. "A guy I know was the plumbing contractor two years ago on a job on Tweak Island, off Long Island in the Atlantic. He did the job for a company, LMM Corporation."

LMM. Last Manly Man.

"Know who owns this island?"

"The LMM Corporation, offshore registry, Cayman Islands, I think. I'm gonna fax you the coordinates."

"Thanks, Les."

For a moment, I toyed with tracking down this LMM Corporation. This would take a long time, and I wasn't sure what good it would do. It was no doubt a holding company of a holding company of a holding company.

As soon as I got the Tweak Island coordinates from Les, I beeped Jason.

"Found island," I said. "Am at work."

Five minutes later, he beeped back, "Blue coming. Half hour."

Jason was waiting for us with another man at a table at the Bog, an environment- and cannabis-friendly club in downtown Manhattan. It was an eco-club, where you could pick up the latest literature on boycotts, swig a brew, and watch *The Wizard of Oz* with the sound turned down and the soundtrack from Pink Floyd's *Dark Side of the Moon* turned up. If you're around my age and you want to really feel your age, stop by this place on a busy night. You never saw so much baby fat. And what an anachronism. It was the 1960s here, black light, glow-in-the-dark peace signs, and R. Crumb "Keep on Trucking" posters, girls with frizzy hair in Indian muslin skirts and tunic blouses (some of them born post-MTV, all born well after the Beatles broke up).

The bar was carved out of half a psychedelic school bus, once used to transport deadheads from Grateful Dead concert to Grateful Dead concert. Plastered around the walls were signs exhorting people to help save this animal or those indigenous people, to free Animal Liberation Front activist Rod Coronado, to boycott this company or that company.

Today, Jason was wearing a coral pink and yellow sundress with pale pink, closed-toe sandals. He looked pretty as a picture.

"This is number twenty. He's a liberation specialist," Jason said, introducing Blue and me to a short, skinny white man in his thirties. "This is Robin, the journalist I told you about, and this is number seven."

"You can call me Blue," Blue said.

"Good to meet you," he said, spreading a Long Island map out on the table and checking the coordinates of Tweak Island against it. "Okay, Tweak Island is right . . . here."

Jason spread his copy of the hand-drawn map of Tweak Island next to the larger map. "We think the bonobos are being held there," he said, pointing.

Number twenty studied the hand-drawn map, then the Long Island map. "We're going to need to reconnoiter the island, confirm its location, and make note of all visible security," number twenty said. "Let's take a little trip out there."

An hour later, Jason, Blue, number twenty, and I boarded a fishing boat moored at the northern end of Manhattan. There was a six-person crew in addition to us, all members of the Organization, two dressed in loose cotton pants and shirts that bore the name Islander Fishing Expeditions. Three others were dressed as tourist fishermen, in Bermuda shorts and short-sleeved shirts. The last member of the crew, named Ethan, was a young, bearded redhead wearing a knit cap and a big un-bleached apron over baggy, rough-weave clothes. He looked like he'd just stepped off a Greenpeace recruitment poster, and he smelled like a burlap bag full of potatoes.

"We are a couple hours away, so just relax for now. When we get close, we'll want you to stay out of sight, inside the cabin, in case they have lookouts who might recognize any of you," number twenty said.

Jason knew Ethan from a previous operation, and they renewed their acquaintance with bear hugs.

"Wow, you make a good-looking woman," Ethan said to Jason. "I almost didn't recognize you."

"Most people don't until I open my mouth," Jason said. "What are you doing on this operation?"

"I'm the chief cook and bottle-washer. Come on down to the kitchen. Bring your friends," Ethan said.

We followed him down to the galley.

"I'm making a big batch of couscous," Ethan said. "You all like couscous, with veggies and broiled tofu?"

"Robin doesn't like vegetarian food." Jason sneered.

"You're not a vegetarian?" Ethan asked me.

"I'm a minerarian."

"What's that?"

"I don't eat any living things, animal or vegetable. I eat rocks. Only rocks. I wash them down with water," I said.

"She's a meat-eater. She thinks she's funny." Jason scowled.

"My couscous is excellent. People sign on to our crew just for the cooking. You'll like it," Ethan said. He was a sunnily optimistic counterpoint to Jason's cynical self-righteousness.

Blue pulled out a deck of cards and we sat at the table and

played hearts while Ethan cooked. We all helped ferry food to the rest of the crew, then sat in the sun and ate it. Ethan, Jason, and Blue discussed various endangered and extinct species—the harelip sucker, the long-jaw cisco, the Wabash riffleshell, the spectacled cormorant, the Tasmanian wolf, the dusky sea sparrow, the hairy-eared dwarf lemur, and so forth. They all had such colorful names. Being interesting was no defense against obliteration, evidently.

It was warm in the sun, and it made me sleepy. I dozed off, visions of long-jaw ciscos dancing in my head. Some time later, Jason awakened me. We were getting close to Tweak Island and had to go into the cabin.

Inside, we were handed binoculars. The fishing boat pulled up near Tweak Island and stopped. We were about a hundred yards offshore. The island was surrounded by a chain-link fence topped with coils of razor wire. Behind the fence was a large, one-story brown building. There was a pier and two speedboats were tethered to it, bobbing in the water and bumping against each other.

For the first half hour, we saw no visible activity on the island. Then a helicopter rose up from behind the building and circled above it. It flew out to us, hovering above us momentarily before flying off.

After that, there was nothing for another half hour, when two men got into one of the speedboats and came out toward us.

"Get down, away from the windows," said Jason.

Outside, we heard the speedboat motor approach, then cut to idle.

"Who are you?" asked a man.

Number twenty explained he was the operator of a fishing tour. Two of our crew, posing as tourists, said something in some foreign language, and then one of the men in the speedboat said, "This is a private beach. Could you please take your fishing elsewhere?"

The speedboat left, heading out toward another fishing boat, a few hundred yards or so back of our boat. Number twenty came into the cabin and said, "We're going to head out a little farther so we're less conspicuous."

Number twenty sat down and began marking up a copy of the hand-drawn map with notations, while another member of his crew looked on. He called Jason over.

"We see from this map that the electricity connects here and here. The alarm system has to be disabled here. The map says the bonobos are held here, unless they've been moved. There are guards here and here. The entrance is double-bolted and requires a pass code. That might be these numbers down here. Just in case, we'll have to bring explosives to blow our way in. In addition to firearms, we'll need tranquilizer guns and nonlethal doses of knockout drugs."

He pulled out an almanac.

"The full moon is waning, but we still have the problem of too much moonlight. What is the weather forecast?"

"Clear tonight, partially cloudy by morning, with possible rain showers, progressively cloudy until the weekend."

"Cloudy is good. Rain is good," said number twenty. "We'll have to work fast to catch this cloudy weather."

One of the "tourists" came inside. "Another helicopter patrol above the island," he said. "The chopper goes out on the hour, the speedboat on the half hour."

"All right. Let's head back to land. The crew and I will make a few quick passes of the island tonight to check out the nighttime security. We'll rendezvous tomorrow morning, eight A.M., at the Bog to discuss our options. That'll give Jason and me time to consult with some other specialists. We're going to need backup on this job."

"I definitely want to be at the liberation, with my own camera," I said to Jason as we sailed back.

"I told you that you could have the story when the bonobos were liberated. I don't break my promises," he said. "I'm meeting with Karen Keyes at the women's conference later. Do you want to join us?"

"Yes."

"Eight P.M., by the Diogenes booth. There's a rock band performing, so the room will be dim, but try to disguise yourself anyway," he said.

"Eight P.M.," I repeated. That was good. The conference was only a couple of blocks from the Metro Grand Hotel, which meant I could stop by and see Gus, try to smooth things out with him.

I didn't have much time for smoothing, as it turned out. It was after 7:00 by the time Blue dropped me off at my place. I just had time to change quickly, put my hair up under a scarf, and run back down to Blue.

"Where to?" Blue asked.

"The Metro Grand Hotel," I said. That's where Gus was now staying. Gus only stayed at the Plaza when he wanted to play the newlyweds-from-the-Midwest game. "Where are you going?"

"I have a bunch of deliveries backed up for this evening," Blue said. "But I'll be on beeper if you need me."

Gus was in the bar of the Metro Grand, unshaven, drinking whiskey.

"I'm so glad you came," Gus said when he saw me. "Can we talk?"

"I don't have much time. I have to run to the women's conference," I said. "I just stopped by to see how you were. . . ."

"Why do you have to go? Are you giving a speech or something?" he asked, clearly annoyed.

"No, I have to meet some people for work. . . ."

"I'm going with you then."

"No, don't do that."

"Why not? What's going on? Look, you keep running off, I can't get a straight answer out of you. . . . It's like you can't wait to get away from me. You owe me some answers, Robin," he said.

It stung when he used my real name.

"It's not you . . ." I said, regretting the words as soon as they came out. I sounded like I was getting ready to dump him.

"It is me! I can't get a part, I can't keep a woman around. . . . What is my problem?"

"It's not you. I really like you. I want to see you. I just . . . have to go," I said, and walked out of the bar.

"I'm going with you," he said, following me out.

"Go away," I said. Man, oh man, I hated to do that, to hurt him.

"Not until you tell me what's going on," he said, sticking with me.

Quickly, I speeded up, walking well ahead of him, but he continued to follow, seething. He followed me right into the women's conference.

The convention floor was packed with people there to watch a rock band called the She-Wolves. The lights were dimmed except around the peripheries of the hall, where booths representing different women's groups and causes were set up. In the low light, I was able to lose Gus.

I couldn't see Jason or Keyes. When my eyes adjusted to the dimness, I saw that the audience was only about half women. The rest were men, of all ages, but primarily young men of various races, some in She-Wolves T-shirts.

On the stage, four women in tight white T-shirts and jeans sang sexually aggressive songs about men, songs originally done by men about women. At the moment, they were singing their slightly rewritten cover of "Little Red Riding Hood," a Sam the Sham and the Pharaohs song. In this throaty, hard rock version, they are the she-wolves and a young man is Red Riding Hood.

"Where's Jason?" someone behind me asked.

It was Karen Keyes.

"I thought he was with you."

"I haven't seen him. Oh, by the way, someone else from ANN called me today. Reb Ryan from . . ."

"Investigative Reports," I said. "What did he want to know?"

"If I knew anything about some missing bonobo chimps. I feigned ignorance, of course. . . ."

"Damn. That means they are getting closer to the real story," I said. "Shit."

"I told Jason I didn't have much time," Keyes said. "I have a symposium at nine I haven't finished preparing for. Can you have him contact me after the symposium?"

"Yeah, if I find him," I said.

After she left, I wandered the conference floor, moving through the darkened hall under corporate banners for soft drinks, menstrual analgesics, clothing lines, automakers, and so on, past the birth control booths, the displays exhorting women to join one women's group or another, the causes— Amnesty International, Globofeminism, Universal Health Care, etc. The Mrs. Degree girls, followers of Suzy Hibben, were handing out brochures next to hosiery company reps handing out free pantyhose. At a booth to promote women's boxing, you could put on padded gloves and hammer a punching ball.

Between the Lesbian Parents booth and a cosmetic company display, my beeper went off.

"Trouble," said the message. "I am coming to get you. Blue."

CHAPTER SEVENTEEN

Something has gone wrong?" I said, jumping into Blue's car.

"Not exactly," Blue said.

Before he could explain, the back door opened.

Gus jumped in.

"Gus, what are you doing here? Go home! For God's sake!" I said.

"So this is who you blew me off for," Gus said.

"No, Gus . . ."

"I'm not leaving until I get an explanation," Gus said. "I'm tired of these wild stories. I want the truth."

"Okay, the truth," I said. "This is my lover. I didn't want to tell you. You're a nice guy, Gus, and it was fun, but my heart belongs to Blue here."

"I thought you were different," Gus said, and he sounded deeply hurt. "It felt special to me. . . ."

"No, I'm like all the rest. I'm a bitch and I was just using you. Now go home, get on with your life," I said.

"I'm going," Gus said.

As soon as he was out of the car, Blue squealed away.

"Want to tell me what that was about?" he asked.

"I can't very well tell him the truth. I mean, I did tell him the truth, and he didn't believe it. He'd rather believe I'm ditching him for another man."

"You broke his heart," Blue said. "He had tears in his eyes."

"Did I? Boy, I hated to do that to him. But what choice did I have? I really liked him too. He's really sweet and . . ."

"Maybe you can make it up to him later," Blue said.

"I hope I get the chance. I really do like him. He's a lot of fun and he's really sweet. Shit. So what's up?"

"Our boy Dewey has spoken some more. Apparently, arrangements had been made with yet another cell to create a diversion on one side of Tweak Island to facilitate the liberation on the other side. It is impossible to reach the diversion squad now. The liberation would have to take place Wednesday night. That means we are going to have to work tonight to be ready to go out tomorrow. We're going to the hospice now. Jason's there. Number twenty and some of his crew are meeting us over there."

"Okay. What will I need . . ."

"Damn," Blue said.

"What?"

"I was supposed to call my ex-wife. Do me a favor?"

"Sure."

"Look in that box of CDs. There's a Robert Mitchum calypso CD."

"Robert Mitchum doing calypso?"

"It sounds strange, but he was pretty good."

"Found it."

"Good," he said, dialing his cell phone with one hand. "Plug it in, forward to the last track, I think it is number fourteen, "My Baby's Loving Arms." Hit the pause button. When I nod my head, hit the play button."

"Okay."

"Honey?" Blue said into the phone. "I'm sorry I forgot to

call you. Business. But I'll see you this weekend and I'll be thinking of you."

He nodded at me and I hit the play button. Blue held the phone to a speaker. After the song was over, he put the phone back to his ear and said, "Love ya, baby. Good night."

"Gotta keep that woman happy," he said to me after hanging up.

"How come you date your ex-wife?" I asked.

"Aw, hell, I'd remarry her, but she wants it this way. Peculiar woman. She thinks it's the only way to keep me faithful. If I step out on her, she's free to step out on me. Know what I'm sayin', Robin?"

"It's unconventional, but I can see the logic to that."

"She's a mean woman that one, when she has reason to be. But I love her. Crazy, huh?"

"I've heard of crazier things," I said. "A friend of a friend is a bisexual woman who only dates married couples she meets through personal ads in the back of upscale magazines."

"Bet that gets messy when it doesn't work out. But then, it's usually messy when it doesn't work out."

"How long have you been divorced?"

"Four years. You been married?"

"Yeah, for five years. He's remarried now, has a kid and another on the way. You got kids?"

"A married daughter in California and two grandkids. They all think we should get married again. They're on my side. Think you'll get married again?"

"I dunno, Blue. My life is too crazy and I'm too busy," I said, as Blue turned into the hospice parking garage. "I'd like to think so though, because I have this terrible vision that I'm going to end up alone except for the male nurse I pay to change my diapers and listen to my life story."

As if on cue, Horton the male nurse was waiting there for us in the garage.

"They're waiting for you upstairs," Horton said.

Jason, a couple of the boat crew members, and some people I hadn't seen before were sitting on the floor at the foot of Dewey's bed. Dewey was unconscious. Number twenty was writing on a blackboard.

"Hi," Jason said.

"Hi," I said. "Has Dewey said anything new?"

"Nothing you have to worry about right now," number twenty said to me. "Listen up. The rest of the crew is scoping out the island right now. We're going to have to go in tomorrow night. That doesn't give us much time."

He drew an arrow to the far side of Tweak Island.

"The diversion squad will be operating here. According to Dewey, they are going to light an old boat on fire in the water here at midnight. At that time, saboteurs must be in place to cut off power and disable the alarm system. Those carrying out the actual liberation of the bonobos will land here."

He drew another arrow to the north side of the island.

"We'll cut through here, and enter through this door." He turned to me. "I understand you'll be bringing a camera."

"An undercover camera, concealed in a purse," I said.

"You've never gone on an operation like this before, have you?"

"I've gone undercover lots of times. I've never gone on an animal liberation."

"I'll want you to stay close to Jason, pulling up the rear. You'll do everything he says. Your job is to stay out of the way and just film. We don't have much time to pull this off, so we'll need to be extra careful. Okay?"

"Okay."

Number twenty handed me a thin, pulpy, dog-eared booklet, entitled simply *Liberating Lab Animals*.

"Read this, it'll bring you up to speed on the basics. I've highlighted the things you need to know in yellow. Blue, I want you to stay behind on the mainland to look after transportation. We'll need a school bus."

Horton the male nurse came in with ginseng sodas and vegetarian sandwiches. We ate while we went over the maps and the drawings and all the plans. Maybe it was because I was really hungry, but I thought those sandwiches were really tasty.

After number twenty was finished with Blue and me, he said, "Go ahead and take Miss Hudson home. Read over that booklet, Miss Hudson. Assemble all the equipment you need, and get a few hours sleep. We meet at the boat landing in north Manhattan at six A.M. sharp. Synchronize your watches."

We did so.

"Tomorrow we prepare the boat and firm up everything. Tomorrow night, we free the bonobo chimps."

"Come on, darlin'," Blue said to me. "I'll take you home."

We stopped off at ANN, so I could pick up the undercover camera, Purse-Cam as we knew it in Special Reports. It was a big women's purse containing a small camera with a fish-eye lens and a rechargeable ni-cad battery pack.

When I got home, my neighbor Sally was in the foyer. She was damned surprised to see me.

"You're okay!" she said.

"So far," I said.

"You got away from the men?" she said.

"What men?"

"Mrs. Ramirez saw some men grab you on Avenue B tonight."

"It wasn't me. It must have been my doppelgänger."

"But Mrs. Ramirez said she was dressed like you, in the pink suit. . . ."

"I gave her that suit," I said. "It's a long story. . . ."

"Ramirez called the cops about it," Sally said.

Unfortunately, the cops were unlikely to believe Mrs. Dulcinia "Cry Wolf" Ramirez, so I called the precinct on the cell phone I borrowed from Sally, let them know about the abduction of Miss Trix by unidentified thugs. How ironic that our alleged resemblance caused more trouble for Miss Trix, a convicted drug dealer and exploiter of small handicapped immigrant children, than for me. Miss Trix had some serious bad karma to clear. I halfheartedly hoped she was safe, though I didn't really have time to waste feeling sorry for Miss Trix right now.

After I fed my cat, I read over the highlighted sections in the booklet number twenty had given me.

"You must pack a duffel bag in advance and keep it with you at all times, until you get the signal that the raid is to begin," it said. "Wear clean, comfortable clothes, and quiet shoes or boots. Over these, you should wear a clean jumpsuit, which can be discarded after a raid. Dark colors are best. You will need gloves. If you will be using wire cutters or other such tools, bring work gloves, or wear two or three pairs of regular gloves.

"All tools must be thoroughly wiped clean, first with soap and water, and then a dry cloth, to make sure there are no fingerprints in case a piece is dropped at the scene of a raid.

"Flashlights should be covered with colored plastic to dim their light.

"It is often a good idea to carry some sort of anti-mate, the kind used by hunt saboteurs to put hounds off the scent of game. Apply liberally every time you cross a road or a stream.

"Arrive two to three hours beforehand and hide out in a wood or other sheltered area.

"After a raid, all clothes must be thoroughly washed immediately to remove all traces of the raid scene."

There were a few other interesting tidbits, such as the information that wearing a mask for long periods can cause dry throat and coughing, so lozenges and water should be brought along, and spraying water on masonry can quiet the sound of a saw. When cutting through barbed wire, only the bottom wires should be cut, because if you're pursued in the dark, your pursuers may not see the uncut top wires, and they'll get caught in them.

These people had put a lot of time, energy, and effort into rescuing lab animals. I was damned glad of it, even though I didn't necessarily support them in all their causes and still thought they were loons.

I packed my duffel bag, arranged for Sally to keep Louise for the next couple of days, left a message at work on the voice mail saying I was going to be out for the day on a personal emergency and delegating more work, and fell into bed to get some sleep.

It was a fitful sleep, never quite gelling into a dream, and my alarm went off far too early. I was a bit dazed from lack of sleep, and without thinking, I hit the snooze button. When the alarm went off again, I awoke with a start. Now I was running late and had to rush around to get it together to meet Blue downstairs at 5:30 A.M., as we'd arranged when he'd dropped me off the night before.

I got downstairs early. There was a white van parked in front of my building. I poked my head out the front door to get a better look. When I did, the interior light flicked on and off.

I ran out, thinking Blue had again changed vehicles.

In a split second, I realized I'd made a mistake. But it was too late. Two men jumped out of the van, grabbed me, threw me in the back, and squealed away.

As one thug duct-taped my mouth, another tied my hands. The man in the front, on the passenger side, turned around.

"You've been so much trouble, Ms. Hudson," said Benny Winter.

CHAPTER EIGHTEEN

We've been waiting for you for two hours," Winter said. "I'm so glad you obliged us by coming down early to go to work. Tie her up."

One of the goons took my duffel bag. My feet were tied and my eyes covered with more duct tape, which the idiot taping me wrapped around my head mummy style. After that, a bag of some sort was put over my head. My mouth was ungagged.

"What have we here?" Winter said. "It's some kind of camera, in a purse."

"Yeah, and look at this, dark clothes, flashlight," one of the goons said. He was listing the contents of my duffel bag. "Oh, and get a load of this, a book on liberating lab animals."

"Where was this operation going to take place, Miss Hudson?" I heard Benny Winter ask.

"I don't know."

"Where were you meeting the others involved in this?"

"I don't know," I said. "I missed my ride thanks to you. He knew where we were going. That's how it works on an operation. A person only gets as much information as she needs."

"Who was your ride?"

"I don't know his name. You know, people are going to be looking for me."

"I don't think so," Winter said. "We're taking care of that."

"How?"

"Can't tell you that. You only get as much information as you need from me too," Winter said. "I believe you know more than you're letting on."

A gun was jammed into the side of my head.

"Where were you headed today?" Winter asked.

"Oh, just shoot me," I said, knowing he wouldn't until I talked.

"Perhaps we will," Winter said. "But not right now. We'll get the truth out of you, later, at the lab. Tape up her mouth too."

Mandervan. Sure, in hindsight that made a certain sense. Benny Winter had seen the address, seen the hat, known I'd run into Hufnagel. I had asked Mandervan, via Winter, about Mandervan's book on the Man of the Future, about what it meant to be manly, as I had asked all the potential interview subjects. Benny Winter may have learned from Morton, a former employer of his and Mandervan's, that I was going to be on the Morton estate on Sunday. Mandervan, in his paranoia, must have suspected I knew something about the Last Manly Man Project.

They were shrewd, he and Benny, promising Solange the future exclusive with Wally Mandervan to throw her and Reb off their trail.

It had never occurred to me before that my crazy hero, Wallace Mandervan, could be this crazy, though it happens to visionary-type people now and then—they become too confident in their own vision and go mad, get messianic.

I don't know how long we drove, but we eventually

stopped. Someone grabbed me and hauled me outside, into the open air. My feet were untied and I was led down some sort of wooden platform—the hollow sound of it made me think of a pier—and then down another, creaking wooden platform that sloped downward. Water was sloshing against wood.

"Sit," a man commanded. A short time later, a motor started up and we were moving. We were on a boat.

"I'll be glad when this job is done," I heard one of the goons say in a muffled voice. "I'm ready for a vacation."

"Where you gonna go?" asked another goon.

"Florida. See my mom, do some fishing. Relax. What are you doing for vacation?"

"I'm going to Vegas. I feel a hot streak coming on."

"You like roulette?"

"I like craps."

"This has been a tough job, Benny," the first goon said. "We oughta get some hardship pay or something."

The goons were quiet for a while. The grinding of the engine, the smell of gasoline and salt water, the rocking of the boat made me feel queasy, and I worried I was going to throw up behind my duct tape and choke on my own vomit. Instead, I fell asleep, and slept until the boat stopped.

I was hauled up a plank and down another wooden pier. A metal gate creaked open.

"Thanks. Take her into the bunker," said an unfamiliar man's voice.

I was taken down some stairs, through a tunnel that smelled like peat, into some kind of space, and was cuffed to a chair.

"Take the tape off her," yet another man's voice said.

Someone held me, while someone else ripped the duct tape off my face and head, taking chunks of hair and probably my eyebrows with it.

"Yee-ow!" I screamed.

"Pipe down, woman. What do you need?"

"Water," I said hoarsely. My eyes wouldn't focus.

Water was poured into me, too quickly. I almost choked.

When my vision cleared, I was sitting across from Wallace Mandervan.

The stories were true. He was a bearded, twitchy recluse with neatly trimmed fingernails.

"You've made a terrible mistake . . ." I said.

"Oh, I don't think so," he said.

A door opened behind him. Gill Morton came in, followed by a man in a white lab coat.

"You got her, huh? I knew she was snooping around the Adam project," Morton said.

"Give her the shot."

A man in a white lab coat came at me with a needle.

"What are you doing?" I asked.

"Sodium pentothol. Truth serum," Mandervan said. "We'll just give it a little time to work. . . ."

"Why are you doing this?" I asked.

"Miss Hudson, someone has to restore the natural order so people can be happy, so men and women can get along again. That's all we want to do, make people happy," Mandervan said. Jarringly, his voice was kind and gentle.

"We don't expect you to understand, because you've been brainwashed," Morton said, in his dubbed foreign movie voice. "But sometimes, sacrifices have to be made in order to move history forward. That's something women don't understand."

Ah, it was for the good of *man*kind.

As the drug worked its way through my already exhausted system, a weird feeling of relaxation came over me, followed by a feeling of detachment. Time lost all meaning. Suddenly, I was speaking involuntarily, but my own voice sounded like it was coming from somewhere else. The truth came spilling out of me.

"You're all nuts," I said. "You can't get women to do what you want, despite your money and power, so you have to fuck with the entire gender. You're a bunch of assholes. And I think you're latently homosexual."

With whatever faculties remained, I kept myself alert enough to just keeping talking, just keep telling the truth, any truth but the truth they wanted, and loud enough to drown out their questions.

Onward, I spewed forth my stream-of-consciousness rant.

"My sort of boyfriend is sleeping with a trapeze artist. He is dumping me for her. I've been sleeping with another guy, Gus, but he's mad at me now. I like him a lot. When he was a kid he had this pet salmon, Harry. Harry was hairy. I just farted. I really do like Hanson. . . ."

"Shut up!" Morton yelled at me.

"My nose is itchy. I'm not a very good reporter. I screen my phone calls. My favorite Monkee was Davy Jones. My second favorite Monkee was Mike Nesmith. . . ."

I was winding down. The energy was draining from me. My voice grew faint.

"Tell us about the liberation," Morton shouted.

I couldn't help myself. Everything I knew about the diversion squad, the liberation squad, and the saboteurs came spilling out in a river of increasingly slow, quiet sentences.

After I had finished, Mandervan said, "How did you know about the Adam project? Why did you start asking Morton and me about the Man of the Future?"

"A coincidence," I said feebly. "I was doing a series on the Man of the Future. Jack Jackson suggested I use Gill, and when I found out Gill knew you, I asked him to help me out. . . ."

"Who knows about this?"

"Just the people involved in the liberation tonight," I said. I couldn't speak anymore. I was hoarse and spent.

"Take her away," Morton said.

The goons uncuffed me, helped me to my feet, and half-dragged, half-carried me out, down a hall, and into another room lined with jail-like cells, all empty. The goons threw me into one and locked it.

I passed out.

When I came to, I heard a man's voice.

"Robin Hudson?" he whispered. "I hear you've been looking for me. . . ."

In the next cell was Harris Hufnagel. The man in the hat.

CHAPTER NINETEEN

Hello," I said. "What . . ."

"Speak quietly. There's a guard posted outside this door. I am assuming you know why I gave you the hat."

"Yeah, the map, the formula, found 'em. You could have made the map more detailed."

"I wasn't sure where we were. When we were given liberty for a day or two and left the island, on land we were transported in the back of a van with blacked-out windows, let off in Montauk, took the train in from there."

"So how exactly did you and I end up here together?"

In breathy bits and pieces, halting every time we heard a noise in the hallway, Hufnagel gave me his story.

During a bad time in his life, due to a gambling problem, Mandervan's people had approached him about working for them on a pheromonal project involving bonobo chimps. Not knowing what he was getting into, wanting to escape the mistakes of his past and avoid prosecution for embezzling research funds, Hufnagel agreed. He found himself in this bunker, working with other scientists like Bondir, who thought they had escaped their pasts by working for Mandervan and Morton, only to find themselves in a different kind of prison.

The plan, he told me, was to devise some chemical that could be secreted into air fresheners, cleaning products, grooming products, and ventilation systems, a chemical that would return women to contented submission and make men stronger and more aggressive. Morton then planned to cut his prices to get those products into even more households around the world and get women hooked on the chemical, cleaning, and resurgent male domination.

"Morton figured that, eventually, it would prove profitable for him financially, as well, but Mandervan was more motivated by philosophy than money," Hufnagel said.

As the project progressed, there was a need for a test group that wouldn't speak about the effects and possible side effects of the chemicals. Bonobos were chosen because they were close relatives to humans, and female-dominated. It was after the bonobos were chosen that Hufnagel was approached because of his work in the area. For the first six months, the bonobos were studied, until their social interaction was known inside and out. By that time, the first version of the bonobo equivalent of Adam 1 had been developed and could be tested. Through continuous testing, refining, retesting, they developed a version of Adam 1 that worked on the bonobos. Through continuous pheromonal therapy, the bonobos' roles changed. The males became chest thumpers, the females became timid and submissive.

Throughout this, Bondir and his team were developing the human version of the chemical. Now, they were ready to test the human version on people.

Bondir had long grown disenchanted with the project, and at Hufnagel's urging, had approached an animal rights activist on the Internet and, wary of a trap, used anonymized E-mail and encoding. That animal rights activist was Dewey. Bondir, whom Morton trusted, arranged a meeting with Dewey and Hufnagel in the city. Hufnagel only went to the city when accompanied by Bondir, because Morton didn't quite trust Hufnagel. The cover story was they were going in for a couple of days of much-needed R&R, shopping, hookers, movies, and so forth.

They took the formula with them after destroying the copy in the lab computer. Bondir was worried because Morton told him I'd been asking questions of him and Mandervan about the Man of the Future, and Dewey was supposed to look into it.

Before their meeting with Dewey, they had drinks with Benny Winter, at his insistence. Again, Bondir was asked if he knew anything about this reporter, Robin Hudson.

"Winter must have slipped something into our drinks, because when we left, we both felt woozy. We cabbed it to the meeting place, and as soon as we got there, we asked Dewey about you," Hufnagel said. "He made a phone call to your office at ANN, but you had just left for a dinner meeting at Wingate's."

It turned out Winter had had Bondir and Hufnagel followed, and before they could exchange any further information, they were jumped by thugs. Bondir was grabbed, Hufnagel got away after being knocked in the head.

"Dewey was taking a beating," Hufnagel said. "They probably would have killed him and grabbed me, but a passerby came along and started shouting. They caught up with me though, just after I found you."

"You were pretty out of it."

"I was drugged," he said.

"And Bondir? How did he die?"

"They had him in the car when they grabbed me. We were on a boat, coming back to Tweak Island, and Luc Bondir got away, jumped over the side. The boat went back to look for him, but they didn't find the body."

"I'm glad you're alive," I said. "I was worried about you."

"They've kept me alive just to reconstruct the formula and oversee the manufacturing. I've had no choice. They threatened to kill the chimps if I didn't cooperate. During the day, I work in the lab under strict supervision. At night, they lock me up in here."

"The bonobos are still alive?"

"Yes. Morton wanted to kill them. Mandervan wants to keep them alive and use them for further experiments. They make excellent test animals because they're so close to humans genetically."

"Why am I still alive?"

"They're planning to test the Adam 1 on you. That's not all. They are planning a secret field test Saturday, at the women's conference."

"That's the last day. Oh jeez, my CEO is giving a speech that day. And tonight some people . . . What time is it?"

"I'm not sure. It's nighttime, maybe ten P.M. I'm just guessing. They don't let me wear a watch anymore."

The door opened and two goons came in with plates of food. After unshackling us, they watched as we ate a dinner of lean beef, potatoes, and broccoli on a plastic plate with plastic tableware. My stomach felt queasy.

"Eat a little," Hufnagel said. "Keep your strength up."

A little was all I was able to eat.

When I asked the guards to let me use a bathroom, they escorted me to a small facility adjacent to the room where we were being held. The guy in the lab coat who had given me the truth serum earlier made me answer some questions about my menstrual cycle, then gave me a plastic cup before he permitted me to empty my bladder.

"Please bring me your urine when you are finished," he said.

"Why?" I asked.

He did not answer.

After I was done, I was given another shot. I don't know what it was, but when I got back to my cell, I passed out.

When I came to, sometime in the middle of the night, all the cells in the room were full. Each held a member of the team sent to liberate the bonobos. Jason was in a cell across from me and number twenty was next to him. They'd all been captured, all except Blue Baker. They were all unconscious.

Despite this, all was not lost, I thought. Blue Baker was still out there somewhere. Someone would notice my absence, surely. Someone would come looking.

CHAPTER TWENTY

In the morning, Hufnagel was gone and the others were still passed out in their cells. I was taken into a bright, clinical room, told to strip, and given a paper gown to wear. Two attendants strapped me to a gurney and left me there. It was hot, and I was sweating. Every now and then some guy in a lab coat would spritz water into my mouth or scrape sweat off me with a paper strip, which he then dropped into a jar.

After the first hour, I thought I was going to lose whatever was left of my mind. I tried to stay alert by observing my surroundings, looking for a chink in the armor. I found none.

Fresh, cool air began to blow into the room. And then, the strangest feeling came over me, a feeling of relaxation, calm, acceptance. I felt quite good actually, my fate resigned, and if I'd been thinking clearly, I probably would have realized I was being affected by the Adam 1.

Soon, the lab coats returned to scrape more sweat off me, spritz more water into my mouth, and stick a big needle in my arm.

"What is that for?" I asked.

"We are feeding you intravenously," a lab coat said, and wouldn't answer any of my other questions.

Jason was the only person there when the goons brought me back to the room of cells.

"Hi," he said. It was weird, after dealing with him dressed as a woman for some time, to now see him back in male mode.

"Where are the others?" I asked.

"They moved them to another part of the building," Jason said. "I don't know where. They've been using us as lab animals."

"Me too. How'd they capture you guys?" I asked, not wanting to admit that I was the one who had given them away.

"We were about to break in and begin the liberation when they caught us."

"How come you didn't cancel the liberation after I went missing?"

"Oh, you didn't know? We thought you were dead. We heard a news report that you were killed in an explosion. Then we heard you weren't dead, but you were in critical condition and unable to speak. So we decided to seize the day, go through with the operation, as everything was in place for it."

"You heard I was dead? Oh fuck. Miss Trix. They grabbed her to use as a decoy for me, buy them some time."

"Poor Miss Trix," Jason said.

"Don't feel too sorry for her. At least she's in a hospital somewhere getting good drugs," I said. "Someone will find us. Blue is still out there."

"Maybe," Jason said, but didn't sound hopeful. They'd probably given him truth serum too, and he'd told them about Blue. For all we knew, Blue was somewhere in this complex, being dosed with mind-altering chemicals.

"You must have left notes or something somewhere."

"We don't leave records or information of liberations behind, in case the police find them. People go to jail for animal liberations, Robin. It's a crime, trespassing, breaking and entering, theft, vandalism . . ."

"So theoretically, nobody knows we're here."

He nodded glumly.

Dinner, the same meal I'd had the day before, came, and a guard watched us while we ate, wouldn't let us talk. More needles were given and Jason and I both fell asleep before Hufnagel returned.

The next morning I went to the lab again, sweated, gave blood and urine, and had my vital signs monitored as I was gassed with more Adam 1. I was out of it most of the time, either asleep because of something they gave me or in that contented state brought on by the Adam 1. But there were side effects. After the drug wore off, there was a crash, a cold, gray depression and a headache.

When I came to back in my cell, I was close to out of my mind. I couldn't remember what day it was; I'd lost track of time completely. My head hurt. I barely ate, and when Hufnagel started to speak to me, I hallucinated that I was at home, in my bed, with my cat, Louise Bryant, and my relatively normal life (all things considered). I passed out again. When I came to, I was clearer. Hufnagel was gone. As I lay there in my cell, it was all I could do not to just burst into tears, like a girl.

Sometime later, I woke up, and someone was standing over me with a gun.

Behind the gunman were two other dark figures, both with guns. This is it, the firing squad, I thought. This seemed as good a time to scream as any, but before I could, I saw the two dark figures stick the guns to the throats of the guards.

"You are under arrest by the global police of the Organization," said one of the camouflaged figures to the guards. Two more camouflaged figures entered, followed by Reb Ryan, who had a small video camera. I'd never been so happy to be scooped, even by Reb Ryan.

A tall man in camouflage makeup came forward. "Thank God you're alive, Robin. I heard you were dead, darlin'. We don't have much time," he said. It was Blue Baker. "Morton has helicopter patrols over this place every hour and the sun is going to come up soon. We have to get everyone out before the chopper passes over again. Put these on."

He handed us black jumpsuits. Though I'd stripped in front of strangers several times recently, I made them turn around while I changed.

Hufnagel and Blue led the way through a series of tunnels to the area where the other liberators were being held. We waited in the hallway, until Jason, number twenty, and the rest came out, followed by Reb and a number of other camou- flaged men. Some of these men, I later learned, were old sanita- tion cop buddies of Blue's. The others were army intelligence friends of Reb's. Once again, the old boys' network was coming to the rescue.

"The bonobos?" Blue said to Hufnagel.

"This way. There are two guards, armed, inside that room. That's where the bonobos are held."

"Two guards," whispered Reb. "Piece of cake. When I give the signal, Jason, you and Blue tie up the guards. Then the rest of you come in, grab as many bonobos as you can."

The shooters crept into the room. There was the sound of a struggle, things bumping, something being knocked over. A moment later, Jason waved us in. The bonobos were in cages and looked dopey, as if they'd been sedated. Working quickly, we broke open the cages and grabbed a bonobo apiece.

Jason looked into the hallway.

"All clear," he said.

"We'll go to the left," Reb said. "Follow me."

Our arms full of chimps, we padded carefully down a series of tunnels and up a staircase to a trapdoor. Blue opened it and climbed through, helping the others and the bonobos through.

When we were all outside, he pointed to a boat about a hundred yards away across a grassy field and said, "Head for the boat."

The bonobos slowed us down—they couldn't run. They just kind of loped awkwardly. We were ten yards from the shore when we heard shouting in the distance behind us. There was shooting.

Don't trip, I told myself. Get to the boat.

The chimp clung to me. My left foot hit the gangplank and I stumbled and slid, but regained my composure and continued with Jason's help.

There was a second boat behind ours, with a full-fledged ANN camera crew aboard. When the guards chasing us saw the cameras, they immediately turned tail and ran in the opposite direction. Say what you will about the news media, but it scares the bejesus out of bad guys. The people most afraid of it are the people with the most to hide, nine times out of ten.

Reb said to me, "Take this camera. Record the entire trip into the city. We're going to call the coast guard and the state police and wait here for them to arrive. And take this tape with you for the afternoon news shows."

"Thanks, Reb," I said. Though grateful, it was still hard to get those words up. "Where's Solange?"

"Had to cut her out of the story. She's tight with Benny Winter. I couldn't trust her not to give it away."

"How did you know we were here?"

"It's a long story, Robin. Mike told me part of the story, and then Blue Baker contacted me, after the rest of you went missing, and filled in a few of the gaps," he said, blinking rapidly.

"How did Mike know? All I told him was about the dead Frenchman, Luc Bondir."

"He knew about the missing bonobos. . . ."

"I didn't tell him that."

"Well, he knew," Reb said. "Hey, Blue, good job."

"Couldn't have done it without you, Reb," Blue said.

"I'm going back into the bunker to help finish the job," Reb said. "We've got reinforcements coming."

He pointed to a number of boats closing in on the island.

"Just a few of my friends, coming to help out," Reb said, and waved good-bye.

As soon as everyone was aboard our boat, the crew threw off the moorings and pulled up the plank and we pulled away, shifting into high gear so quickly that I and a few others lost our balance and landed on our asses in a pile of chimps.

"Go like God, guys," Blue shouted at the crew.

"You called Reb Ryan?" I said to him.

"Yeah, when the animal liberation crew didn't show up."

"I thought maybe you'd been captured too, Blue."

"I'm a former undercover sanitation cop. I'm hard to catch," Blue said, and smiled.

We were away from the island now. Jason and number twenty were, with the assistance of some of the others, trying to keep the chimps in order while Hufnagel sedated them.

"Now what do we do?" I asked Blue.

"There's a school bus waiting for you on the North Shore," Blue said. "It'll take you into the city."

"What day is it?"

"Saturday."

"Last day of the women's conference. Oh shit. That's when Morton and Mandervan were going to test the Adam bomb on the feminists at the conference! My boss is giving a speech there this afternoon," I said. "On national television."

"Here," Blue said, handing me a cell phone. "Go ahead and make some calls."

Jack wasn't anywhere to be found, nor was Dr. Karen Keyes. I left messages everywhere and called the conference center. It was noisy at the conference center. Jack wasn't there yet, so I asked to speak to the head security guy, explaining that we were on our way to the hotel with a bunch of chimps and that a mood-altering bomb was going to go off there sometime today.

"You're nuts," said the security guy, and hung up on me.

"Fuck," I said. "We'll have to go straight to the hotel. Keyes will be there, we can give her the chimps, warn everyone about the bomb. I hope we get there in time."

The sun was coming up. It looked like clear sailing now. One of the animal rights nuts plugged in Johnny Nash, "I Can See Clearly Now." We all had a good nose blower of a cry. I collapsed to the deck with my bonobo in my lap. It chose that moment to take a leak all over me.

CHAPTER TWENTY-ONE

When we got to the mainland, we were met by a male bus driver and a woman, who smiled at the large chimp urine stain on my clothes and said, "We have diapers for the chimps."

Too tired to talk beyond agreeing that we had to go to the convention center immediately to find Keyes, we just sat, trying to keep the chimps under control as we headed toward Queens, relieved that the worst was over.

Or so we thought, until we were driving through Queens, around Jackson Heights, and the bus sputtered, slowed down, and broke down. Murphy's fucking Law.

"What should we do?" Jason asked.

"Fuck. Well, we can try a car service to get another van . . ." I said.

"What time is the conference finale?" Hufnagel asked.

"The last round of speeches begins around noon," I said.

"Might take too long for a car service, if they take us at all."

"Our other choices are the subway or taxis," I said.

"We can't take a dozen bonobo chimps on the subway.

We'll have to try taxis. We're going to need more diapers though," Hufnagel said. "Jason, there's a drugstore up here, you buy a bunch of Pampers, and Robin and I will try to get cabs. The rest of you, watch the chimps, okay?"

Even as we were walking down the avenue, looking for cabs, I was thinking that this was like a Letterman bit, i.e., can a handful of disheveled humans and a dozen chimps get a cab in New York City?

The answer? Yes. I got a cab before Hufnagel. Had the guy roll down his window.

"Hi, what's your name?" I said.

"Pardap."

"Look, Pardap, this is going to sound nuts, but my friends and I just liberated a bunch of apes, and we need to get them to Manhattan. Can you radio for about five cars to take us into Manhattan? If you do, my boss, Jack Jackson, will pay you a thousand bucks each. I swear to God!"

"Hey, I've seen you on TV," he said.

"That's right. But I'm not who you think I am. . . ."

"You're Robin from ANN," he said. "We thought you were in the hospital, in bandages!"

"What? No, I'm okay. You recognize me?"

"The video club in my village in India watches ANN all the time, by satellite. They know all about you in Balandapur, and how unlucky you've been in your life. Didn't you get their letters about your last haircut?"

"Haven't had time to read through my mail lately. . . ."

"We know all the ANN people in our village in India, and I watch all the time here, too, when I'm not working or studying. Dr. Solange Stevenson is a goddess in my village in India."

"That's lovely. We're in a hurry. Can you do this for me? I can actually introduce you to Dr. Solange Stevenson if you do."

In well under ten minutes, five other cabs, all driven by

men from the same village in south India, were there. The apes were freshly diapered, and we all piled in and drove off like maniacs to Manhattan.

By the time we made it to the Queensboro Bridge, the sedation was wearing off, the chimps were really starting to act up, and we were drawing more than a few looks. On the edge of the city, our procession of chimp-stuffed cabs excited a double-decker bus full of tourists, but nobody else seemed to notice. New Yorkers are still, all in all, the most self-absorbed people on the planet.

When we pulled up to the Jackson Hotel and Convention Center, I didn't even wait for the taxi to come to a complete stop.

"Stay here," I said to the driver, and I flew out the door and into the hotel, tearing through the lobby, while Jason, Hufnagel, and Blue followed with the bonobo chimps, herding them as if they were sheep through the lobby.

"Stop!" yelled a hotel security guy.

I kept running, up the stairs to the main ballroom, where Jack would soon be delivering a speech. Quickly, I scanned the room and saw Liz, with her Seeing Eye dog, and the camera crew.

"Liz, where's Jack?" I asked.

"Robin? Is that you? You're out of the hospital?" she said.

"Do you know where Jack Jackson is? He's speaking today."

"In a room down the hall. But . . ."

"It's out that way, to the left . . . why?" said Jim the cameraman.

"No time to explain. We have a bunch of bonobo chimps. This is very important. Find Karen Keyes and let her know they're outside the door," I said, heading back out and down the hallway to the green room. It was locked, no doubt for security purposes.

"Jack, Jack, it's Robin. Let me in!" I screamed, banging on the door. I could hear the chimps squawking and the pounding of people's feet coming up the stairs.

The door opened a crack and Larry, Jack's ethicist, peered out. Couldn't wait for him—I practically kicked the door open. Jack was sitting with his lawyer, a couple of bodyguards, and Solange Stevenson.

"You're out of the hospital. . . ."

"No time for that now. Jack, we've just liberated a dozen bonobo chimps," I spit out rapid-fire. "We had to take cabs to get them here. We promised the cabbies a lot of money . . . and that they could meet Solange and have their pictures taken with her."

"Reb was on that story," Solange said. "Why didn't he call me? Where is he?"

"He stiffed you," I said.

"Slow down," Jack said. "The bonobo whats?"

I repeated as much of the story as I could.

Then I inhaled again.

"How many cabs?" Jack asked.

"Five. I think. Promised them a grand each."

Jack turned to his lawyer. "Where's my petty cash?"

The lawyer patted a briefcase.

"Go down, give them two grand each, and take Solange down with you."

"Come on, Jack, we have to go into the ballroom . . ." And rather than finish explaining, I took him by the hand.

Security had formed a cordon at the top and bottom of the mezzanine stairs to hold the chimps in. Keyes had come out of the ballroom and she and everyone else were all screaming at once. A couple of the chimps had slipped through and I scooped them up handily, as if I did it every day of my life.

"Let them in!" Jack bellowed, just as the human wall broke and the chimps flooded through. This motley group ran into the ballroom, interrupting a heated debate between Alana De-Witt and Belle Hondo.

Just then, I caught sight of the whistling white man and several other goons up on the mezzanine. "Uh-oh," I said.

"What is it?" Jack asked.

"No time," I said. "Call the cops or someone. . . ."

The goons were making a run for it. Blue and I ran up opposite staircases to the mezzanine, trying to corner the bad guys. Blue stopped one on his end, but me, I'm a mere slip of a girl. The whistling white man handily shoved me aside, and I crumpled onto the steps as he and another goon tried to run past me. I was knocked on my ass, but I wasn't out of the fight yet. Quickly, I stretched a leg across the steps, and the goons went tumbling over each other, coming to a stop a dozen steps below me. Security guards grabbed them.

But it was too late. Air was blowing into the room along with, I guessed, the Adam 1.

The voices in the room got quieter and slower, like records winding down on an old hand-wound Victrola. There was a tremendous calm. All was silent. On the dais, Alana DeWitt and Belle Hondo were standing, confused. They turned to each other. DeWitt started crying. They hugged.

Unfortunately, this human-aimed gas had no effect, or at least a different effect, on the bonobos, who were now out of control, some of them tearing around the room, pulling off their diapers, some of them loudly copulating. I saw Liz's dog trying to maintain his composure as bonobos romped around him, beginning to strain against the leash, and abruptly breaking free and following instinct, barking loudly. Liz went flying and landed in a knot of now docile, weepy feminists, who fell into

[236]

Suzy Hibben's booth, bringing it and several of her Mrs. Degree girls down.

Jack, meanwhile, was feeling his oats.

"Open some damned windows," he shouted angrily, followed by the rest of the men. "Round up the damned chimps. Let's get control of things here."

Twenty minutes later, the chimps were subdued, the men were calm, and the women were starting to come to their senses. Karen Keyes got to the dais and explained for the cameras what had gone down, who the bonobos were, and why we needed to save them, as maintenance staff scooped up diapers and overturned chairs. Keyes ran her short film. When the credits started to roll, loud applause erupted and weepy women were whipping out their checkbooks.

After that, Solange gave a speech introducing Jack, although it may have been the aftereffects of the Adam 1 that made her so sweet. Jeez, I wish I could get some of that stuff. It could come in handy.

"My boss, my hero, my mentor, Jack Jackson," Solange said, wrapping it up.

Jack took the podium and winked, though he resisted slapping Solange's ass as she handed the stage over to him.

"Well, we've had some excitement here today," he began. "It all kind of confirms my theory. People are surprising. But women are the most surprising.

"Not long ago I watched *2001: A Space Odyssey*, and it was so farsighted. Predicted a lot. But it, and every other accurate sci-fi thing I could think of, missed one big thing. Almost all the women in these movies and books are in subordinate, traditional roles. Few of these visionaries envisioned feminism."

E.g., Wallace Mandervan, I thought.

"It has been a big surprise for a lot of people. Men,

generally speaking, kind of got caught with their pants down on this one. Since the women's lib stuff really hit, the surprises have just piled up. Someone says, 'A woman can't do this or that,' and right away, some woman will come along and do it. You know that saying, The only thing a man can do that a woman can't is pee standing up? It turns out that isn't even true. As one of my female employees tells it, all a woman needs is a proper-sized funnel to accomplish that. A little technology. And hey, we got a lot of technology these days, so who knows what else we can do? So where does it go from here? Probably, women will continue to surprise, and men will too."

There was some stuff about male conditioning, and female conditioning, and how men and women helped keep each other and themselves in their consigned roles in the past.

"Things have changed, from the days of the modern Stone Age family," Jack said. "Another one of my female employees called it the Flintstone Paradigm, based on an episode of the *Flintstones* (which incidentally, Jackson Broadcasting owns). In this episode, Wilma and Fred decide the other has it better, so Wilma goes to the quarry and Fred stays home to look after the house. Long story short, they discover that each has a difficult job, and they are happy return to their traditional roles. Well, we aren't cavepeople and there is no going back. But it is true that men have now taken a greater role, not big enough, mind you, but a bigger role in housekeeping and child-rearin', and women have joined the workforce in greater than ever numbers and shoulder more of the economic burden. And I think the result of this is that we all understand each other a little better, having walked in each other's shoes, and we can use this to get along a little better in the future.

"Men need your support as you need theirs. It seems like women want us to be strong and protective, but not too strong, not too protective, and we don't know what the hell you want sometimes. Guys who aren't tough enough might be called weak by women, as well as by other men. If we hold the door we're patronizing, if we don't we're unchivalrous. It's still harder for a man to quit his job and stay home with the kids. He faces a greater social backlash than women who left the hearth do. It takes guts to buck the prevailing thinking. Men are supposed to be so gutsy. In some ways, we are. But in some ways, men are much bigger chickens than women. No offense intended to the chicken.

"Speaking of chickens . . ." he said, and proceeded to relate the story of Mr. Chicken, our favorite peg-legged chicken martyr who died protecting his hens and chicks from stronger enemies.

"Mr. Chicken illustrates the pressure on men to provide for and protect their families, especially the women in their families. Sometimes, this protection crosses the line to control. Men are confused.

"But that Mr. Chicken story has lessons that go beyond male or female. It's a story about persevering despite handicaps, and a story about transcending a stereotype, because Mr. Chicken, whose breed is synonymous with cowardice, made of his little chicken life a testament to bravery. That's what we all have to do, transcend those stereotypes we impose on each other and ourselves, see each other not only as men and women—and vive la différence there, hubba hubba," he said, and winked. The rascal. "But as whole human beings. That's my modest commitment to women, to see them as whole human beings, and I'd like women to see men that way too. Toward that end, I'd like to announce the formation of the Worldwide Women's Network, a cable and satellite network that will debut early next year, bringing intelligent, provocative, and, yes, entertaining programming to men and women all over Planet Earth. Solange Stevenson, stand up again, will you? Solange is going to be the president of this new network."

Applause.

Then he said, "And I hope women have a lot of great sex in the future. Women not enjoying sex just causes more problems for men. I know men have some problems in that regard, but you could do a lot by loosening up a little, having some *fun*!"

CHAPTER TWENTY-TWO

Only after the conference ended was I told the details about my "death" and subsequent hospitalization. A woman bearing a startling resemblance to me, with my NYPD press ID, was found following an explosion in an abandoned warehouse in Long Island City. The initial report that she was dead went out before paramedics were able to revive her. In the meantime, my death had been announced on television, and Robert Huddon's obit had run by mistake. It had been a banner day for Murphy's Law.

Miss Trix, covered in bandages, unconscious and then unable to talk because of smoke damage to her throat and painkillers for her first-degree burns, wasn't able to tell anyone who she was. Despite how lousy she was, what with the deaf-mute orphans she had employed in her drug operation, I probably would have felt a little bad for her under normal circumstances. But I just didn't have the time.

When I finally got home that day, Mike was waiting for me. What a sight for sore eyes he was, that complex, dark-witted, moody, and faithless Irishman.

"Thank God, you're okay," he said. "Girl, I don't know how you do it. . . ."

"People who live in glass houses, Mike," I said. "How did you know about the missing bonobos?"

"Well, when I heard you had died from Susan Brave and Claire, I immediately hopped on a plane and came out here. By the time I got here, you'd been upgraded from dead to critical condition, Girl. So I went to the hospital."

He paused and bit his lip.

"In the waiting room I struck up a conversation with another guy there, who introduced himself as your boyfriend, Gus."

Without revealing his own status, Mike managed to find out a little about what a hot number I was, as Lola.

I had my head to his chest and could feel him inhale deeply.

Gus had also related some of the "lies" I'd told about fist-fighting thugs, missing bonobo chimps, and animal rights nuts.

"I was at a loss, Girl, didn't know who to talk to, so I called Reb Ryan."

Back in Mike's heyday as a cameraman for ANN, before he went out on his own, he'd been Reb Ryan's cameraman. They'd covered wars and had been kidnapped together in Beirut.

"Reb started putting the pieces together, and then he was contacted by some animal rights guy."

That would be Blue Baker.

"How come you weren't with Reb at our liberation?"

"I have a daughter, Robin, remember? I no longer think it's fair to her if I put myself in dangerous positions on dangerous assignments. Reb seemed to have it under control."

He held me for a while, quietly. He was troubled.

"What is it, Mike? Are you mad about Gus? I'm sorry you found out that way. . . ."

"Now probably isn't the time to talk about all this, Girl."

"Oh hell, in my life, there may never be a good time," I said. "Say it."

"I'm getting older. I need to settle down," he said.

"You think you can settle down with Veronkya, that crazy trapeze girl," I said, lightly snorting her name.

"Veronkya? She's eighteen and makes you look like a paragon of sanity. God, no. The truth is, Girl, I hadn't had another woman in over a month . . . that's what I wanted to tell you."

"That's your big confession?"

"There's more. I got tired of unfamiliar women, of crazy, unfamiliar women and all the nutty consequences and scenes. Seemed easier just to masturbate to porn in my hotel room. And I missed you. I was going to ask you if you maybe wanted to try monogamy."

"Mike, I've been down that road with you, and with other guys like you, and that pathology never changes for too long. . . ."

"I know all your logic, Robin," he said. "You might be right. And I know my history of other women would make it hard for you to trust me. All the same, I want to try. But not with you. The Gus thing, it hurt me. I know you were hurt by the other women in my life too. I don't know if we could ever really trust each other."

"So what are you telling me?"

"I'm going back to my ex-wife."

"Felicia?"

"Through all the stuff with Samantha, and through the reports of your death, the time I spent at the hospital waiting for you to recover, Felicia was there for me, and I've been there for her. It's as if all the bad things between her and me have fallen away and the love we had can come through. And we have a daughter. . . ."

"You're breaking up with me to go back to your ex? Oh damn," I said.

"Yes. I'm here for you today though," he said. "I care about you, Girl. . . ."

"No, don't say any more. I'm too tired to fight. I think I'll take a pill and hit the hay. Let's talk next week."

"Hey, I didn't let on to your friend Gus about you and me. Figured I owed you that. He seems like a nice guy."

We kissed, chastely, and Mike walked out of my life, temporarily at least.

Mike, who needs you, I thought. But as soon as the door closed, I felt the absence of his warmth and started missing him. I still had some of those cheesy Mecca souvenirs he collects, each one with a story about the pal who gave it to him. There, on the wall above my computer was the Enfield rifle he had given me, with another story attached. There were the news clippings about stories we did together, the photographs of vacations we took. Oh damn.

Surely it wouldn't take Mike long to realize that he couldn't settle down, I thought, even with Felicia. Every few months, he had to hit the road and go off to shoot a war, a circus, an expedition through the rain forest or some damn thing. When lusty people are apart for long periods and lonely, things happen, like affairs. Maybe he and Felicia would work out, maybe they wouldn't. If they didn't, maybe I'd still be here. Maybe not. In a way, I hoped it would work out for him and Felicia, if only because I didn't think Samantha could handle her parents reuniting and then splitting up again.

There was a game when I was a kid, by Parker Brothers, called Careers. You wagered at the beginning on how much love, money, and fame points you would get in your life. Then you went around the board, trying to match those numbers, and the person closest to his wager wins the game. Something like that. When I played, I'd always go for one thing, put all my eggs in one basket, usually for fame, but sometimes love, sometimes money, because it increased my chances of winning—in one area of my life at least. What hubris to think now that I could have it all.

Damn damn damn. But I couldn't deal with this right now,

because if I started thinking about it I might get all sentimental and blue. What was it the Roman poet Ovid said about love? If you're looking for a way out of it, be busy. Love yields to business. Something like that.

After the frenzy of the subsequent few days died down, Jack and I had dinner at his men's club.

"Why didn't you tell me what was going on?" Jack asked.

"One, I was sworn to confidence. Two, after you gave me your support on the Man of the Future series, I didn't want you to know I was chasing another story, and maybe on a wild-goose chase."

"Well, it all worked out," he said. "We got a helluva lot of free publicity out of it. That don't hurt none."

"It hurt a little," I said.

"Yeah, you've been through a lot. You're quite a gal. You know, I actually asked you here to fill you in on a few things," he said, changing the subject.

"Shoot."

"First, it was no accident I came down to Keggers that night and spoke with you, the night we went barhopping. Bob McGravy told me I should talk to you."

Bob McGravy was an executive vice-president at ANN and one of my far-flung mentors.

"Bob said that I should talk to you informally, give you a few belts of vodka, loosen you up."

Someone else would have found a wee sexist element in this—you know, getting the girl drunk to loosen her up. Except Jack got guys drunk too.

"It loosened me up all right," I said, ruefully.

"Don't be sorry about it. It's good to do that once in a while. My lawyers tell me I shouldn't . . . but lawyers, sometimes they just interfere with human communication," he said.

"Why did Bob think you should talk to me?"

"We were discussing women and feminism. Some of our biggest stockholders are prominent suffragettes and feminists, but I always felt a little uncomfortable around them. So I called up some feminists to find out what was going on with them these days, somehow rubbed them the wrong way. Got me thinking. And Bob, he says, there are a lot of different feminists. I asked him for a name, and he gave me yours. Said you called yourself a feminist, but you didn't have a stick up your ass about it, and you'd know the right people to talk to."

"That was good of Bob."

"I like your ideas. Not all of them, but a lot of them. People have to think globally now, Robin, beyond the group."

His eyes were bright and the pupils had shrunk to dots.

"The thing is this: Big things are happening with women all over the planet. Even women who stay home these days aren't like women who stayed home in my day."

"Now they're soccer moms with power."

"Right. And, hell, there's money in women. Look at all the corporate sponsorship that lined up for that conference, and the coverage. So I figure, this new network will have an audience, if we do it right."

"And Solange will be the president."

"What do you think of her?" Jack asked.

Solange Stevenson is a passive-aggressive asshole who, under the guise of sympathy, probes for people's weaknesses and then delivers a toxin-dipped stiletto to those vulnerable points. But as I get more, you know, mature, I play my cards closer to my chest and say the polite, politic thing when I absolutely have to.

"I respect her a lot," I said. "She had to kick down the doors to break into broadcasting. That made it easier for the rest of us to come through."

Jack smiled. "Good answer. The truth is, she's a manipulative bitch sometimes, but we need some of that at the top."

"I'm a bitch too," I said.

"Not enough of one sometimes," he said. "But enough of one to stand up to Solange Stevenson."

He smiled slyly, and I realized then that he had seen what was really going on between Solange and me at his cocktail party.

"And you got ideas. What I'd like you to do is be in charge of programming for the new network. It's a lot of work, a lot of travel, a lot of risk. But somehow, I think you'll do okay. You'll be number three in the network. That's a big leap up for you."

"Who's number two?"

"Your old boss in Special Reports. Jerry Spurdle. Solange will be president, he'll be vice president, and you'll be the programming executive," Jack said.

Jerry Spurdle was my old archnemesis, who had been running the Berlin bureau into the ground for the last couple of years. He believes women are just vehicles for the transport of their breasts.

"Jerry is number two all right," I said.

"The guy knows how to handle advertisers. You'll be a good team. So what do you say?"

Life. Man, the choices sometimes. Here, have a great job, working for two people you can't stand. But come to think of it, I've had a fair bit of experience with that situation in the past. It was a good gig, no doubt about it. A chance to make up my own programming and maybe foment a little rebellion out there in the wider world.

"I'll take it," I said.

"Good," he said. "Boy, I can't get over it. Morton and Mandervan, conspiring together. I always thought they were nuts, but I thought they were nuts like me. You know, nuts in a good way."

"Jack, the world has too many insane people in it, and too many of them have money," I said.

"Power can corrupt," Jack said. "You can start thinking you're a demigod, that you know better than other people what is good for them, and what the future holds. You watch out for that, Robin, now that you have a little power."

"Yeah, hubris. But I've got a curse on my head. Whenever I start thinking I'm hot shit, a man leaves me, or I fart in a private pre-interview with a handsome actor and there are only two of us in the room, so he knows it's me, or a dead body turns up in my life. . . ."

"I was just reading this thing by Benjamin Franklin, *Fart Proudly*, about how much pain and embarrassment is caused because we can't fart freely without offending others. Benjamin Franklin proposed creating some drinkable tonic that would perfume people's intestinal gas, so we could fart without offending others with an unpleasant odor."

"You know, with America's appetite for deodorants, it's amazing someone hasn't invented and marketed just such a thing," I said. "People would be a lot happier if they could fart perfume."

"But you'd still have to do something about the sound, wouldn't you?" Jack said. "It's worth looking into though. I've got me an ethicist now, may get an anthropologist, why not a biochemist?"

"Why not, Jack?"

"Now I have to run. I have a date."

"Oh? With whom?"

"Shonny Cobbs," he said.

Something about the way he smiled just then made me wonder if all of this—Jack trying to understand and empathize with women, his sponsorship of and speech to the women's conference, even this new network—was more about winning back Shonny than making a quick buck off women. Probably it was both. Two birds, one stone.

I had to run too. Had to stop by Litigious Liz's house and make sure she was okay, despite that broken arm, and head over to the Bog to meet Jason.

"More soda?" asked the Rasta bartender.

"Thanks," I said. "How is Dewey?"

"Much better," Jason said. He was dressed like a man again. "But he is disappointed he wasn't part of the actual bonobo liberation."

"He was a big part of it overall though," I said. "How's his vocabulary?"

"Improving. So, you want to join the Organization?"

"I'm a journalist. I have to try to be objective. Besides, it sounds nice in theory, Jason, this Disney utopia of happy animals and happy indigenous peoples, with no sexism or racism and all that. But I don't know if I want to live in some multicultural unisex world where everyone speaks Esperanto. I kinda like people's differences, you know?"

"I may yet convert you to the shining path," he said, taking a swig of his organic microbrew and swallowing hard. "Are you still going to eat meat, in spite of everything?"

"I'm giving up meat," I said.

"Really?"

"No. I'm just kidding. I like meat. My body absolutely craves it at least once a month," I said. "Don't you ever miss it?"

"No."

"Have you ever had a Beauchamp Inn ham?"

"God, no."

"They poke holes all over it and then cover it with an inch-thick crust of bourbon, brown sugar, and spices and then they slow-bake it so the ham absorbs all but a quarter inch of the crust. The meat is so juicy, and the mixture of the apple-smoked ham, the bourbon, the brown sugar, the spices . . . it is heaven."

"It's a pig's ass."

"And so tasty. What about bacon? The smell of hickory-smoked bacon and coffee when you're out camping. . . . C'mon, don't you ever miss having a big juicy steak at a barbecue or a ballpark hot dog and a beer at a baseball game?"

"Eat a cow? Ugh."

"You want everyone to stop eating cows, don't you?" I asked.

"Yes."

"I could go for everyone cutting back to once or twice a month, for health reasons . . ."

"And because, for example, valuable rain forest is cleared to provide grazing land for beef cattle," Jason said.

"True. But no more beef, ever?"

"If I were dictator of the world, yes," he said.

"But if we stop eating beef, what are you going to do with all the cows? Kill the ones who can't be dairy cows? Can't have them just standing around gobbling up valuable land, breeding . . ."

"You could neuter the males."

"Don't kill 'em, just maim them . . . so they can't have sex! But give them a long useless life chewing the same patch of grass in the same field day in, day out, emitting methane gas into the air and screwing up the atmosphere."

"You could put them to work. . . ."

"Doing what? Train them to be watchdogs? Or circus cows? I guess a few dozen of them could haul Amish plows, but what kind of life is that? Hauling a plow all the time. I believe in giving them quality of life, and then slaughtering them humanely, and then eating them."

"Eating them is the humane option? Please. How would you feel if some superior species landed on this earth and because it ranked higher in the food chain, it got to eat you?"

"Well, presumably, I'd win them over with my endearing personality," I said. "And they'd make me a house pet while they ate all the animal rights activists and vegetarians."

He laughed.

"Endearing personality? You'd be lunch," Jason said. "They'd keep the vegetarians as pets, because we are more highly evolved."

I laughed. "And too skinny to make good eating."

"You know, I'm a nice guy," Jason said. "You bring this nasty side out in me."

"Way to take responsibility."

He just smiled at me. Wow. Jason and I were finally at a point where we could discuss this stuff without any antagonism and name-calling. There was hope for the world yet.

EPILOGUE

So, you see, I saved the world from the past, saved the world from returning in the future to a time of docile, contented women and overly aggressive men. Oh, I'm not saying I did it alone. Reb got the official credit, along with "unidentified animal rights activists," and I don't mean to deny Reb or the others their due, seeing as they saved my life and all. But they couldn't have done it without me. If I hadn't stopped for the man in the hat, if I hadn't gone to 7 Mill Street, if I hadn't stumbled into a story and unwittingly led Reb and Solange in that direction. . . . Well, you know.

Miss Trix has now fully recovered. Most of the damage was from smoke inhalation, but there was some facial scarring and she required plastic surgery on her face to erase signs of the fire. People who have seen us both say we no longer resemble each other. I never thought we did to begin with.

The first thing Hufnagel did after the conference ended was file a patent for Adam 1, not because he wanted to market it, but because he wanted to keep it off the market. The patent ties it up for a long time. Nobody else can make the stuff now without his permission. Hufnagel is going back to face the embezzlement charges against him, and it looks like he'll probably get probation or a pardon.

Mandervan is in jail. Gill Morton, meanwhile, escaped and at this writing has not been located. Escape is easy when you're rich. It's tougher if you're a regular slob like me. However, one of his men turned state's evidence against the guy who shot at me, another of Morton's men, despite their assurances at the time that the bullet had come from elsewhere.

Though hindsight is not always twenty-twenty, sometimes things do seem clearer later, after you have more facts. Morton's motivations for being involved in Mandervan's scheme, aside from the moneymaking potential involved in making women more docile and getting them to use more cleaning products, became clearer to me after I again read through all the Morton materials I had. One old ad struck me, a Morton ad that ran in the back of *Popular Mechanics*, circa 1957. A dejected-looking man, wearing a short-sleeved plaid shirt and high-waisted trousers with a perfect crease, was eavesdropping on a circle of boys. Underneath was the caption: "When the other boys ask 'What does your dad do?' how does *your* boy answer them?" Then, in smaller type: "So your job isn't what it should be, maybe you had to leave school early, maybe the war interfered. Don't let these things stop you. Start a dynamic new career and be your boy's hero. Be a Morton Man!"

Below, it showed a man in a hat and a suit, carrying his Morton Products sample case, which came free with the purchase of a "starter kit." The man was smiling confidently and looking slightly upward toward the Gleaming White Future, while his boy stood beside him looking up at his dad worshipfully.

"All it takes is a small investment and the desire to be a business success. Have you got what it takes?" it asked.

Hard to believe now that any man who had the brains and

ability to be any kind of business success would be naïve enough to fall for this manipulation. But hundreds of thousands of men did over the years, and many succeeded.

That man in the ad, and all the men he represented, made me so sad. How could he know that in just a few years, chances were his boy would either be off fighting in Vietnam or wearing his hair long "like a girl" and protesting the war. The son might look at him not as a hero but as an Establishment toady who compromised his values for the sake of a dollar. The man couldn't know that in another decade, his wife might be burning her bra and exploring her own sexuality and raising her consciousness. The future he'd been promised by the Morton Company, which was also Gill's vision, had been betrayed.

It just served to underscore that old saying, that when people make plans, God laughs and cries. Or, to put it more succinctly: Murphy's Law.

Whatever can go wrong, will. That had certainly been true in my life, time and again. After you've seen enough evidence of the law in action, you find it hard to put much faith in anything, even evolution.

After all this, I took a little time just to try to figure out what life lessons could be pulled out of all this. You know, it's a curse to be as smart as me. I'm not boasting—I'm just smart enough to know how stupid I am, and that's a curse. Isn't there a saying that man is the only animal who knows how stupid he is? If there isn't, there should be.

You just don't know what to expect, do you? Who knew, at the end of the millennium, that bowling and square dancing would be "hip"? Did you ever in a million years think you'd hear a newscaster say the phrase "money-laundering Buddhist nuns"?

It's a strange new world. Today I read that a scientist has found a way to implant the natural behavior of one animal into another species, creating a chicken that acts like a quail. Last week, I read that in the Khansi tribe in northern India, roles are completely reversed. Women are considered the more successful businesspeople, and so they have always run the outer society while men have stayed home to cook, clean, and look after the kids. But the Khansi men are rebelling, and the women are trying to keep them to their traditions.

Maybe I'll do a program on them.

Going completely behind the scenes as a programming exec, and going off the air, should make me more anonymous. I'm looking forward to that. On the other hand, it has put Solange Stevenson directly in the firing line as president of the new, risky network. I hear Lynn Hirschberg from *Vanity Fair* wants to interview her.

Solange and I have had a few preliminary meetings, and I can foresee some trouble down the road. After all this, I went to her and said, "Look, I know I haven't always been fair to you, and I really respect what you've done and how you've succeeded despite the ill will of slobs like me." I meant it too. And I figured she'd respond by saying, "Yes, I haven't always been fair to you, and I respect what you've done, etc." A little give-and-take, is that so much to ask? But instead she said, "I'm glad you're strong enough to acknowledge that, Robin." That's it. No give on her part. And I have to work with her, and my oily former boss, Jerry Spurdle.

But I'm going to give Solange her due, because she's taking the heat with the new network, and I'm having all the fun . . . for now.

Dewey and Jason disappeared with the wind, off to rescue animals somewhere, before I remembered to ask Jason to help me find the mad cow hoax culprits.

The bees disappeared almost as quickly as they arrived, following their queens elsewhere.

Blue Baker is still dating his ex-wife.

Among the perks that resulted from this whole thing was

that I got to hear some of the stuff people said about me when they thought I was dead. It was very Tom Sawyeresque. Louis Levin made a dub of the on-air report, including the Huddon obit and the president's relieved comment that Robert Huddon was not dead, Robin Hudson was dead. Louis also gave me a copy of the rumor file postings during "my" death and hospitalization. People called me brave, outspoken, funny, and several men I'd never dated claimed they had dated me. Life is great and people love ya when you're dead.

Things like this happen and your life changes almost completely. Take Mrs. Ramirez. Now she likes me, which is a curse in and of itself, because every time she sees me, she wants me to come sit in her apartment, drink tea, and listen to her tell me, as a member of the media, everything that's wrong with the media, the world, the younger generation, and whatever else has lodged up her backside.

But . . . sometimes I listen, because she's an old lady all alone in the world, with her own point of view, and I respect her because she has persevered on her own, like Mr. Chicken, despite her handicaps and despite the risks.

In the end, after all that, I only did one piece of the Man of the Future report, the summation, a collage of visionaries from DeWitt to Nukker to the At-Home Dads. Liz wrote and voiced the rest, and that makes her the first blind reporter on network television. She's coming to work with me at the new network, and not only because she has promised not to sue me ever, but because she's pushy and perseveres beyond her limitations. My friend Louis Levin and a few choice others are also coming aboard. I never did demote Jim the cameraman, adhering to one of the important management lessons I learned along the way: Pass the buck to someone else. He's working in the Fashion Unit now, gets to shoot pretty young models all day.

Some things may never change. I bet, fifty years from now

in winter, you could walk down Fifth Avenue between the Plaza and Saks and see a succession of fat, bald guys in expensive overcoats, each with a much taller, much thinner, much younger woman in a fur coat. There will always be unattractive, piggish, control-freak men who use their wealth and/or power to obtain and control attractive, underfed women, and there will always be attractive, submissive young women for sale or rent. Funny thing is, these guys consider themselves to be the elite, the upper crust. And they are just so caveman, the great white hunters with their nubile young women wrapped in dead animal skins.

As for men and me . . . God/dess knows, I'm not gonna figure it all out. About all I hoped to figure out about men was: What is that mysterious thing good men have that makes me overlook all sorts of annoying shit, and will they have more of it in the future as they evolve? Whenever I try to give it a name, I think of women with the same quality, and this is a distinctly male thing. I never find it in women. It remains a mystery.

As Jack said, "Vive la différence, hubba hubba."

Gus got a part in an off-Broadway play and is moving to New York. All of a sudden, I see Gus, really see him for who he is, and I like what I see. I know so much about him, and I didn't realize it. I know about his single working mother, raising him alone, looking for a husband and father. I know about little Gus taking his pet fish, Harry the hairy salmon, out in a pail for a walk. Who knows, maybe he and I can try being real, though I may have to kiss his butt a bit to make up for blowing him off earlier.

Or someone else may come along. As Paul Newman says to Joanne Woodward in *The Long Hot Summer* (a movie that is hotter than porn, incidentally), "Life is long and full of salesmanship."

If that or something else doesn't work out . . . well, somewhere out there, a young man is being born, a young man who will hear the call of male nursing, and destiny will take it from there.

Like I said, I know I can't figure it out completely. The more answers I get, the more questions those answers spawn. It makes me think of an old Burns and Allen routine, which goes something like this:

GRACIE: I make up riddles.

GEORGE: Tell me one.

GRACIE: What's the difference between a man and a pickle?

GEORGE: I give up.

GRACIE: I give up too.

GEORGE: You give up too? I thought you said you make up riddles.

GRACIE: I said I make up riddles, not answers.

ACKNOWLEDGMENTS

They say it takes a thousand old books to make one new book, or something like that, but in my case, it takes about a thousand people. After all these folks have done to feed, inspire, cajole, protect me, make me laugh, or whatever, it's the least, the very least, I can do, to thank them.

Information on the bonobo chimps was obtained via the Anthro-L listserv; *Bonobo—The Forgotten Ape*, by Frans de Waal; a Natalie Angier article that appeared in the *New York Times;* and the Save the Bonobos Foundation. I am also indebted to the folks on the Utopia-L, Forteana-L, and Dorothy-L listservs for their advice and other contributions.

Thank you, Russ Galen, my agent, who really worked his ass off and got me through some crazy times; Danny Baror, my foreign rights agent, who brings his Israeli tank commander experience to his battles on behalf of me and his other writers; Claire Wachtel, my editor at Morrow, and a long-suffering angel; Paul Fedorko of Morrow, for his enormous faith and encouragement; Susan Isaacs for all her good advice, encouragement, and for being such a good sport when I got us kicked out of the University Club; Paul Mougey, who came up with the name "Sad Marquis"; David Bernknopf, who coined the term "squirrel on waterskis"; Simon Brett, for turning me on to humorous mysteries and going out of his way to meet with me in London; Gerrit Kuilder at the American Book Center in Amsterdam; Ion Mills and Pam Smith of No Exit Press in the U.K., even though they are terrible slave drivers and, frankly, insane; Adrian Muller at Crime in Store, London; Geoff Mulligan, for taking me to No Exit; Otto Penzler of Mysterious Book Shop; Scott Sellars at Penguin Canada; and Charlie Gillett of Oval in London for providing a soundtrack for the last revisions!

At the Chelsea Hotel, Scott Griffin, John Wells, Arnold Weinstein, and Nile Cmylo made inestimable contributions to the writing of this book, and, as always, the staff and management's faith sustained me.

Also, thanks to Jed Sutton—everyone needs a friend who will hold their hair when they throw up; Eddie Dixon; Bill the IMC handyman; Stu who became Blue; and X, the handsome young man who unwittingly gives me a recharge every time he walks below my balcony.